BODY

+

SOUL

MARIO DELL'OLIO

While every precaution has been taken in the preparation of this book, the publisher assumes no responsibility for errors or omissions, or for damages resulting from the use of the information contained herein.

Body and Soul
First edition. May 15, 2019.

ISBN: 978-1-7330750-0-8

Body
+
Soul

This is a work of fiction. Names, characters, events and incidents are the products of the author's imagination. Any resemblance to actual persons, living or dead, or actual events is purely coincidental.

"For all of us as we struggle with our own human frailty. For all who have struggled to find love and who have been marginalized because of who they are and who they love. May all find peace in knowing that that are good and worthy of love just as they are."

CONTENTS

PROLOGUE

Our first touch sent shivers down my spine as he gently pulled me closer; I can still feel the hairs at the base of my neck rising as our cheeks grazed. The scent of him still lingers in my memory, enchanting me as if I were inhaling in his very essence. Before him, I didn't know that it was possible to desire another person's touch so desperately, or to need unconditional approval and adoration so helplessly.

Before him, I couldn't comprehend the impact another man could have on my life and my future. I was 18 years old and it was the most intense relationship I had ever had. I had never encountered such intimacy. He consumed my every thought, my every desire. The gravity of each struggle and the euphoria of each joy surpassed any that had come before. Arguments were more heated; sadness, more poignant; and the delight was ecstasy. I experienced and fiercely savored the depth of each and every new emotion.

Somewhere in my mind I knew that this was forbidden. Guys don't kiss other guys. But desire prevailed and pushed that thought, along with all others, far from my consciousness. I let my senses take over and guide me the rest of the way. My lips tingled with anticipation until they met his—not urgently, but tenderly exploring. What is this unfamiliar sensation? They were lips like any others I had kissed, yet they felt completely different and I was reeling with unexpected passion. That first tentative kiss was almost reverent, drinking each other in as if from a sacred vessel. Once I had tasted, I longed for more, and our kisses became more fervent and hungry. I wanted to consume this man like no other being I had ever known. My need frightened me, but I could do nothing but acquiesce.

I had never entertained the thought of being with another guy, and I had never felt any sexual passion for girls; I believed I wasn't meant to be coupled. This served as confirmation that I was meant to become a priest. I came from a traditional Catholic family and I was always drawn to the priesthood. I also knew that the Church taught against pre-marital sex. Though many of my friends ridiculed the idea that a person shouldn't have sex before marriage, I was not bothered by it. It didn't seem so arduous to me, and I wondered what all the fuss was about. I was not as obsessed with sex as most other adolescents. That all changed when I met him.

I couldn't comprehend my fascination with him, and I began to understand how a sexual relationship could become totally consuming. Though there were many kisses before him, none reached more deeply into my mind and my heart than his. I could have never imagined how this relationship would change my life.

✝

CHAPTER 1

LUCA
WINTER TO SPRING 1978

I had many girlfriends throughout my high school years, yet no relationship lasted very long. I was fully engaged in the chase: each budding romance brought excitement and challenge. My attention was easily captured and I enjoyed every playful encounter I had with girls. They seemed to connect with me more easily than my male friends. We would chat endlessly and laugh without guile. My female friends would readily confide in me and I in them, creating a familiar intimacy in each successive relationship. This led to my numerous, but short-lived romantic flings.

My best friend John and I made a quick study of flirting with any girls who were receptive. Sitting in the school library, one of us would look up from our homework.

"Hey, I'm bored. Do you want to go flirt?"

"What, and give up this fascinating history essay? Twist my arm! There's Susan. Let's go."

At that, we would run off to chat and joke around with our classmates. It was always good-natured fun and we always found a receptive audience. We were playful and silly, and our targeted audience was quite entertained. The girls we interacted with knew we were harmless: John had a girlfriend, and I was always with one girl or another. They just enjoyed the silly banter, stupid jokes, and over-the-top compliments we gave them.

"Hi Susan. What are you doing?" John would begin.

Then I'd jump in. "Wow, you look great in that blouse. Don't you think so, John?"

"Luca, Susan always looks good!" John insisted.

"Good one, John," Susan interjected. "You guys are crazy, completely shameless! Go bother someone else, I have work to do," she said as she laughed out loud.

"Oh, come on Susan, how could you be so cruel?" I asked plaintively.

"Now you've done it. Luca is crushed by your rejection," John said.

"Alas, Luca, my heart is taken by another," Susan said, playing along.

"I'll never forget you Susan! I will wait a hundred years for you," I replied.

"We'll be back again tomorrow!" John shouted, and off we'd go to another friend.

"Oh, I'm sure you will be," Susan said as she chuckled and waved goodbye.

Connecting with a new, pretty girl filled me with excitement. The dance would begin subtly with eye contact, and then a bit of flirting, followed by a mutual expression of interest. I fully enjoyed the deepening of each friendship as we shared our inner thoughts and emotions. Friendships with other guys didn't offer the same kind of emotional connection. John was my best friend, but we rarely, if ever, shared our feelings. I longed for deeper relationships, and the girls I dated gave me my first taste of emotional intimacy.

Even so, I was largely indifferent as each relationship waxed and waned. I quickly became infatuated, but my heart always seemed to ache for some new love interest just as swiftly. There was always something missing, but I couldn't figure out what it was. I recall looking over at one of my girlfriends and thinking, Why don't I want to be with her anymore? She's absolutely gorgeous. She's smart and funny, and I really like her. But I just don't feel like going any further with her. I guess we're just not right for each other. Other times, though, I would simply ask myself, What's wrong with me? Why am I never satisfied with whomever I'm dating?

In some ways, my dating experience was completely normal. I felt exhilarated by kissing my date and caressing each other in my car at the end of the night. I enjoyed the euphoria of being with a new girl and looked forward to our time alone. But I never sought more. I simply wasn't that interested in having sex.

One particular instance is burned in my memory. I had been dating Beth for a month or so, and we were getting along well. She was a sophomore and I was a senior. She was adorable with brilliant red hair and green eyes, and hung onto my every word. We were always playful and silly with each other. I reveled in her admiration, and enjoyed the fact that I could simply be myself with her. With Beth, I didn't have to act like a certain kind of macho guy.

Often, a whole gang of friends would go out together, and by the end of the evening many of us would pair off with our respective dates. There was always a certain amount of showmanship that accompanied our social interaction. There was competition to see who would be the first to make out in a dark corner. Looking back, I recall being more interested with what my buddies were doing than with the girl I was dating. Were they making out? How far did they go? What were they doing now?

I was still dating Beth by the time my senior prom rolled around. She was elated when I invited her. Not many sophomores got asked by senior boys. Always an event planner, I had organized a pre-prom gathering at my house. It was a non-alcoholic gathering, but my mother made fresh homemade pizza, baked ziti, and many other delicious treats. No one seemed to mind that there was no beer.

It was a warm June evening, and the patio in our backyard provided the perfect backdrop to our gathering. Being an amateur photographer, I staged each couple in front of a rhododendron that was in full bloom. After everyone had their individual photo session, I arranged all the girls on the deck looking down on their dates lined up below. They laughed at my stage direction, but happily complied. John ribbed me mercilessly, saying that I was worse than a wedding photographer. But I relished every moment. It was my senior prom: I knew that it was a rite of passage, and I wanted it to be perfect.

At the prom itself, I danced with many of my friends and bounced from table to table, chatting with everyone.

Beth clung to me the entire evening and pouted each time I chose to dance with someone else.

"Come on Beth, it's not like you're sitting alone," I said to her. "You've been dancing every time I have. We'll have some alone time later. For now, let's be social, OK?"

"But I'm your date. You should be dancing with me, not all these other girls," she whined.

"Seriously, Beth? Everyone is dancing with their other friends. That's just what we do," I explained impatiently. Her neediness was annoying me, and I was beginning to realize that I was bored with the relationship.

After the prom, it was customary for couples to go down to the shoreline and park, with the goal being to watch the sun come up after fooling around in the car all night. After Beth and I said goodbye to our friends, we drove down to the river. The Hudson was beautiful, and there were numerous hidden spots to park away from prying eyes. I had found a clearing in the trees where we could see the moon reflected in the water. It was incredibly romantic.

It was approximately 4 a.m. when we settled in. Beth scooted over to me and removed my bowtie. I leaned in and began to kiss her as she unbuttoned my ruffled shirt. We were getting hot and heavy, and yet I felt as if I were simply going through the motions. As things progressed, Beth became more and more assertive. She placed my hand on her breast, while her hand reached between my legs. As she became more aroused, she slid her spaghetti straps down her shoulders and lowered the top of her gown. It was pleasant enough, but I began to lose interest. I just wasn't into it, but I knew that this was what was expected, so I played along. However, I wasn't making any moves to go further.

Beth decided to take the lead as she unzipped my pants and tugged at my briefs. Though I was aroused, I had no desire to have sex with her.

"I need a breather," I said as I began to pull away.

"I don't. I've been waiting for this for a long time," she said as she kissed my neck and down my chest.

It felt good, but I just couldn't go any further. I wiggled out of her embrace and put my hand on her shoulder.

"Hold on Beth. It's 5 a.m., and I'm exhausted. Let's just call it a night, OK?"

She lifted her head and look at me in disbelief. It sounded like I was rejecting her affection. She had trouble taking no for an answer and continued to caress me. With a mischievous smile on her face, she unfastened my pants, and her hands reached down to grabbed hold of me. I jumped at her forceful grip and pulled away immediately.

"No, Beth! Let's not. I think it's time to head home."

"What's the matter, Luca? Don't you like me anymore?" She said as she placed her hand on me once again. I gently put my hand over hers and moved it away.

"Look, it's not that. I'm just tired. It's been a very long night and I need to get home."

She knew I was lying, but couldn't understand why. Any other boy would have jumped at her willingness to have sex. I could practically hear the questions running through her head: Is there something wrong with me? Why is he treating me like this? We were silent for the entire drive home.

In the weeks that followed, she began to resent me. I had rejected her and she felt humiliated. She could tell I wasn't attracted to her anymore. I knew there was no hope of repairing our relationship, and we broke up shortly before graduation. In my mind, there was nothing unusual about how we ended things. Every relationship I'd had with a girl had ended in a similar way. At a certain point, I just began to lose interest. Never did I suspect that I might be more interested in boys. That concept was completely foreign to me.

I didn't reflect on my feelings all that much. I was enjoying the end of my high school years and looking forward to new adventures in college. Worrying about girls wasn't at the top of my list. Little did I know that there would be cataclysmic changes ahead of me. College life would bring many new experiences that would capture my attention and rock my small, comfortable world.

CHAPTER 2

LUCA
1978 TO 1979

Like every freshman, I looked forward to starting college with a combination of fear and excitement. I had been accepted at the Hartt School of Music in Hartford, Connecticut, and it was an accomplishment beyond my wildest dreams. After a whirlwind of orientation events, I settled into my new reality of living in a dorm and eating bad food at the campus dining complex. I was lucky, though—there was a burger bar that was open until 2 a.m., and it became my home away from home. When the pasta served in the cafeteria looked like flattened water hoses, or if mystery meat was on the menu, I survived on double cheeseburgers and fries.

I was a music major. But since my interest in music began late in my high school career, I had no formal training in voice or piano. In fact, although I had been accepted into the high school concert choir during my junior year, I had struggled with my audition for the honor choir, which was comprised of the advanced singers.

John's sister, Rita, had helped me work on my voice part for the audition. It was a 16th century piece by Thomas Tallis called "If Ye Love Me." It was a cappella and had a very high tenor part. Rita sat at the piano in the cramped practice room and played my part over and over again. I had little trouble with the notes, but my counting and rhythm were off. Not being able to read the musical notation well enough to count, was a substantial disadvantage.

The evening of the auditions, I was a wreck. John and I arrived together with our music and sat in a corner to practice. Soon, the choir room was filled with singers creating a cacophony of sounds in all four voice parts. I felt my anxiety mounting. John was nervous too, but when he turned to look at me he was taken aback. My usual bubbly personality was gone. I was somber and white as a ghost.

"Dude, what's the matter? You look like you're going to a funeral. Lighten up!" he said.

"I should have never let Rita convince me to do this. I'm not nearly as good as everyone else in here. I can't do this."

"Sure you can. What's the worst that could happen? You don't get in. So what? Who really cares? Seriously, you need to calm down, Luca."

"Yeah, but that would suck. I'd be so embarrassed."

"Obviously you've never been cut from a team, have you?" he asked.

"No, of course not. You know I don't play sports," I said.

"You get used to disappointment after a while. It's just part of life," he reassured me.

"You're right," I replied. "I just need to breathe, and try to remember everything I went over with Rita."

"Like I said, who cares if you don't get it? It's not the end of the world. You still have concert choir," John reminded me.

John and I always looked out for one another. We met in gym class freshman year. I had just transferred in from another school district, so I was the new kid. Most of the other guys knew each other from elementary school. Since I was short and skinny, I had always been uncomfortable in gym classes.

The day we met, the class was divided into teams as usual. The coach selected the team captains and left the gym to sit in his office. When they began to choose their players, I bowed my head and got ready for the usual ridicule that came with being chosen last. I hate this so much, I thought. When will this torture ever end?

"Who's gonna get the queer?" one of the team captains bellowed.

"Not me! You got the last pick, he's yours," the other kid responded.

The first one turned to me and barked, "Don't screw things up for us, faggot. My team never loses and we're not going to start now."

I got up from the bleachers and walked over to his crew. To make matters worse, the captains informed the class that we would distinguish the teams by "shirts and skins." One team had to remove their t-shirts, and I prayed it wouldn't be mine. But some prayers go unanswered. My humiliation was complete when we were instructed to take off our shirts. As I lifted mine above my head, everyone could see my pronounced ribs poking through my torso, and some of them began to taunt me.

That's when John quietly turned to me and said, "They're assholes. Don't listen to them. My name is John." He stuck out his hand.

"Luca. Thanks, John," I said as we shook hands.

From that moment on we were fast friends, and stuck with each other throughout high school and college. While I didn't have an athletic bone in my body, John seemed to be good at everything. Yet, he never treated me like the other guys did. In his eyes, we were simply friends.

Back at our audition, everyone went silent as the director entered the room and warmed up the choir. I was intimidated by Mr. Dickinson from the moment I met him. He was so arrogant, and unless you were one of his stars, you were treated with disdain. However, once we began to sing, I started to feel better. We were separated into voice parts, and then into octets. We sang "If Ye Love Me" again and again, with different combinations of people, and one by one, students were eliminated. After the fourth round of eliminations, Mr. Dickinson put us into quartets, and we started the whole process once again.

It was here that my musical weakness began to show. I began to miss entrances or sing during rests. There was one particular part that I continued to get wrong with each quartet configuration. Each time I made a mistake, I became more and more nervous. In the end, I was cut in the final round.

I was crushed. My disappointment was even more

bitter because five singers were left in each voice part, except for the tenor part—mine. Everyone could see that the tenor part had fewer members than each of the others. They knew that I was the one who couldn't cut it. I tried to be positive and went over to congratulate John, whose bass voice could be heard loud and clear in each quartet.

"Congrats, man. You did great, John."

"Thanks, Luca. You did well too, buddy. You made it to the final round. Sorry you didn't get in."

"It's OK. I did my best," I responded half-heartedly. "But you must be really psyched."

"Yeah, whatever," he said, punching my shoulder as hard as he could. "Let's go to Mario's Pizza. I'm starving!"

Soon we were laughing and joking like we normally did. John didn't allow himself to celebrate his victory because he knew it might hurt me. In fact, he would always downplay his membership in the honor choir, and I always knew that he did that for me. That was a signature characteristic of our friendship. There was so much that was left unspoken, but neither of us ever doubted our bond.

Mr. Dickinson, however, never treated me the same after I was cut from the honor choir. I felt as if he blamed me for not being good enough. I was so down on myself that I barely sang during the following concert choir rehearsal. Dickinson stood directly in front of me as we attempted to sight-read a new piece. "Sing, Luca, sing! What's wrong with you?" He shouted. I was mortified. I was already ashamed of my performance during the auditions, and his public shaming drove me deeper into self-loathing.

After that, I was determined to improve. I knew that I had to learn the basics of reading music. A good ear and a pretty voice were not enough to be considered a good musician. I had to study musical notation and some basic theory. Rita became my music tutor; each day, we would hang out in the practice room as she taught me the basics. She even gave me a few piano lessons. If anyone was looking for me during any of my free periods, they could find me there.

"Luca, you're obsessed! Take a break. Let's go to the commons and flirt," John would say when he saw me there day after day.

"Nah, I really have to get this down. Your sister is a slave driver. Do you understand the circle of fifths?"

"The circle of what? I'm dragging you out of here. Let's go." John took my books and pushed me out of the practice room.

"Seriously, John, I want to learn this stuff," I pleaded.

"Enough learning. It's time to slack off. We're going to the commons to find girls!"

When Mr. Dickinson programmed selections from Handel's Messiah for the concert choir, I was smitten. I had never heard such beautiful music before, and immediately went out to buy it. Since it was a pack of four records, it was way more expensive than any music I had ever purchased. I must have worn out the grooves in those albums by Christmas. I just couldn't get enough. When it came time to apply to college, I started thinking about majoring in music.

I looked for colleges and universities that were in the tri-state area: New York, New Jersey, and Connecticut. I didn't want to travel too far from my family—my Italian roots were deep—and narrowed my decision down to five schools. For most of them, applicants didn't have to declare a major, unless it was to apply to specialty programs like engineering. At the University of Hartford, whose music school had a great reputation, there were a whole series of steps to be taken to apply to the music program. I was overwhelmed and knew that I needed help. I swallowed my pride and walked into Mr. Dickinson's office.

When I showed him the school's audition requirements, he laughed. "There's no way you'll be able to work up three songs in different languages by the audition in February. What gave you this crazy idea?"

I was taken aback by his dismissive approach. He was a sarcastic man who didn't hold back his scorn for those of us who were not musical geniuses. In fact, we used to call him Mr. Dick because, more often than not, he was one. I ignored the fact that he had just laughed at me and pressed on.

"I love music, Mr. Dickinson. I know I'm not the best singer you've ever taught, but I want to try." I said honestly. "What do I have to lose?"

"OK, Luca. I will help you, but I recommend applying for music education. You don't have the time to put together a portfolio of songs to audition to the voice performance program."

"Do you think I'd have a better chance of getting in as a music education major?" I asked.

"Yes. You could always audition for the voice program after you are accepted. But remember, there are no guarantees. Music is a very competitive field."

Even though Mr. Dickinson's sarcasm wounded me, his advice was good. A few months later I received a thick envelope from the University of Hartford. I tore it open and screamed with joy. I was accepted into the music education program at Hartt. At school the next day, I ran to tell Mr. Dickinson. He was his usual sarcastic self in response.

"Well, I guess they saw something in you that I didn't. Good luck, Luca, you're going to need it."

I didn't let his mockery dampen my high spirits. He was a dick, after all. But getting into music school gave me the boost of confidence that I needed.

I had also been accepted at St. Robert's College, which was close enough to home for me to commute. It was run by the Jesuits, a Catholic religious order that are often called the intellectuals of the Church, and was ranked as a highly competitive university. I always admired the priests in my parish and my faith was deeply engrained in me. Going to a Catholic university run by an order of priests seemed to be a natural fit for me.

I secretly hoped if I attended St. Robert's, it would prepare me for the seminary when the time came. Though I told no one, I had always dreamt of becoming a priest someday. But at this point in my life, I was consumed with my new-found passion for music and still tempted to attend Hartt.

A decision had to be made. I weighed the pros and cons of each school but could not make a decision. I agonized over the choice and talked about it incessantly. John was sick of hearing me vacillate.

"Luca, what's holding you back? The answer seems obvious to me," he said in frustration.

"What do you mean, it's obvious? If it were, I would have made the decision already!"

"Come on, Luca. Sometimes you can be so dense.

You've been holed up in the music room all year. You've been obsessed with learning everything you can. How is that not obvious to you?"

I was silent for a moment, sitting there with a bewildered look on my face. He was right, of course. But he didn't know my secret desire to become a priest.

"But St. Robert's has such a great reputation. Didn't you decide to go there? We'd be at the same school," I replied.

"Yeah, I love St. Robert's and I'm psyched to go there. But I'm not a music freak like you, Luca. You got into a music school. Don't be stupid."

"Yeah, you're right. I still can't believe I got in. I'll hate myself if I don't give it a try."

So, there I was, a freshman at the Hartt School of Music. However, my lack of music education during my youth placed me at a distinct disadvantage. I found theory class to be unendurable, and I struggled to understand material my classmates found to be easy. On the other hand, I thoroughly enjoyed the concert choir and my performance courses. The repertoire was grand and I was thrilled to be singing major works by classical composers. If not for all the opportunities to perform, I would have been lost.

My roommate, Craig, was a vocal performance major with an outstanding tenor voice. He encouraged me every step of the way, and I basically worshiped him for his talent. He was also very handsome, and I was completely obsessed with him. Craig exuded confidence and my feelings for him continued to intensify. Thankfully, he was completely oblivious to my infatuation. I, myself, didn't quite understand it.

The semester flew by and I was immersed in my

studies. Though I still had trouble with music theory, Craig proved to be an effective tutor. But he was the only one I could reach out to. So many of the performance majors at Hartt were incredibly competitive. Anytime they found out that I was an education major, they would visibly discount my musicianship. Performance majors thought those of us in music ed were second-class citizens, since we obviously hadn't made the cut to be one of them. Few, if any of us, were considered for solo work in the choir.

The worst part was that these attitudes made it difficult for me to make friends. My first semester of college was surprisingly lonely, which was a departure from my high school experience. Back then, I had always been at the center of my group of friends, and had numerous events and activities to keep me occupied. As a college freshman, I was starting from scratch. I ended up coming home almost every weekend to hang out with John at St. Robert's.

To add to my unhappiness, I began to feel the absence of a religious community as the year wore on. Although I wasn't obsessed with religion, I missed our youth group back home, and longed to be with people of like mind. There was no chapel on campus, and I was incredibly disappointed with the local parish church. Very few people attended Mass there, the music was horrible, and the homilies were worse. Since I was visiting John almost every weekend, I began attending Mass with him at the St. Robert's chapel. He was very animated when he talked about how much he loved the school and, sensing my unhappiness, he encouraged me to transfer.

"If you don't like it at Hartt, transfer. Hell, you're here practically every weekend anyway!"

I wasn't completely sure yet. "St. Robert's doesn't have a music major, which kind of sucks. But maybe that's OK. Didn't you say that the choir and a cappella group are really good?"

"They're amazing. Their concerts are great. If you transfer, I can audition for the choir too and we could sing together again. Just do it. You know you want to be closer to home again. Plus, you said all the music people are stuck up snobs. You don't need that."

"I do hate it there," I admitted. "And Mom and Dad would be thrilled to have me home again."

"That's cool, Luca, sounds like you've made a decision!" John said. He grinned with satisfaction as he punched my shoulder hard.

"Wow! I sure do miss that, John. What have I done all year without a sore shoulder?"

I re-applied to St. Robert's and was accepted as a sophomore, on the condition that I fulfill some of the core curriculum I had missed during freshman year. I knew it was the right decision and couldn't wait to get back home. What I didn't know yet was that I would meet someone at St. Robert's who would completely transform my life.

CHAPTER 3

LUCA
AUTUMN 1979

I didn't understand true desire until I met Brad. I was instinctively drawn to him: his eyes, his lean body, and especially his self-confidence. It seemed like he could talk to anybody. He exuded charm with his infectious smile and jocular way of making physical contact. It seemed so natural. From our first handshake onward, I responded to his touch viscerally. I was confused by my physical response to him, but I didn't over-think it. However, every time he threw his arm around my neck or playfully punched my shoulder, I was brought more deeply under his spell.

It seemed like Brad was always a part of my college life, but in reality, we met at the beginning of my sophomore year. I had just transferred from Hartt to St. Robert's College. Since there were no dorm rooms available at that time, I lived at home with my parents, ten miles away, and commuted to class each day. Unfortunately, there weren't any orientation events for transfer students, so I found it difficult to break into the community of residential students. They had established friendships and hung out together in the dorms. The commuter lounge offered little opportunity for interaction with those housed on campus, and many commuters always seemed to be rushing home or to jobs in the area.

The one comfort was that John commuted as well. Unfortunately, he was one of those guys who had to rush off to work each day after class. There were many days when our paths didn't cross at all. To remedy my lack of community, I immediately joined the concert choir and the folk group at the campus chapel. Participating in the folk group and campus ministry were activities that John didn't care for, so I struck out on my own. I hoped that I would find a home there and meet people who were similar to my friends from our parish youth group. I wasn't pious or overtly religious, but I always felt at home in church-related environments. Considering my ultimate goal of priesthood, it was a logical fit.

That is where my path first crossed with Brad's. We both volunteered for the campus ministry department. I helped lead the music and Brad read at Mass. Every week, I would play my guitar and sing the contemporary hymns that I loved so well. The university folk group led the music at Mass every Sunday night. One week, early in the semester, I was packing up my guitar after Mass when Brad passed by. He caught my eye and flashed his irresistible smile.

"The choir really sounded great tonight. You have a beautiful voice," he said as walked up to me. He and I were about the same height; he was slim, built like a swimmer, and handsome with his thick head of blond hair and hazel eyes. He beamed when he smiled, exposing his brilliantly white teeth. There was an air of confidence about him that drew me in right away. It seemed as if he were saying, "I've got this." His every movement was assertive and authoritative.

"Thanks," I responded shyly. "I really love that closing song."

"Yeah, I do too. You gave me chills when you sang the solo parts. I'm Brad," he said as he extended his hand.

His touch was electric; the warmth of his hand radiated up my arm and I was immediately entranced. I could feel my voice shake a bit as I introduced myself.

"Hi, I'm Luca."

"I don't remember seeing you here last semester. Are you new to St. Robert's?"

"Yeah," I said. "I just transferred in."

"Cool, what's your major?"

"English. I want to be a teacher someday. What about you?" I asked.

"Finance. I want to be a millionaire someday!"

We both laughed at his candor. I liked this guy; he was funny.

"So where do you spend your free time when you're on campus? I haven't seen you before tonight," Brad asked.

"I'm usually at the commuter lounge or at the library between classes," I responded.

"Ah, so that's why we've never run into each other. I'm never at the library and I have no idea where the commuter lounge is," he chuckled. "Who do you hang out with? Maybe we have some mutual friends."

"I really haven't met too many people because I'm a commuter," I said. "It kind of sucks."

Brad put his arm around my shoulders and said, "Well, we'll just have to do something about that! What are you doing right now?"

"I was just going to jump in the car and head home to study."

"Well, I'm meeting up with some friends at the pub for dinner. Why don't you join us?"

"Sure, that'd be great. I'm starving and really don't feel like going home yet," I responded enthusiastically.

We were inseparable from the start. Although I was a commuter and he lived in the dorms, we could be seen together all over campus. Brad drew me into his social circle, and they quickly became my friends as well. It turned out that a number of them volunteered for campus ministry activities or sang with the choir, so I ran into them all the time. From that point on, I was on campus and in the dorms more that I was at home.

After a long day of classes or hours of studying, one could easily count five to ten people hanging out on the couches in the reception area of the campus ministry office. It was a gathering place for many of my new friends. Many of us developed strong friendships with the Jesuits and the rest of the staff, and our laughter and animated discussions could be easily heard down the halls of the dorm where the office was located. This was the kind of community that I longed for, and I finally felt like I had found a home at St. Robert's. I didn't miss the anxiety I had felt each time I entered the music building at Hartt. The competition and endless put-downs from other musicians kept me on constant guard. At

St. Robert's, I hardly felt any loss of music in my life because I was singing and playing guitar so much. I had no regrets about giving up my coveted spot in the music school.

More importantly, I had Brad. He was unlike any friend I had ever had before. I couldn't define it, but I felt closer to him than I did with any other guy in my life. We would talk incessantly about our hopes and dreams, and share our deepest feelings with each other, in a way my other male friends and I never did. I was comfortable being vulnerable around him. We were very physical around each other, always hugging or playfully wrestling. Sleeping over in Brad's room was a common occurrence.

Since Brad was an only child, his parents doted upon him. He was treated as the crown prince of his household, which gave him an attitude of self-assurance and fearlessness. He radiated personal power, and people were naturally drawn to him. Everyone just assumed that Brad would succeed at anything he put his mind to. For me, who had often struggled with self-confidence, Brad's bold attitude toward life was like a drug. I couldn't get enough.

Although our friendship was unique to my experience, I never dreamt that it would evolve into anything else. I honestly didn't know there was any other direction our relationship could go. I never considered that we might become romantically drawn to each other. It simply felt as if we belonged together, as if I had found the best friend I had ever had. I never questioned our friendship or physical contact. It just seemed natural.

CHAPTER 4

BISHOP DE SANTO
SPRING 2015

Bishop De Santo didn't use social media regularly, but certainly understood its necessity in reaching a wider audience. His office used it to disseminate the latest news, share information regarding educational events and, of course, promote the diocesan fundraising efforts. His own Facebook account was benign. He filled it with descriptions of the many events he sponsored and quotes from his homilies at Mass. It was also a great way to keep in touch with friends. His Facebook friends consisted of parishioners from each of his previous churches, as well as classmates from college and his seminary years.

He was used to getting friend requests from people he hadn't thought of or heard from in decades. On this day, however, he was shaken by a friend request that he had just received. It was an unwelcome intrusion into his present-day life. The bishop was all for connecting with people from his distant past, but there was no reason to invite painful memories back with them. Feeling a bit disconcerted, he deleted the friend request and posted a quote from his latest homily. He closed his laptop and got up from his desk. He needed some air.

He drove to St. Mary's by the Sea, a beautiful sea wall along Long Island Sound. There was a mile-long walkway there with beautiful mansions on one side and the water on the other. De Santo came here often to clear his head or to connect with God. Today, he needed to put his past in perspective.

Bishop De Santo's path had been meticulously planned years before. He always knew that he would enter the Catholic seminary after college and be ordained a priest. But there were times when the idea of celibacy threatened to derail his plans. His struggle to make sense of his past relationships and to move on from them was an arduous task.

He thought about the friend request he had just received. Just the day before, his friend Diane had texted him a photo of the same person, who she ran into while visiting a mutual friend. She captioned the photo, "You'll never guess who I ran into!" Why did she feel the need to send that? What was she implying? It unnerved him. He had no desire to relive that heartache, nor did he feel the need to reconcile with someone who had nearly destroyed him. No, his priesthood was the most important calling of his life: it had led him to his post as bishop. He resolved to keep his past safely tucked away. He needed to forget about the painful memory, which had invaded his peaceful day and disturbed his equanimity.

Bishop De Santo was happy and fulfilled. In his heart, he knew that he was on the correct path. He had felt the calling long before adulthood. In fact, when he was in elementary school, he used to say Mass every Sunday morning. His mother was a seamstress at a lingerie factory, and had sewn a set of priestly vestments for him from scraps of leftover fabric. The young priest loved that his cassock was ruby red, just like a Cardinal's garb. De Santo would line up each of his stuffed animals in an orderly fashion in front of his altar. From his mother's kitchen, he took a slice of white bread and cut it into the shape of a disk using a juice glass. To top it off, his grandfather poured a drop or two of wine into the goblet holding his ginger ale. Even back then, he knew the parts of the Mass, and after his homily he would bless the bread and wine and give communion to each of his congregation.

Though his four older siblings poked fun at him, his parents treasured his weekly ritual. Their Catholic faith was central to their family life. None of the children ever complained about getting up early every Sunday morning to go to Mass. They always sat in the same pew on the right side of the church, and De Santo would go with his mother to the side altar of Mary. Together they would light a candle for his deceased grandparents. He'd been drawn into the mystery and ritual of their faith for as long as he could remember. The Church was a second home to De Santo, and he had been fascinated by each mystery that the nuns taught him in school.

Certainly, the greatest influence on his faith was his

mother. As the youngest child, De Santo spent a great deal of time with her. She was a storyteller and would regale him with tales of her life growing up in Italy that highlighted her dedication to the Church. One of the most poignant stories she shared with him was about the period after her mother died. She was only 10 years old when she lost her mother and father, and was lovingly raised by her aunt, who accompanied her to Mass each day.

"Tesoro," De Santo's mother said to her son, calling him her treasure. "I knelt at the altar of the Blessed Virgin each day. I would say to her: You took my mother and my father, I have no one. Mary, you are the mother of God and now you must take my mother's place." Signora De Santo looked at her son and said, "And that is just what happened. Whenever I was in crisis, the Madonna helped guide me along the proper path." She reached out and placed her hand on his. "She will do that for you as well, figlio mio. All you need to do is ask. Your faith will always lead you."

His mother had instilled a strong sense of faith in him, and as he grew older, his dream to become a priest grew progressively stronger. However, De Santo never shared this dream with anyone, especially not his parents. This was between him and God. He had to follow each step without positive or negative pressure from his family.

He could always picture his dream vividly, though. Glowing candles adorning the altar of a Gothic cathedral. The pipes of a grand organ heralding the start of Mass, as he processed up the aisle in his vestments. The scent of incense mingling with the warmth of the wooden pews. Hues of scarlet red and cobalt blue glowing brightly, as rays of sunlight filtered through the stained-glass windows. The light created a jewel-toned prism upon the gleaming white altar cloth. He would genuflect before the altar and kiss it before intoning the opening rites of the Mass.

Though his friends and family could see that he was devout and passionate with regard to his involvement in church ministries, no one suspected his private desire to serve the Church as an ordained priest. Everyone simply assumed that he would marry and start a family.

During high school, De Santo basically grew up at his best friend's house, and was friends with each of his three siblings. As a result, it seemed completely natural when he and his buddy's older sister Catherine began to have romantic feelings for each other. She was a year older than De Santo, and he was smitten. They were both active in the church youth group, where talking about personal struggles and faith was an integral part of the weekly meetings. He and Catherine participated in many other activities like basketball, softball, or even Twister. They laughed easily together. She was refreshingly candid and didn't buy into the common mind games of adolescence.

One evening, they were standing by his car after the youth group meeting had ended. When they hugged goodbye, De Santo kissed her gently on the lips. He slowly pulled away to evaluate her reaction. She smiled at him, leaned in, and returned the kiss. Their feelings were mutual.

As boyfriend and girlfriend, their relationship seemed to change very little. They still laughed at the same things, hung out with her siblings, and went to youth group events. The only difference was their physical contact. Since both of them were devout Catholics, the idea of sex was out of the question. They didn't even need to talk about that. Without the pressure of sex, De Santo was much more relaxed with her when they would make out in the car or at home. He never felt pressure to go any further, and they often stopped before either of them got too aroused. However, he truly enjoyed the simple pleasure of holding her close. When she went away to college, De Santo grew lonely. Catherine was pulling away emotionally, and they found that maintaining a long-distance relationship was taking a toll on both of them.

Catherine broke up with him when she came home for Christmas vacation that year. He was devastated—he had never felt so comfortable with any other girl. He pined after her for months. But with the passage of time, he moved on and dated other girls. In many ways, he led a normal teenage life.

As beautiful and painful as his relationship with Catherine had been, he knew in his heart that it was only temporary. He planned to apply to the seminary after college and be ordained a priest, just like Uncle Pete, his father's brother. The family never called him Uncle Pete, however. It was always Father Pete. His mother loved to tell the story of Fr. Pete's first Mass.

"You were only three years old and you were mesmerized. You looked up at the choir and the pipe organ in the loft with your mouth wide open. You turned your head when the altar boys processed up the aisle holding the candles and the incense. You never took your eyes off of them."

"Yeah, Ma, I've heard this all before." he'd say with a smile.

"But the best part," she continued, undeterred, "was during the consecration. You finally recognized Fr. Pete as he lifted up the host. The altar boy rang the bells and you looked up. The church was silent, and then you yelled out, 'Why is Uncle Pete standing up there all alone?' Everybody turned and giggled, because it was the most sacred part of the Mass and we were supposed to remain silent. Other than your Uncle Pete, you were the star of the show!"

Bishop De Santo smiled. His mother still told that story whenever she met some of his priest friends. Looking back, he realized that he had been true to his plan. He secretly entered the seminary program during his junior year of college. The only person in his family who knew about this was his Uncle Pete, who was a pastor of a wealthy church in New York City. De Santo didn't tell his parents because he didn't want to feel any pressure throughout the process. They would be over the moon with joy at the news, and he just couldn't bear disappointing them should anything cause him to change course. Of course, he told none of his friends. He continued to carry on like an average college student.

He never imagined that his plan to enter the seminary would take a unique and exciting turn. In the spring of his senior year, the vocation director of the archdiocese called him in for a meeting to discuss his future.

"Good afternoon, Mr. De Santo. How is your final semester in college going?" the director asked in his booming baritone voice.

"It's been great, Monsignor Ryan. I really love it there," De Santo replied enthusiastically.

"Well, don't like it too much. We wouldn't want the Jesuits to get their hands on you!" the Monsignor said jokingly. "We have big plans for you."

"No worries, Monsignor. My uncle would kill me if

I became a Jesuit. He has visions of us serving at the same church someday."

"Well, who knows? That is certainly not out of the realm of possibility. For now, however, we must turn our attention to your immediate future. It is time to decide where you will be studying theology. Have you given that much thought?"

"I know that you send men off to Washington, D.C. or Baltimore—and isn't there a seminary in Yonkers?" De Santo asked. "I guess I'd prefer Washington, D.C. But I am happy to go wherever you send me, Monsignor," he added earnestly.

"Yes, we do send men to each of those places. They are all reputable seminaries." He paused for a moment and then continued. "Are you aware that every so often, we send a select few to Rome, to the North American College?"

De Santo stared at Monsignor Ryan with wide eyes. He was speechless.

"Did you hear me, Mr. De Santo?"

"Yes, yes of course. What does that mean for me?" he finally replied.

"Let me be frank with you. You have excellent grades, you have studied the Italian language for eight years, and you show great leadership qualities. The Cardinal believes that you are a perfect candidate for the North American College. What do you think about that?"

"Wow! Monsignor, I would love to study in Rome. I have lots of family in Italy. It would be a dream come true. I don't know what to say. Thank you for considering me for this."

"To be clear, this is quite an honor. You would have

to work hard to live up to the Cardinal's expectations, Mr. De Santo. Are you willing to do that?" the Monsignor said sternly.

"I won't disappoint you or Cardinal McGuire. I promise."

"Then it's settled. You will get the paperwork within the next few weeks."

"What steps do I have take to apply?"

"Mr. De Santo, you don't need to apply. You've been appointed."

De Santo was silent as he let the gravity of the Monsignor's words sink in. Although he didn't fully grasp the enormity of the appointment, he understood that it was a significant honor. Monsignor Ryan continued to speak, but De Santo barely heard a word.

"You'll have to get baptismal records and a marriage certificate from your parents, as well as your sacramental records. If you have any questions, please feel free to make an appointment with me. Good luck on your finals. We will be in touch very soon."

De Santo's head was reeling. Seminary in Rome! It didn't get any better than that. But how was he going to get his parents' marriage certificate without them knowing? They had been married in Italy. Of course, he could simply ask them, but he wasn't ready to tell them yet that he had decided to become a priest. Before he could tell anybody, he needed to wrap his head around this new development. He decided to talk with Fr. Pete, who would be so happy with his news. De Santo called him as soon as he got to his dorm.

"Hi Fr. Pete, how are you? I'm sorry that I haven't called in a couple of weeks. It got so busy."

"Carissimo! You just brightened my otherwise difficult day. No worries. It's good to hear your voice."

"I wanted to fill you in on the latest developments. I just got out of a meeting with Msgr. Ryan," De Santo said with excitement.

"Yes, the Monsignor told me that he would be meeting with you. Tell me, what's going on," Fr. Pete responded.

"I know it's last minute, Fr. Pete, but can we get together for dinner tonight? I have so many questions."

"Of course, caro. Can you get to Vecchia Roma by 7:00 p.m.?"

"I love that place! Yes, see you soon. Ciao, Zio."

Vecchia Roma was their usual meeting spot. De Santo recalled many evenings spent together as Fr. Pete counseled him through his many adolescent traumas. Nothing seemed insurmountable when discussed over an authentic Italian meal with his favorite uncle; Fr. Pete was one of his most significant mentors. That evening De Santo launched into his story before the waiter took their orders.

"You're never going to believe this, but they want me to go to Rome for seminary."

"Bravo! Monsignor Ryan told me that he was considering you for the North American College. Congratulations!"

"Thanks, or should I say—grazie."

"Auguri, caro nipote." Fr. Pete said, giving his nephew his best wishes.

"Grazie, Zio! I only have one problem. I'm not ready to tell Mom and Dad, and Msgr. Ryan told me that I need their marriage certificate. How do I get that without them knowing?"

"Do you know the name of the church where they got married?" Fr. Pete asked.

"Yes, they brought me there on my first trip to Italy after high school graduation. It's a tiny parish in Venice."

"Perfect. You speak and write Italian, so all you have to do is write the church a letter explaining why you need the certificate. I am sure they will be happy to send it to you."

"I guess it's not as complicated as I had made it out to be. See, this is why I need you, Fr. Pete."

"Is that all you need me for, my dear nephew?" he chuckled. "Listen, you're going to be a priest soon. Enough with this Father Pete business—call me Pete, or Uncle Pete, but let's dispense with 'Father.'"

"Sorry, it's just a matter of habit. It may take some time."

As the evening wore on, De Santo began to feel his dream of priesthood was within his grasp. Fr. Pete, who had been his personal hero since he was a young boy, had indeed become a colleague after his ordination to priesthood. But he never ceased being his mentor.

CHAPTER 5

BISHOP DE SANTO
SPRING 2015

The bishop was relatively new at his job. Although he had been a Catholic priest for 30 years, he had only been ordained a bishop a year earlier. As a priest, he loved the pastoral work at each of his church assignments. He cherished being there to support people in their greatest need, to help people through struggles of faith or the loss of a loved one. The joy-filled occasions, such as weddings and baptisms, allowed him to be present at some of the most significant moments in his parishioners' lives.

Bishop De Santo was proud of his accomplishments within the church and was secure in who he was and his life choices, even though during his early years as a priest, he was passed over when prestigious assignments opened up.

Back then, he had never worked at wealthy or prominent churches—never those that were noticed by the archdiocese. Although he had studied in Rome during his seminary years, De Santo was not ambitious. But most of his colleagues assumed that he would climb the hierarchical ladder with ease.

As a seminarian, studying in Rome was a great adventure. With his Italian heritage and facility with the language, he felt quite at home. The culture and the food brought him comfort, and he made many new discoveries when out exploring the ancient cobblestone streets. Artifacts of ancient history were literally around every corner, and the beauty and grandeur of the many churches nourished his love of art and architecture. The slower pace of life seemed natural in contrast to the ever-hectic rush of the New York area.

He loved living in Rome, but he was not prepared for the overt clericalism within the seminary and in the city itself. All he ever wanted was to be a simple parish priest, to teach and work with young people. This was in striking contrast to the clerical environment in the shadow of the Vatican. It was a given that Rome was the training ground for the future leaders of the Church. The Roman seminarians were supposedly the chosen ones, and they were openly told as much.

De Santo scoffed at his classmates who joked about their futures as bishops and cardinals, and watched with a cynical eye as they vied for favor with each bishop who visited the seminary. They gossiped and speculated about who was being considered for cardinal and thus get to elect the next pope. Often, he would get up from the table and exit the conversation soon after it started. While gossiping about church politics was a favorite pastime for many of the seminarians in Rome, it held no interest for him. In fact, he found it aggravating. It had nothing to do with why he wanted to become a priest. He couldn't care less about Church politics or which powerful dignitary was visiting the North American College at any given moment. On those occasions, he usually planned to be out at a local trattoria, feasting on his new favorite pasta dish.

His volunteer work allowed him to see beyond the blatant clerical attitude that surrounded him. While in Rome, each seminarian was asked to work at a local church in order to get pastoral experience. De Santo volunteered at a church that was a five-minute walk from the seminary. There, he helped lead the youth group by organizing activities, youth Masses, and service work within the city of Rome. He was drawn into the community and immediately felt like he was part of the family. He knew that this was what he was meant to do. During his ordained ministry, De Santo was not considered a company man, so his prospects of advancing within the Church hierarchy were slim. Nonetheless, he would be quite fulfilled as a parish priest and enjoyed spending time with the families he'd come to love.

When he was ordained a bishop, he left New York for Connecticut. Fairfield County was just a stone's throw from Manhattan, but it was a completely different world. Being along the coast of Connecticut, De Santo felt more connected to nature, and to God.

As De Santo walked along the Long Island Sound, he mused over the fact that he was actually a bishop. How could that possibly have happened?

He thought back to when he was first made a pastor. He was sure that politics came into play when his appointment was made. He had no illusions that he would be selected as pastor for a wealthy church in the city. Those posts were reserved for priests who were high on the hierarchical ladder—those who had always played the game right, or didn't challenge the status quo. More importantly, those posts were reserved for men who championed the Church's stance on one or more of the hot button issues of the day–contraception, abortion, or gay marriage. That was not his style, nor did he agree with the Church's hardline approach to those issues.

Due to conflicts with his superiors a few years after his ordination, De Santo was certainly not one of the favored ones, and he believed that he was set on a course towards ecclesiastical mediocrity. But it hadn't always been that way. There was a brief moment in the sun for Bishop De Santo during his first assignment.

His return to New York after his ordination was delayed by several years while he completed his doctorate in Sacred Theology. He was thrilled and surprised when he heard the news that he was assigned to St. Patrick's Cathedral. Roman seminarians were often given plum assignments on their return to their home diocese. Fr. De Santo got along well with the Cardinal and was tasked with serving as his master of ceremonies during all major liturgical events. De Santo loved the pageantry of the Church and was more than happy to serve in such a visible role. If nothing else, he knew how to put on a good show. His first few years flew by, and there was a great deal of chatter regarding the positive trajectory of his career. He took all of this in stride, always putting his mind to the next event. During the work week, he found himself saying Mass and hearing confessions at the neighboring Catholic high school. He loved working with teenagers and hoped that he'd be able to teach full-time someday.

As the years passed, he began spending more time at the high school and had gotten permission to direct the choir. Fr. De Santo couldn't contain his excitement as he recounted his rehearsals and performances at the dinner table. The Cardinal took note and remarked, "I have rarely seen you this animated, Fr. De Santo. Teaching really seems to suit you. Can you picture yourself teaching full-time?"

"I love it, Your Eminence!" De Santo replied, his eyes shining. "Each day brings a new adventure. During each rehearsal, I feel as if I am painting a landscape with their voices. Each measure of the music is like a brushstroke. The performance is like the exposition of a masterpiece that we created together."

"Well, that was certainly a colorful way to describe a choir rehearsal," the Cardinal teased. "Perhaps we should chat about the possibility of teaching full-time."

"I would love that, Your Eminence, but I wouldn't want to let you down. I really enjoy serving as your MC. That would be difficult to give up."

"Don't worry about that, Fr. De Santo. It's important that we place our priests where they can have the greatest impact, and our young people certainly need to be inspired. It seems that you have that gift. I will have a talk with Monsignor Devlin at St. Theresa High School. It will all depend upon their needs, of course—but in the meantime, pray on it, and we will just let it evolve naturally," the

Cardinal said.

"Thank you, Your Eminence. I will," Fr. De Santo replied.

+++

Monsignor Devlin heard from Cardinal McGuire the very next day. Devlin was always on guard when he received a call from the Cardinal. It usually meant that there was a complaint from a parent or a financial problem. The Monsignor took his role as Headmaster quite seriously and wore it like a badge of honor. He despised having anyone interfere with the running of his school, and made it clear to the faculty that his authority was never to be challenged. They lived in fear of his temper and made sure to follow his directives to the letter.

"Good morning, Monsignor," the Cardinal began. "How goes the shaping of our young minds today? Have you discovered the future president—or better yet, the future pope?"

"Good morning, Cardinal McGuire. What a surprise to hear from you," Devlin said guardedly. "As of yet, I am still searching for the next captain of the baseball team. Up to this moment, I am not convinced I have met a future pope at St. Theresa's!"

They both chuckled awkwardly.

"To what do I owe this honor, Cardinal? What's on your mind?"

"Right to the point, Monsignor. That's what I like about you, Devlin—you don't suffer small talk, do you?"

"I never have," he responded.

"How is Fr. De Santo doing at St. Theresa's? Are you

happy with him?" the Cardinal asked.

"I'm sure he's fine. To be candid, I don't pay much attention to the music and arts programs. They certainly won't get our students into college, will they? But with regard to Fr. De Santo, the students seem to like him. Why do you ask?"

"I believe it's time for him to teach full-time. His talents are being wasted at the Cathedral. I believe that he would be an asset to your faculty."

"I see." Monsignor Devlin hated when the Cardinal interfered with the hiring of his staff, even if it turned out to be a good fit. Devlin felt that it was a challenge to his authority and autonomy, both of which he guarded fiercely. He continued with caution. "Well, Your Eminence, I am pretty certain that we don't have the budget for a full-time music teacher for the next academic year. I think it's best to have Fr. De Santo remain as a part-time teacher. I have always believed that it is important for these young priests to have experience in parish ministry."

How bold of him to counsel me on the needs of a young priest, McGuire thought. He needs to show a little more respect and learn his place.

"I see, Monsignor," the Cardinal replied. "You do realize that Fr. De Santo has a doctorate in Sacred Theology from the Pontifical Gregorian University in Rome. I'm sure that you will be able to put together a full-time position that combines his many skills and talents. I'd like him to receive an offer letter before I post the clergy assignments for the archdiocese in June."

There was a pregnant pause during which Cardinal McGuire could hear Msgr. Devlin take a deep breath. His message had come across loud and clear.

"Of course, Your Eminence. Is there anything else I could do for you today?" he replied stiffly.

"Thank you for asking, Monsignor. No, I believe we are done here. You have a good day, now."

When Devlin hung up the phone, he was fuming. How dare the Cardinal foist a new priest or teacher on him after he expressly told him that he had no opening? Obedience was one thing, but Devlin felt that he had been bullied into hiring De Santo. In addition, the Monsignor despised the special treatment that the Roman priests received. Many of them lorded it over the locally educated priests. What's wrong with the seminary at Dunwoodie in Yonkers? he thought. It was good enough for me. At least there, we know what's being taught. It made his blood boil just to think about it. I'm sure he's a fine young priest, but I'll be damned if I'm going to make it easy on him, he thought. There was more than one way to assert his authority.

CHAPTER 6

FATHER DE SANTO
AUTUMN 1991

The following September, Fr. De Santo began teaching theology at St. Theresa High School and continued to direct the choir. He couldn't have been happier with his new job. Within the theology department, he taught a junior class called, "Ethics and Family Life" that was right up his alley. The course covered interpersonal relationships, dating, marriage, and sexuality. He found that he was adept in facilitating animated discussions with his classes, and he did away with long, boring lectures and rote memorization of Church teachings. His students were actively engaged in discussions and looked forward to his classes. The faculty was friendly and welcoming, and he began to form significant friendships with a few of them. He could see himself teaching there for many years to come.

But as the years passed, the Church became more and more conservative under Pope John Paul II, he felt that his dedication to the poor and work with young people was valued less and less. It was strange–although much of his style was grounded in the Gospels, the institutional church switched focus, giving him a growing sense of disconnect. The sermons he heard at Mass, as well as the directives issued from the Cardinal, spoke primarily of the evils of abortion, premarital sex, and homosexuality. It seemed that these topics were the only focus for the Church, and they were growing into obsession. One couldn't escape the constant condemnation of certain expressions of sexuality, and the elevation of sexual morality above all other teachings.

This was a significant departure from the heart of Fr. De Santo's faith and his own personal journey. Even though he had taken a vow of celibacy, preaching against homosexuality was disturbing to him. He preached about compassion and kindness, challenging both his parishioners and students to work toward social justice and equity. As the Church was becoming increasingly rule-oriented, it seemed evident that his pastoral style was valued less and less. Some even questioned his orthodoxy, saying that he was not in line with the Pope. Although that was ridiculous, Fr. De Santo began to watch his back among the newly emboldened conservative Catholics—not only because of his pastoral approach, but also because he himself was gay. Only his closest friends knew about his sexual orientation, but Church rumors could ruin his reputation.

The hardline atmosphere spread into the Catholic school system. Religion curricula were being revamped to include more Church history, with a heavy emphasis on doctrine. Seminar courses were being reexamined, and free-flowing discussions that departed from official Church teaching were not allowed.

Despite these unsettling changes, Fr. De Santo continued to teach as he always had. He believed that open discussions on controversial topics helped his students to grapple with their own understanding of right and wrong. Ultimately, each individual had to make his or her own ethical choices. He hoped that his approach would at least encourage them to be more reflective about their decisions.

However, his more pastoral approach to sexuality got him in trouble with the school administration. In their eyes, abstinence was the only acceptable approach to sex outside of marriage. When he was at last called into Monsignor Devlin's office to discuss his teaching methods, De Santo couldn't help but defend his approach. After all, he was an ordained priest who was educated in Rome. That should hold some sway, he thought. But he had no idea how much contempt Devlin held towards Roman-educated priests.

The Monsignor was in a surly mood and glared at him. "Father," he said, "I understand that you continue to have class discussions that allow students to argue with the official Church teaching on matters of sexuality. You understand that the diocese has given specific guidelines regarding our religion curriculum. Why haven't you complied?"

De Santo drew a deep breath before beginning. "Monsignor, how can we in good conscience eliminate any discussion of the use of condoms when teenagers are contracting HIV at an alarming rate? Of course, the best option is to abstain from sex, but these are teenagers. They are having sex no matter how much we teach about waiting for marriage. How can we reconcile their health and safety with this approach? Shouldn't we give them all the information they need to make responsible decisions?" The Monsignor seemed unmoved, but De Santo pressed on. "Ultimately, their moral decisions are a matter of conscience. I strive to give them the tools to discern what is right for them, within the guidelines of the Church."

"Look, Fr. De Santo," Msgr. Devlin began. It was never a good sign when the monsignor used his proper title and last name. De Santo could tell the man was not happy with him, and began to feel uneasy as Devlin continued. "You don't seem to understand that you are the adult here. These children need you to tell them what is right and wrong."

De Santo believed that there was a rational argument to be made in his defense. Maybe he could help Devlin understand where he was coming from. "But Monsignor, I do give them official Church teaching in all of these areas," he said. "They have a clear understanding of what the Church sees as right or wrong. However, in allowing them to discuss opposing opinions, I can help them to understand the reasoning behind these teachings. A healthy dialectic will help them to make good decisions if and when they find themselves in a morally compromising situation. Believe me Monsignor, I do not teach anything that is against Church law," Fr. De Santo added, in an attempt to defend himself.

"Fr. De Santo, you can be quite tiresome at times," the Monsignor snapped. "You don't seem to understand that this is not up for discussion; it is a matter of obedience. The Cardinal has been very clear in his directives. You will teach abstinence only. The rest is God's will. You may go."

Fr. De Santo was aghast. For a moment, he sat in silence as Devlin stared him down. Finally, he rose from his chair and turned to leave, his thoughts racing. *I've been dismissed! He won't even consider having a rational discussion about the pastoral and educational rationale behind my approach. This is not the Church I was raised in. It has become a Church of rules and regulations, not one of mercy and love.*

He was so angry as he walked out of the office that he neglected to say a proper goodbye to the Headmaster or his assistant. The staff couldn't miss his tight expression, though. As he made his way to his classroom, his usual smiling and open face was shrouded with anger and disappointment. When the students saw him, they gave him a wide berth and exchanged questioning looks. "What's up with De Santo?" one asked her friend in a whisper. "I've never seen that look on his face!"

Once he reached his empty classroom, he closed the door behind him and rested his head in his hands. Although he knew in his heart that he was in the right, De Santo felt an overwhelming sense of shame. He had been treated like a dog that had made a mess and was whacked on the snout with a newspaper. It wouldn't have been a stretch to hear Devlin say, "Bad boy!"

De Santo believed in the need for order and rules, but not as an end unto themselves. He believed that Church teachings existed to help guide and instruct, not to scold and punish. He was so disappointed, both in his Church and his school. *What am I to do now?* He thought.

Toward the end of the school year, Fr. De Santo asked to be transferred to a parish. Parish ministry would include providing spiritual direction, which would allow him to counsel people in discerning their own moral path. Plus, there was much less scrutiny there. Unless he preached with open disdain for Church teaching, he would be ok. He would be able to effect change without compromising his integrity. While his heart ached at the thought of leaving his beloved students, he knew that he had to extricate himself from this toxic environment. At least in a parish, I'll be able to maintain my dignity and advise people to do what is truly right for themselves, he reasoned.

Monsignor Devlin accepted his resignation with a smug look of victory on his face, and De Santo was not surprised when his transfer request was immediately granted. Even the Cardinal, with whom he had a friendly relationship, was cool to him. De Santo was certain that Msgr. Devlin gave the Cardinal an earful regarding the heretical goings-on in his classroom. When his assignment was posted, Fr. De Santo found himself assigned to St. Bernard, a poor suburban church in White Plains, far from the more favored parishes within the archdiocese. He had obviously ruffled some powerful feathers. Although he felt the sting of his loss of status, he hoped that he would find a home in his new parish and get back to the work that originally drew him to his priesthood.

The pastor at St. Bernard Church was a simple man of few words. They got along well enough and, best of all, the pastor had a laissez faire attitude toward Fr. De Santo, letting him do as he pleased as long as there was no controversy. This independence was just what he needed after being under Msgr. Devlin's thumb at the high school. He soon found himself at home once again.

The years of parish work that followed were very fulfilling, far from Church politics and hierarchical scrutiny. However, De Santo understood that under the reign of Pope John Paul II, he was a persona non grata in the halls of Church power. So much for the Roman seminarian becoming a prince of the Church, he thought. Some of the in-crowd considered him to be on the edge of heresy and excluded him from important social gatherings. Fr. De Santo just kept his head down and threw himself into his work.

He would become heavily invested in community outreach, care for the elderly, and leading the parish youth group. He became a true advocate for social justice and marginalized communities, and although that wouldn't bring him political favor, no one could accuse him of acting in a manner that was contrary to Church teaching.

This state of affairs continued under the papacy of Benedict XVI. However, when Pope Francis was elected in 2013, it was like a breath of fresh air flowed through the dusty halls of the Church. The doctrinaire approach to Church teaching was discouraged in favor of a more pastoral approach to ministry. Pope Francis communicated that the Church was no longer a place of judgment and exclusion; everyone was welcome. Even so, the Cardinal in New York was still very conservative on social issues. Because of that, an older and more seasoned Fr. De Santo was circumspect, and continued to act with an abundance of discretion.

In many ways, De Santo felt vindicated. This was the Church that drew him to ministry so many years before. He held his head higher and acted with more confidence. He continued to work with the poor and stand up for those in his community that were marginalized. Although there was still no change in Church teaching on homosexuality, he felt that he was now able to begin active outreach to gay and lesbian Catholics who struggled with the Church. Up until now, he was only able to do individual counseling for people grappling with these teachings.

Nonetheless, Fr. De Santo did not feel safe coming out as a gay priest. There were still too many risks from the Church hierarchy. As for the people in the pews, many wrongfully associated gay priests with pedophilia. So De Santo continued his outreach ministries, but tried to stay as discreet as possible.

For most priests of his age, becoming a pastor was pretty much a given. Considering the lack of men entering the seminary, there simply weren't enough priests to staff the many parishes in the diocese. Most became pastors by the time they turned 40. When De Santo was made pastor at the age of 41, he assumed that he had risen as high as he could within the ranks of the Catholic Church, especially given his fall from grace.

After many happy years at St. Bernard, Fr. De Santo was made pastor of St. James Church in White Plains. It was another struggling parish with a very diverse congregation. It was exactly the kind of community in which he felt most comfortable. Although he spoke Spanish with an Italian accent, the parishioners loved him. He was thrilled to have his own church to lead and, best of all he had no one looking over his shoulder. As pastor, he was responsible for the budget and could allocate funds to his most valued the projects. As a result, he was able to establish official outreach programs and support groups. During the era of John Paul and Benedict, Fr. De Santo had sought to fly under the radar. With Pope

Francis now leading the Church, he felt emboldened to pursue his passion to minister to communities on the margin.

CHAPTER 7

LUCA
AUTUMN 1979

The retreat center was on the New Jersey shoreline, with an extensive beach facing the Atlantic Ocean. I loved retreats. Time away from my classes in an atmosphere of quiet reflection and loving interaction with friends centered me. I've always been a worrier, and retreats took me away from my battles with anxiety and self-doubt.

I waited for the bus in excited anticipation. This was going to be my first retreat since high school, and Brad was going too. I was grateful to have found such a good friend so quickly. Transferring to a new school and establishing new relationships from scratch had been difficult. I rarely saw John on campus and I hated being alone. I craved a circle of friends to hang out with. Brad was the answer to my prayers.

Each time I looked into Brad's eyes, I felt something within my chest swell, growing warm and tingling. If our arms or legs touched when we stood or sat beside each other, it was as if his warmth pulsed throughout my body. Whenever that occurred, he would lean into me and I responded in kind. I welcomed the feeling of his warm skin against mine. If our cheeks happened to touch, it was electric.

On retreats, everyone was incredibly affectionate and physically demonstrative, much more so than usual. Throughout the weekend, both students and faculty were effusive as they expressed their feelings and care for one another. This provided numerous opportunities for Brad and me to get even closer, and our embraces lingered longer than most.

I was never one to look for deeper meaning in the moment. I followed my instincts and accepted what I felt as natural and good. Although I realized that I was physically attracted to Brad, I didn't consider the fact that I might be gay. In 1979, the gay men I saw on the news and the character actors I saw on TV were effeminate or dressed like women. While I believed that everyone had the right to simply be himself or herself, these people bore no resemblance to me or my desires.

I also knew there were risks for people like that. I clearly remember Anita Bryant, the former Miss America, leading a campaign against these vile deviants whom she believed threatened traditional family life. Her hateful words were deeply ingrained in my psyche. According to Bryant, gay men were out to recruit young children to molest them. These words, and the unfortunate effeminate boys at my school who were interminably tortured by bullies, were the only frame of reference I had for being gay. New York City was only an hour train ride away, but it might as well have been across the country. On the rare occasions when I traveled into the city, I found it overwhelming and somewhat frightening. I was quite sheltered from the wider world around me.

With Brad, I never questioned what my feelings could mean or what significance they might have on my life. I simply followed my heart, and we continued to be very affectionate. We hugged a lot, and whenever we would sit near to one another, our legs and arms touched. I was drawn to him; I needed to be as physically close to him as possible. I had never had such a physical relationship with any of my other male or female friends. And although that should have raised some questions for me, I didn't think twice about it. I remained in deep denial regarding the implications of our intimacy. It was simply the way we were when we were in each other's company. He was my best friend and when we were together, nothing else mattered. We were completely focused on each other.

My friend Irene later revealed to me that she often felt left out, or uncomfortable when she was alone with us. She said that there seemed to be an invisible wall that kept everyone else out. Of course, neither of us was aware of anyone else but ourselves. We were totally infatuated.

As the events and activities of the retreat began to unfold, Brad and I found plenty of free time to relax and bond with our classmates. As was my custom, I pulled out my guitar and began to play. I sat on the floor, and soon a crew gathered around me and began to sing. Nerds that we all were, we sang through the entire repertoire of our folk hymnal. We knew all the words by heart, and those of us in the folk group sang in harmony with sensitive dynamics. Although I was lost in the beauty of the music, I was keenly aware of Brad's knees behind me. He was seated on a chair and I leaned my back into him. Though I couldn't see him, I knew he was enjoying this.

When it was time for the next activity, I began to pack up my guitar as everyone scattered. Brad hung back to speak to me.

"Luca, that was so much fun. All you had to do was take out your guitar and everyone just came over. You were like a magnet. I wish I could play guitar," he added wistfully.

"I can teach you, Brad. It's not that hard. We have some free time after dinner. Do you want to give it a try?" I offered.

"That would be awesome! I've never played an instrument before. This is going to be so cool," Brad responded excitedly.

"I have to warn you, Brad—this is a steel string guitar. When you first start to play, it can be a little painful on your fingers. After you develop calluses, it doesn't hurt at all," I said. "It actually feels kind of good."

"I am at your mercy, Luca. If you cause me pain, I'll probably enjoy it!" Brad said. He winked at me and nudged my shoulder. "In any case, I know you'll take good care of me." I wasn't quite sure how to react to his overt flirting. It was the first time I realized that our attraction to each other could be more than friendship. I could feel my cheeks flush red, so I smiled and looked away. I didn't know what to think as my repressed desires began to rise to the surface.

Later that evening we had our first guitar lesson.

Brad had trouble holding down the strings hard enough to form chords. This was normal for a new learner, but Brad was very impatient with himself. The sound he produced was anything but pretty, and that made him even more agitated. As the lesson went on and his fingers became sore, the music sounded even worse.

"Damn it, Luca! I'm never going to get this. How do you make it look so easy?" he blurted out in frustration.

"Take it easy, Brad. It just takes time and patience."

"OK, yeah, you're right." He drew a deep breath and composed himself. "I can get this. Show me that chord again," he said with determination.

"Your pointer finger goes on the second fret on the third string, middle finger on the third fret, then your ring finger on the second fret. The bottom three strings, like this," I said, demonstrating.

"It sounds so good when you play it. This is way harder than I thought it would be," he admitted.

"Don't sweat it, Brad. Each time you pick the guitar up, it will get easier. Your fingers will know where to go on their own, and when your calluses build, your fingertips won't turn blue."

"Let's keep trying. I know I can get that D chord." He made a final attempt before abruptly pulling his fingers off the neck of the guitar, as if he'd been stung by a bee. It looked like a blister was beginning to form on his ring finger. "Ouch, that really hurts!"

"I think it's time to stop now, Brad. The good news is that your blister will turn into a callus pretty quickly and then the pain will go away completely."

"Man, I suck! I don't know if I want to keep at this,"

he groaned.

"Hey, don't give up so easily, Brad. This is the first time you've ever touched a guitar. Give yourself some time," I said encouragingly.

"True, but I hate not being good at something. It's embarrassing."

"Don't worry. No one else is watching you but me, and I love teaching you," I said.

"Luca, you are so damn patient. Thank you, buddy," he responded, giving me a big hug.

"Anything for you, Brad," I said. Then I looked around the darkened room. We were completely alone. "Where is everyone?"

"I think everyone went to bed. We may be the only ones up." Brad's eyes lit up. "Let's go take a walk on the beach before we turn in. It's beautiful out there."

Although there was a hint of a chill in the air, the Indian summer sun had warmed the beach throughout the day, and the sand continued to radiate that heat. We sunk our feet into it and felt the warm grains of sand between our toes. During the day, Brad and I found ourselves with solitary moments to stroll along the shore, sharing our dreams and aspirations. But we had never gone out at night. It was strikingly beautiful, with the din of the crashing waves and thousands of stars twinkling above. Although we didn't hold hands, we walked closely enough together that my fingers grazed his.

After our long walk on the moonlit shore, he and I sat on the beach animatedly chatting, pausing every now and again to look out at the ocean. Neither of us was tired. It had been hours since the others had gone off to bed, but we could not tear ourselves away from each other. There was so much to say, so much more to share about our history and our dreams of the future.

As the night wore on and turned into early hours of morning, I began to feel the chilly air and shivered. Brad suggested that we throw a blanket around us to ward off the cold. He ran inside and grabbed one to sit on and one to wrap around us. Cozy and warm underneath the blanket, we continued to talk about anything that came to mind. Our bodies were almost intertwined, but neither of us acknowledged the intimacy. At one point, I yawned and looked at my watch in shock.

"Oh my God! It's 4 a.m. I can't believe that we've been huddled out here for three hours."

"Well there's no sense in going to bed now," Brad replied. "Why not wait for the sun to come up? The sunrise on the water should be beautiful."

I turned to him and said, "You know, I've never been awake for sunrise."

"Me neither! OK, then let our very first sunrise be together," he said, smiling back at me.

We pulled the blanket around us a bit more tightly. I looked at him and said, "I can't believe that we've only known each other for less than two months."

"I know! I feel like we've always been friends. I love you, Luca!"

"I love you too, Brad!"

No other boy had said that to me so frankly, and in return, those three words flowed easily from my mouth. There was not a hint of hesitation. My whole body was flush with warmth. Looking into each other's eyes, we embraced each other tightly, as had become our custom. I could feel the warmth of his chest and neck. But somehow, this time was different. His hands gently caressed my back and it felt so good. One of my hands held his head against mine and my fingers were laced through his thick blond hair. That familiar warmth within my chest grew in strength, and I could feel myself becoming aroused.

This had never happened to me before. I was startled by its intensity, but I simply let it happen. Stirring within me were feelings that I had never imagined or knew existed. Strangely, they didn't scare me or raise any red flags. My body pulsed with desire and I felt my heart rate quicken. Each touch was cautious yet deliberate, as if we were waiting for permission. It seemed that time had stood still and we were counting each movement with steady anticipation. Our cheeks brushed against each other and I could feel the stubble of his unshaven face tickle mine. I breathed deeply and took in his smell: masculine and inviting.

Rather than move away, our faces moved closer to each other. He kissed my cheek softly. When I kissed his in return, I let my lips linger against his face. Slowly, our heads turned inward toward each other until we were face to face, our lips barely apart. Our eyes met. His seemed to grow wider just before they closed and we kissed for the first time.

His lips were unlike any I had kissed before; they were softer, fuller, and masculine in a way I just couldn't describe. There was no urgency as we kissed with full lips and responded to each tender caress. When his lips parted and I tasted the warm silkiness of his tongue against mine, I was transported beyond any of my previous experiences. First soft and tentative, our kisses became heated and passionate.

Meanwhile, our hands explored and caressed each other with yearning and passion. I found myself in completely unfamiliar territory, and let myself give in to the moment. My hands stroked his arms and explored his chest with wonder. It was the first time I had ever touched another man in such a way and it felt as natural as could be.

When we finally broke for air, we gazed into one another's eyes.

"I've never done this before," I said shyly.

"Me neither. Are you okay?" he asked.

"Yeah, it's just… I don't know."

"I get it. But, Luca, it feels right, you know, because you are so special to me."

"Yeah, I feel the same way," I said softly, leaning in until our lips touched again. I was hungry for more.

What is happening to me? I had never longed for anyone's touch this way. My skin tingled beneath his fingers as I felt the blood rising up from my chest to my neck and face. When my cheek touched his, I pressed closer into him. I couldn't get enough contact. There was an unexplainable euphoria that consumed my entire being. I felt fully alive for the first time.

We lay back on the blanket and embraced each other tightly. His tongue found my ear and explored it with tender kisses. I was in ecstasy and thrust my entire length against him. My jeans felt tight and I was very aware that we were both fully aroused. It was electric. We writhed and kissed without fear of reprisal. Neither of us wanted it to end.

"Hey handsome," Brad said to me eventually. "We should sit up. The sun is about to come up."

"Oh yeah," I acknowledged. The beach and rolling

waves came into focus as the sky lightened; the sunrise was just moments away. "Wasn't that why we stayed out all night?" I asked.

"Funny, you're a funny guy," he said as he playfully jostled me.

"I try," I said as I pecked him on the cheek.

Our heads touched as we gazed out over the water at the amber glow in the sky. Brad and I turned to each other once again and kissed lovingly. Having given each other permission, our hands explored each other without reproach. There was no fear of rejection. We just gave into our mutual attraction and desire. The physical contact that I had experienced with girlfriends was nothing compared to this. It felt as if I had come home.

The pink and orange sky morphed to bright blue as the sun stretched its rays over the water. As the colors of the sunrise lightened, I turned to Brad.

"We should probably go back to our rooms before the others wake up. I'm not sure they would understand why we stayed up all night."

"You're right. I could use some sleep before we start the day."

"Yeah, I'm exhausted too."

"Hey, Luca. Thank you. It was incredible to spend the night with you."

We kissed once more and then gathered the blankets to head indoors. When we reached the dormitory, we embraced and kissed a bit longer before we returned to our rooms. I hoped to get an hour or two of sleep before the activities of the day began.

Before I nodded off, I lay on my bed, staring out the

window as the sun bathed the beach with its brilliant light. My thoughts were swimming with excitement and wonder. What just happened to me? Can it be true that another guy could feel this same desire for me? Brad filled every space in my heart and mind. When I closed my eyes, all I could see was his face before me. I could feel his full lips touching mine, while his body pressed against me. Images of us together on the beach were like a warm embrace as I drifted off to sleep.

+++

All too soon, the clanging of bells sounded throughout the hall. With zombie-like movements, I made my way to the showers. Once dressed, all I could think about was coffee. Without it I was useless. I sat at the dining room table, looking out over the shoreline and savoring my first sip. As the caffeine pulsed through my veins, images of Brad and me kissing on the beach flashed in my mind once again, and I couldn't help but smile. Slowly, the dining hall filled with other groggy college students who went straight for the coffee—all but Brad. He burst into the room with exuberance.

"Good morning everyone! What a beautiful day!" he exclaimed. He came to my table and sat right next to me, putting his arm around my shoulders. "Good morning, wonderful. How's my best buddy this morning? Did you sleep well?" he asked with a wink. We both exploded with laughter.

We were giddy teenagers all through breakfast. My dear friend Irene noticed our silliness and knew something was up. "What are you so happy about, Luca?" she asked suspiciously.

"It's just a beautiful day on the beach, don't you think? Don't you just love it here?"

"Uh, yeah, but you don't see me jumping up and down at the breakfast table. What are you two laughing about? What's going on?" she asked again.

"Nothing, Irene. We just stayed up late last night solving the world's problems. We didn't get much sleep," I said. I was being honest, but obfuscating the most important details.

"That's all? Well, that's boring," she said as she returned to her breakfast.

"Hey Irene," I said, changing the subject. "We're on lunch duty. I get to make meatballs with you today!"

"If they want authentic Italian food, they had better have us do the cooking!" she replied.

"The biggest challenge will be to decide whose mother's recipe will win out!"

"Mine will, of course!" Irene said with confidence.

"Wait a minute! My mom's meatballs are the best in town," I replied.

"We shall see, my sweet Luca," Irene said teasingly.

My answer and quick change of subject seemed to quell her curiosity, and I turned to Brad and winked. The rest of the retreat passed in a blur of stolen kisses and private looks from across the room. Nothing else seemed to matter. We were so very happy.

CHAPTER 8

BISHOP DE SANTO
SPRING 2015

One of the necessary consequences of expanding outreach programs of the diocese was the constant need for fundraising. Bishop De Santo had gathered an excellent staff that organized numerous events for each charity. There were spaghetti dinners, carnivals, and musical events held all over the diocese. For his wealthy donors, there were golfing expeditions, art exhibitions, and black-tie banquets. There was barely an evening free for the Bishop; he was sure to speak at each and every event.

De Santo was accustomed to schmoozing with the potential donors; in fact, he quite liked it. He could often be found in the midst of a crowd, laughing and telling stories. It didn't matter if the event was a pancake breakfast at a local parish or a lavish reception with influential donors: Bishop De Santo simply loved being with people. It energized him. He laughed easily and knew how to entertain his audience. It also helped that he was quite passionate about each of his programs, and could speak in great detail regarding their positive impact. His belief in the value of fundraising to support charitable activity gave him the energy and drive that he needed.

The dinner this evening was an annual tradition, by far the most prestigious event hosted by the diocese, with over four hundred donors in attendance. The guest list included some of the most notable figures in Fairfield County: investment bankers, Wall Street brokers, and tech industry leaders. These were major contributors to each and every campaign the diocese launched.

De Santo was confident that tonight would be a great success. He hadn't examined the entire guest list, but had been briefed by his staff on some of the key players who would be in attendance. Upon arrival, he took his usual post near the entrance to the banquet hall, so that he could meet and greet the steady stream of guests pouring in. Then, Maria, one of his employees, had to whisk him away once a stretch limousine carrying the mayor of Greenwich pulled up in front.

"Bishop, you should be there to greet him personally as his door opens," Maria counseled him.

"Of course, of course. Let's go. Please make sure that someone is greeting the rest of our guests in my absence," he instructed.

"You know that we always have that in hand. You just upstage us when you wait at the entrance." Maria laughed.

"But aren't I the star of the show?" he teased her in return.

"Money is the star of the show, Bishop—money. You just make it easier for them to let go of it," she responded good-naturedly.

Once the guests were seated, the master of ceremonies stepped up to the podium to give some introductory remarks. Bishop De Santo sat at the head table looking out at the large number of donors in attendance. Everything was going smoothly, and he was delighted with the knowledge that tonight's dinner would pull in millions of dollars for many of his most cherished programs. Unbeknownst to him at that moment, however, was that his life would be forever changed by the end of the evening.

His name was called and he rose to take the podium. As was his style, he made a flippant remark about the impressive gathering of wealthy individuals assembled before him.

"I haven't seen so many bejeweled women and men since last year's fundraiser!" he began. "We will be passing the basket around as we do each Sunday. Please feel free to toss in your most valued gems. I believe that you will sparkle with greater beauty after all those distractions are removed from your fingers and around your necks." His humor was well-known, and after their hearty laughter, he went on to thank them. "What God has blessed you with in your work and your wealth, you have returned to Him through your generosity. Many of you have been faithful supporters of this diocese and our many outreach programs, and I am grateful for your continued participation in transforming the lives of so many people in need. In addition, you have spread the word and brought many new people into our fold. My sincere welcome to all of you who are with us for the first time. I plan to meet each of you tonight to extend my personal thanks. You are now part of something greater than yourselves. Welcome to our family. Now let us bow our heads in prayer as we say grace."

The banquet was an elegant affair. The chef was a well-known owner of several restaurants in New York City and Connecticut, and did not disappoint. The guests enjoyed a delicious menu, from the pasta course of agnolotti with morel mushrooms, ricotta di pecora and black truffle butter, all the way to the sumptuous dessert selection. Profiteroles were Bishop De Santo's favorite dessert—flaky puff pastries filled with French cream and topped with rich dark chocolate sauce. By the time the presentations started, the guests were in high spirits enhanced by the lavish dinner and the warm glow of good wine. Bishop De Santo was having a wonderful evening.

After the formal presentations had come to a close, the Bishop made it a point to stop at each table to greet everyone in attendance. His personal and congenial style was the foundation of his success. He had a mind for detail and tried to make each stop personal by asking about family members and home life. For him, this was the best part of these fundraisers. He loved getting to know new people and reconnecting with those he had come to love over the years.

By the end of the evening, he was satisfied that he had spoken to most of the guests. As the crowd dwindled, he arrived at the last table. A number of guests rose to greet Bishop De Santo and bid him goodbye. By the time he turned to speak to the only new donor at the table, most of the crowd had gone. He recognized him instantly.

CHAPTER 9

BRAD
SPRING TO SUMMER
2015

Brad and his wife Wendy had always been involved with charitable work. It was a major boost to his image and helped with his client base. The couple was new to Connecticut, having lived in Manhattan for most of their married life, and this fundraiser would serve as a critical means by which they could introduce themselves to Greenwich high society. At least, that was how he presented it to Wendy. But Brad had an ulterior motive.

When he learned that De Santo would be sponsoring the event, he knew he had to attend, even though it would be a huge risk. Brad had run into his college friend Diane a couple of months ago, when she was visiting a friend of

Wendy's. Diane asked why neither of them had attended the recent St. Robert's College reunion.

"We had a great time!" she exclaimed. "So many of our choir friends were there. Irene, John and, of course, the most famous of our crew—Bishop De Santo!"

"Are you serious?" Wendy exclaimed. "He's a bishop? That's incredible!"

Brad was speechless. The next day, he sent the Bishop a friend request on Facebook, but weeks went by and he never heard from him. That only served to make Brad more determined to reconnect.

Tonight would be the night. As he drove his Mercedes to the valet, Brad saw the Bishop at the entrance to the venue, welcoming each of the guests. It was perfect. Brad handed his keys over to the attendant, offered Wendy his arm, and began to ascend the stairs. But when he looked up, the Bishop was gone. Brad looked all around and spotted him with the mayor, surrounded by photographers.

"What are you looking for, Brad?" Wendy asked.

"Nothing–well, the Bishop," he admitted. "He's with the mayor," he added nonchalantly.

"My, hasn't he become important," she said in a sarcastic tone.

"Now, now, Wendy. He's done well for himself. There's no need to be catty," he chided. He knew she still felt a bit of resentment about their past.

"I'm not being catty. I am just saying that we have done quite well ourselves too. Haven't we, Brad?"

"Yes, quite well. But we don't need to lord that over everyone. Besides, everyone in Manhattan already knows how rich we are," he said with a chuckle.

Once everyone was seated, Bishop De Santo took to the podium. He was a striking man. His silver hair gleamed under the spotlight and his affable smile enchanted his audience—including Brad. De Santo was as handsome as ever, even more so than in college. He was still trim, too: Brad could see his muscles outlined through his black Armani suit. Brad felt that long-ago excitement return and adjusted himself through his pants. He was immediately taken back to the first time they met at St. Robert's. De Santo was always smiling, and had an irresistible, self-deprecating manner. Brad was immediately drawn to him. He knew then that he just had to be with him. Now, here he was again after more than 35 years, looking even more dazzling. Brad couldn't wait to talk to him, to be near him again.

The rest of the dinner was interminable. All he wanted was a moment alone with him. Brad was sure that the Bishop would be shocked to see him, and relished that idea, but wanted to reconnect even more desperately. After all these years, Brad still felt drawn to him.

Brad watched as Bishop De Santo made his way to each of the tables. He made sure to sit so that he was somewhat obscured by the others at his table. He couldn't wait to see the Bishop's face in that first moment of recognition. When De Santo finally got to their table, Brad was about to burst with excitement. Their tumultuous year as roommates in college was one of the most significant periods of Brad's life. He felt his heart skip a beat when Bishop De Santo got to the table, and his mind flooded with memories from their time together at St. Robert's. Their eyes locked, and after a moment's hesitation, Bishop De Santo extended his hand.

"Brad! How many years has it been? I am so surprised

to see you tonight. How are you?"

"Bishop, what an honor to see you again. This was a lovely event, you should be proud of yourself."

"Thank you, Brad. As you can see, I am very passionate about our good works." De Santo intentionally put on an air of distant congeniality.

"Well you were certainly in your element. You look great! The priesthood certainly suits you," Brad said, a hint of sarcasm in his voice. Bishop De Santo let this jab roll off his back. Brad's humor had not changed.

"Please, Brad, we have too much history for you to be so formal. Call me Luca."

Brad felt Wendy nudge him. He was so mesmerized that he had forgotten that she was there.

"Let me introduce you to my wife, Wendy. You remember her from St. Robert's, don't you?"

"So nice to see you again, Wendy," the Bishop replied. "I hope Brad has been good to you. As you may know, he was quite challenging as a roommate!" All three laughed awkwardly.

"He still is, Bishop Luca! Honestly, I don't know how I put up with him," she joked as she nestled under Brad's arm. She was being overly affectionate, and Brad knew that it was meant to send a message—he is mine. Luca received it loud and clear.

In order to lighten the moment, Brad said, "Wendy, I'm shocked! I am nothing but sweetness and light. And you are lucky to have me."

"I rest my case, Bishop," she said with a satisfied grin.

"Well, in some ways, Brad, you haven't changed," Luca said. It was his turn for a jab.

"As I've always said, Luca: when you got it, flaunt it." Brad's smirk was not lost on Luca, who chose to ignore it. Instead, he asked, "What brings you two to Greenwich? I thought that you lived in New York City."

"We did. I still have an office there. But I prefer to work from our Connecticut location. We recently bought a home right on Long Island Sound."

"Well, that is wonderful. Good for you." Luca responded.

He was clearly trying to bring the conversation to a close, but Brad wasn't ready for this to end. He was determined to see Luca again, soon. When Wendy excused herself to go the restroom, it provided the opening he needed. Finding themselves together again after so many years, they looked at each other more closely. Luca seemed uncomfortable now that they were alone, and Brad felt the need to put him at ease, to bridge the gap. He looked squarely into Luca's eyes and said, "So, Luca, you look very happy."

"I am happy. I love my work and I am incredibly fulfilled. Events like this one keep me out most evenings, but you know that I always loved to be the life of the party," Luca said.

"Yes, I do recall that both of us were at the center of every social event at St. Robert's. That's probably why you keep yourself so busy with all these charitable causes," Brad replied.

"And you—you seem happy," Luca said begrudgingly, surprised by his lingering resentment for Brad.

"Happy enough," Brad responded honestly. There was so much more he wanted to say to him.

Brad took a step closer and put his hand on Luca's arm,

feeling the heat from the firm bicep beneath his grip. Luca did not pull away, so Brad squeezed his arm affectionately and said, "Seriously, Luca, don't you ever get lonely?"

"To be honest, the life of a celibate can be very lonely," the Bishop responded honestly. "But I have good friends that support and love me." He was startled by the effect that Brad's touch was having on him. He could feel tingling throughout his body as he flushed with heat.

"I'm glad to hear that, Luca. Better you than me. I still need someone to cozy up with at the end of the day. Being alone at night must be a constant struggle." Brad softened his hold on Luca's arm, gently caressing it.

Luca smiled sadly. "Yes, nighttime is particularly solitary. But look at you!" he added, as pulled himself away from Brad's touch. "You have done quite well for yourself. You have a family and a beautiful wife. You always told me that you would have two kids and work for a major bank. You wanted to be wealthy, and you had a plan. You did exactly as you said. You must be very happy with yourself."

Brad was taken aback that Luca remembered his detailed plan. He obviously still carried the memory of their relationship with him. Brad reached out to touch Luca's forearm. We're making a connection, Brad thought.

"I am, Luca, but you may remember that I was never fully satisfied when I reached one of my goals. There was always something more, something new to set my sights on. I don't think I have ever rested on my successes. I never let myself simply be happy," he said.

"And how about now? Are you happy now, Brad?" Luca asked.

That was the Luca Brad knew, always asking the most

significant or poignant questions. He always knew how to get at the heart of the matter. He hasn't changed a bit, Brad thought. He knew this encounter had thrown the Bishop off balance, but even still, Luca was reaching out to him. Brad answered as honestly as he could.

"I'm not sure I know what happiness really means. Even with my children and my wife, I still feel lonely at times. I feel as if I am searching for something, but I never seem to find it."

"Well, that sounds a bit like a self-help book, The Ubiquitous Search for Meaning" Luca joked, trying to lighten the mood. "Perhaps you should try your hand at writing." This was getting much too heavy, given his unexpected and unresolved feelings for Brad.

"I know that you are a busy man, Luca, but I would love to get together, just the two of us," Brad said as he squeezed Luca's arm again. "There is so much to catch up on. Small talk can only go so far, and we both know there's a great deal to chat about. Can we meet for lunch next week?"

The invitation took Luca by surprise and he backed away ever so slightly, but Brad noticed. He hesitated, then stuttered as he responded. "Well, well… of course, Brad. I will check my calendar and let you know. I am sure that we can set something up," he said evasively.

"Great! Here's my contact information. There's a private dining area in my office. Perhaps we can meet there," he offered. "I'd rather be somewhere private where we can talk. My schedule is pretty open this week. Call me and we'll set a time."

Wendy returned from the restroom and possessively assumed her previous position under Brad's arm.

"So, are you boys all caught up?" she asked with a big smile.

"Only just begun, sweetheart. We're going to get together to reminisce a bit more," Brad said, looking for her reaction. She stiffened but said nothing.

"Wendy, it was such a pleasure to see you after all these years," the Bishop added. "I hope that we will meet again soon."

"Oh, Bishop Luca, you must come over for dinner," Wendy offered. "We'd like you to meet our children, Michael and Maryann. They are wonderful young people and we are very proud of them"

"I have no doubt that they are. I look forward to meeting them," Luca answered.

"OK, Wendy, it's been a long night for Luca. I'm sure that he just wants to get out of here and into bed," Brad said as he winked at Luca. He could see that Luca wasn't quite sure what he meant by the wink, but let it pass. Then the three of them bid each other goodbye and promised to be in touch soon.

CHAPTER 10

BISHOP DE SANTO
SUMMER 2015

Back at the rectory, the Bishop paced in his suite. Though he had gone a bit gray around the temples, Brad looked exactly the same, with a full head of blond hair and a wry smile. His slim frame was accented by the Hugo Boss suit that hugged him tightly in just the right places. When he placed his hand on Luca's arm, the Bishop felt his energy pulse through his body. It was unnerving to still be so attracted to him. Luca could almost picture what it would be like to sleep with Brad again. The very thought aroused him and frightened him. No, that can never happen, he thought.

Then there was Wendy. Brad had started dating Wendy toward the end of their senior year. Luca never fully accepted their relationship as real. When he and Brad were together, he had always spoken of his plan to get married, have two children, and become rich. It was never an issue of Brad being gay or bisexual. Being anything other than straight simply didn't fit into his plan. Luca just didn't believe Brad was being true to himself. He knew that Brad had told Wendy that his relationship with Luca was simply a phase. It had made Luca's blood boil. In his mind, calling their relationship a phase diminished its importance. Now, he was nauseated by how publicly affectionate she was with Brad. Wendy was sending him a message and it was crystal clear—stay away from Brad.

Throughout that entire encounter, Bishop De Santo had been all smiles on the outside, but felt tightness in his chest. Flashes of their tumultuous relationship swirled in his mind. He and Brad did not end on friendly terms. What made Luca even more anxious was that he felt a strong attraction to Brad once again. How is that possible after all the pain he caused me? What do these feelings mean? Could there truly be hope for reconciliation after all these years? So much had remained unresolved. However, given his awakened sexual feelings, he wasn't sure that he should see Brad again.

He continued thinking about his years at St. Robert's College. The painful arguments and constant quarrelling with Brad were blended with memories of soul-searching discussions and a deep loving friendship. It was a time of self-discovery for both of them. They were inseparable college friends who met each new experience with a sense of adventure. Luca could not think back on his years at St. Robert's without recalling how big a splash the two of them made on the campus scene—always laughing, singing, and at the center of attention. Still, their relationship was fraught with conflict. He flashed back to one of their usual fights after they had become roommates.

Luca had been sitting at his corner desk trying to concentrate on the hundreds of pages assigned in his literature course. The reading load was much greater than he had ever had in high school, where he was used to doing well without a great deal of effort. But at St. Robert's, the workload was beyond his expectations. He struggled to keep up with all the reading and the many papers he had due, and worried constantly about his grades. It seemed that the only courses he excelled in were the religious studies and philosophy classes. That didn't really surprise him. But he had to do better in English. That was his major after all, and he couldn't average a B in his English courses.

With a burst of boisterous energy, the dorm room door flew open. Brad was laughing loudly with a friend from one of his business classes.

"Then she asked what all of that had to do with banking! Can you believe it?" Brad exclaimed and they both burst into a fit of laughter. "She is so dimwitted! She'll never make it in the business world," he added.

"Well at least she won't ruin the curve on the next exam!" his buddy said.

"No chance! We should be grateful that she's in our class," Brad responded.

Luca always hated when Brad belittled other people. He could be so condescending, especially towards girls. He had no tolerance for people whom he perceived to be his intellectual inferiors, and he expressed his disdain often. Whenever Luca would challenge him on it, he responded by turning his eye back to Luca. "Oh don't be a pussy, Luca! Besides, you're only an English major. You wouldn't understand." Another of his favorite put-downs was, "Luca, you're such a bleeding-heart liberal. Do you think you can save every wounded bird? Maybe I should call you St. Francis." It irritated Luca to no end. Nothing he could say would stop the onslaught of insults.

Luca raised his head from his books. With a pleading look, he said, "Hey Brad, I'm really trying to study. Are you guys going to be hanging out here for long?"

Brad rolled his eyes at his friend. "There he goes again, raining on our parade. What are you reading, English lit? Why don't you get a real major? You know that you'll never find a job with a degree in English!"

"Seriously, Brad? I'm just trying to get my work done. You'd be pissed if I did this to you when you were studying for a test. Give me a break."

"Why don't you just go to the library? Rick and I need to work on a project for finance," Brad responded dismissively.

"Because I am all set up here at my desk with everything I need."

"Well, we'll only be an hour or so, you can put up with us until we're done. Come on, Rick, sit down."

Luca was seething. This wasn't the first time Brad placed his desires over Luca's, but humiliating him in front of Rick was a new low. The fact that Luca hardly knew Brad's classmate made it even worse. He knew that he wasn't going to win this argument: Brad was never one to give in. Luca slammed his book closed, gathered up his stuff, and left to sounds of them laughing. Brad could be so cruel at times.

Luca confronted Brad about it later on, to the sound of more dismissive laughter.

"Luca, don't be so sensitive. I was just kidding. You need to lighten up, learn to take a joke."

"Look, Brad, it's not a joke when you are constantly belittling my major or interrupting my study time. It's really frustrating."

"Well, I'm right, aren't I? What are you going to do with an English degree?"

"Brad, you know I want to teach high school. What's the big deal?"

"And you'll be poor for the rest of your life. Why spend all this money on education just so you can struggle to pay your student loans and your rent? I mean, I could see Bio or Math, but English with a minor in Religious Studies?"

"It's my choice. I get to decide what I want to do with my life, not you. So lay off, would you?" Luca said angrily.

"Sure, sure, you get to decide that you'll be paid next to nothing to teach impressionable young minds. You're right, I shouldn't let it bother me," Brad jabbed once again.

"I don't know why I even argue with you, Brad. I end up feeling worse than I did beforehand. Just forget it!"

Then Brad's tone changed, becoming fleetingly contrite. "Hey, Luca, come here. I'm just kidding." He locked his arms around Luca in a huge hug and said, "You know I love you, right?"

"It certainly doesn't seem like it," Luca responded, showing his frustration.

"Come on, Luca. We are meant for each other. This is just the way I am. I don't try to please people just to make them like me."

"It's not about pleasing people. It's about treating them with respect."

"Whatever—that's what you do. You're always worried about what people will think of you. You never stand up for what you want."

"So you're saying that I'm a pleaser?"

"Of course you are! That's one of the things I love most about you. You always try to take care of everyone, including me." Brad's tone softened. "I do love you. We just don't have to agree on everything."

"Being kind to each other should have nothing to do with whether we agree or disagree," Luca responded.

Luca would always walk away from arguments like this feeling that there was something wrong with himself— that perhaps he was being too sensitive and just needed to let go. His feelings were never validated and it was beginning to affect his self-image. He even began to question his career path. This pattern lasted for the entire time they lived together.

As he allowed these memories to come flooding back, Bishop De Santo knew he had to get out of his lunch date with Brad. He had long ago put these painful memories aside. In fact, by the time he was at the North American College in the Vatican just a few years later, Brad never crossed his mind. His successes beyond St. Robert's College all but erased the feelings of insecurity he felt during those two years with Brad. So why should he dredge up the past now? They had both grown up and gone on to create happy and healthy lives. They had little in common then—how much less would they have to share 35 years later?

At least, that is what his rational mind argued. The

problem was that he did want to see Brad again. He wanted to talk with him as two adults whose lives had turned out to be successful beyond their own imaginings. What harm can come from having lunch with Brad? he thought. It would simply be two old friends catching up. Or is it more than that?

Bishop Luca had a strange feeling in the pit of his stomach. Whenever he was faced with a personal ethical dilemma, he would get a similar feeling. If he made the correct choice, it would go away. What was it about having lunch with Brad that prompted such distress now? It was because, beneath all of the rationalization, Luca knew what was really going on. After nearly 30 celibate years, he suddenly longed to be with Brad again, to feel that intimacy that he had long ago left behind.

This realization disturbed him even more than the painful memories of their conflicts. But Brad was a married man and had a family. Luca told himself that he was being foolish. It was only lunch with an old friend, and it was long past time to resolve their old conflicts. Despite his feelings, he had no reason to feel insecure or self-conscious. He was content in his role as a priest, and bishop. Nothing could change his commitment to his vocation. There was nothing to fear.

CHAPTER 11

LUCA
AUTUMN 1979

When we got back to campus Sunday afternoon, Brad and I were anxious to get a moment alone again. Ever since our time on the beach Saturday night, I had thought of nothing else but him. It was torture not being able to reach out and caress him and press my lips against his. I slung my duffel bag over my shoulder as we walked across the quad to Brad's room, where we found his roommate studying.

Mickey was a really affable guy, but he lacked social skills. He was a self-professed nerd and loved burying his head in the books. He didn't have many body friends, but was friendly with a lot of people. He never seemed to pick up on the fact that people weren't interested in a particular passion of his or that they made fun of him—or in this case, that we might want some privacy.

"Hi Brad. How was your retreat?" Mickey asked.

"It was incredible! How was your weekend?"

"It was fine. Lots of work to catch up on. I have a huge test in Bio tomorrow. Just trying to study," Mickey responded.

"Wouldn't it be quieter in the library?" Brad suggested. "The noise from the hall is just going to get worse as the evening wears on."

"Nah, I work better at my own desk. There are fewer distractions, plus I don't feel like hiking all the way down to the library with my books."

Mickey's response was final. There was no wiggle room to convince him to leave. Brad and I sat on the edge of his bed and quietly chatted about the retreat. Soon we began to giggle.

Mickey turned to us. "Seriously, guys? You sound like a couple of high school girls gossiping about the school dance. Can you go hang out somewhere else?"

"Hey, it's my room too, Mickey! What the hell?"

"Come on Brad, let's go to the campus center. Mickey needs some space right now," I interjected, trying to keep the peace.

"Thanks, Luca. I really need quiet when I study," Mickey said appreciatively.

"Whatever. Later, Mickey." Brad stood up and left without looking at him.

We exited the dorm and crossed the quad. It was a beautiful autumn afternoon, but now Brad was angry.

"Who does he think he is?" he fumed. "We should have just stayed and let him go to the library."

I tried to defuse the situation. "Yeah, but you don't want to start a war with your roommate. That'll just make both your lives miserable. Just forget it." What did it matter? I thought. We would just have to be a bit more creative to find some time alone.

We ended up at the campus pub and found an open booth in the far corner. The place was pretty empty, so we didn't have to worry about being overheard. We each ordered a beer and French fries and completely forgot about Mickey. Under the table, our legs were intertwined. We were completely infatuated with each other.

"So Brad, what did all that mean on Saturday night? I have never felt anything like that before," I admitted.

"Me neither, Luca. It was pretty intense. All I know is that I want more."

"So what do we do now?" I asked.

Brad squeezed his legs around mine under the table and said, "We have to find some place to be alone."

I looked in his eyes. I could feel the heat rising as my face flushed red.

"Yeah, we do, but where?"

"We'll figure it out, Luca."

"I'm still not sure what to think. Does this mean we're gay?" I asked earnestly.

"You think too much, Luca! We're not gay. Neither of us is effeminate, we don't cross dress. We're regular guys— we're just hot for each other. I don't look at any other guys like I look at you."

I was still very naïve, and had no sense of how homophobic Brad's rationale was. There was a great deal of self-hatred in his definition of gay. As I considered what he was saying, Brad continued talking quietly.

"Just seeing you enter a room makes me hard," he said as his shoeless foot caressed my inner thigh under the table. I jumped a bit at his touch. I wasn't used to such an assertive sexual advance.

"You are so bad, Brad. Someone might see us," I said, looking around nervously.

"Oh, you have no idea how bad I can be, Luca. Wait 'til I get you alone again," he said lasciviously. I moved away in embarrassment. I couldn't resist my attraction to him, but he was making me uncomfortable. I tried to re-focus our conversation.

"It sounds like it's not going to be so easy to find any place private. Does Mickey always hang out in your room?"

"Actually, he has class from 8 a.m. until noon tomorrow, and he never comes back between classes. What's your schedule, Luca?"

"I don't have any classes until later in the day. How about you? If you're free I could come by."

"I have an 8 a.m. class, but I can be back in my room by 9:15. Why don't you come over then? We'll have the whole morning together!" Brad said enthusiastically.

"Yeah, I can make that work." I smiled at him affectionately. "I can't wait."

Since I was a commuter, I reluctantly said good night to Brad and drove home. Even though I had gotten very little rest on the retreat, I hardly slept that night. Though I felt ecstatic about where our relationship might be going, I struggled to understand it. Although he was obviously interested in pursuing a sexual relationship with me, Brad seemed nonchalant about the whole thing. Even when I pressed him to define it or discuss it while we were in the pub, he seemed to simply take it at face value. It happened; we enjoyed it. We should do it some more.

That wasn't enough for me. I needed to understand it. Our physical expression of love did not fit into any category I knew. Did it mean that we were gay? How could it? Like Brad said, we weren't into leather or dressing in women's clothing. However, something about Brad's explanation didn't sit well with me. It didn't ring true—but then, neither did my understanding of what being gay meant. There was so much I didn't know. All these thoughts kept me up all night as I tossed and turned.

When morning came, my desire to see Brad alone reached a fever pitch. After breakfast and a quick shower, I hopped in the car. I couldn't wait to get to campus and drove way too fast. Finally, I turned into the main gates, parked in the commuter parking lot, and sprinted across campus. The dorm hall was quiet. I knocked on Brad's door at 9:15 sharp, and when the door opened, he reached out and grasped me by the back of my neck and pulled me in. He wore only a t-shirt and gym shorts, and looked at me with heavy-lidded eyes. I dropped my backpack and threw my arms around him.

He cupped my face in his hands as he kissed me hungrily. There was a sense of urgency in our touch. I wrapped my hands around his waist and felt his smooth skin under his shirt, before moving my hands up from his belly to his chest to lift off his t-shirt.

We were both shirtless and on his bed in moments, kissing passionately and caressing each other. We seemed needier than we had that night on the retreat. It was like we couldn't get enough of each other. Before long, our pants were off and we lay on his bed in only our underwear. I was afraid to go any further. I didn't even know what to do next.

Brad broke from our kiss and gazed into my eyes while he took my hand and placed it over his briefs. I felt his heat emanating through the thin cotton and I squeezed. Brad let out a moan. Then he slipped his thumbs under my waistband and lowered my underwear. A moment of embarrassment washed over me: I had never been naked and aroused in front of anyone before. I recoiled a bit, but Brad pulled me closer.

"You're beautiful, Luca," he said. His touch sent shivers throughout my naked body. I began to let go of my fear and trusted where he was leading me. There was no need to be afraid; we just did what came naturally.

Before we knew it, the clock read 12 noon. Brad jumped out of bed and began to dress. "Hurry up Luca!" he called to me. "Mickey will be back any minute."

I threw on my pants and was just tucking in my shirt when the door opened. Without skipping a beat, I said, "Hey Mickey, how was your test this morning? Do you think you did well?"

"Piece of cake. I shouldn't have wasted so much time studying," he exclaimed gleefully, before launching into a detailed explanation of the entire exam.

Brad zipped passed us and headed for the bathroom without saying a word. He looked as if he were angry. What's wrong with him? I thought. Is he freaking out about us? I wondered if I had done anything wrong. Just then, Mickey interrupted my thoughts. I hadn't been listening to a word he was saying.

"Are you heading to lunch? I'm starving."

"No, I don't have a cafeteria pass since I'm a commuter."

"Well, that's too bad. Most of us hang out there. It's a fun social scene."

"Don't worry, Mickey, I'll grab something at the pub. See you a bit later."

"OK, see ya." He left the room pretty quickly and I sat down on Brad's bed. What just happened? We almost got caught. Why did Brad take off? So many conflicting thoughts swirled in my mind.

When Brad returned from the bathroom, he looked distracted. "Are you OK?" I asked. "You flew out of here like a bat out of hell." I was concerned that he was feeling guilty about what we had just done. My anxiety level was rising and I didn't know how to relieve it.

"We cut it too close! We have to be more careful next time. If anyone were to find out what we did, we'd be screwed," Brad answered.

"You're right. We just dozed off and lost track of time. But Mickey seemed fine," I said, trying to reassure him. "He didn't suspect anything. He was going on and on about his test. He even asked me to go to lunch with him." There was a short pause as I took a deep breath. I looked up at Brad until our eyes locked.

"So, there's going to be a next time?" I asked tentatively.

Brad sat down beside me, put his arm around my neck and pulled me to him playfully. "Of course there is, stupid! I'm not letting you go!"

So that became our routine. Whenever we knew

that Mickey was at class, we'd have our rendezvous. Mickey began to refer to me as his second roommate, and the three of us would hang out together every now and again.

Although it was working out well, I still worried about the meaning of our relationship. When I went to the 12:10 Mass each day, I prayed for guidance. I never thought I could feel this way about anyone, let alone another guy. I loved Brad, but at the same time, I deeply believed that I had a vocation to the priesthood. I couldn't recall a time when I had ever doubted my future before; I had always felt the calling. In my prayer journal I wrote:

"O God, please help me through this confusion. I know what the Church teaches about homosexuality. I know that it is wrong, but I am not sure who I am or if I am gay. I simply know that I am in love with Brad, with all my heart. My every thought is about him and when we are apart, I long for the next time we'll be together. The physical closeness we experience is born out of our love for each other. I give all of myself to him when we are alone: my heart, my mind, and my body. I want only the best for him. I want him to realize his dreams and I want him to be happy. How can such a selfless love be evil? I know what sin looks and feels like. There is a sense of foreboding and fear of the consequences of my wrongdoing. I don't feel that with Brad. It just seems natural. Deep in my heart, I know that this is not sin. Our love for each other is not evil. Help me to reconcile this with the teachings of the Church. You know that I am a faithful servant and I always seek to do your will. Please, God, give me peace."

Each day at Mass, I would cross myself as I knelt in the front pew of the chapel. I would do what the Jesuits call the examine and list the events of the previous 24 hours. I would thank God for all the wonderful moments with Brad and all the fun we had together. But I would also examine my conscience to see if there was any action or thought that needed reconciliation. Each day, my prayer would end the same way: I love him so much, O God. How can this be wrong? Please give me peace.

My relationship with Brad continued to develop and grow just as most romantic relationships did. I had evening classes until 10 p.m. twice a week. Rather than drive home, I would just stay overnight in Brad's room. Mickey didn't seem to care at all. However, Brad and I had become bold in our physical intimacy, perhaps even careless. When we were sure that Mickey was asleep, we would fool around under the covers. That went on for quite some time until one night, Brad and I were lost in our lovemaking. We must have made a bit too much noise, and out of the darkness, Mickey said in a groggy voice, "Would you guys just knock it off and go to sleep already?!"

We froze, neither of us breathing. "Sorry, Mickey," Brad responded. What did he hear? Did Mickey know what we were doing? Or did he just think we were innocently kidding around? Not likely. After that, we resolved to be more careful. We would simply have to wait until we were alone. That seemed more than reasonable. Luckily, Mickey didn't mention it the next day and treated us as he always did. Brad and I breathed a huge sigh of relief. We had dodged another bullet.

Those first few months together with Brad were like a dream. Though the ordinary routines of college life were much as they had always been, my world sparkled. The colors were brighter, the music more beautiful, the laughter and joys more intense. I recall just hanging out in with him in his room studying. He was busy at work, his desk lamp shining on his calculations. I lifted my head from my reading of Moll Flanders and watched him work. I was mesmerized. How is this guy so important to me? I am so lucky to have found him.

When he looked up and found me staring at him, he asked, "What?"

"Nothing."

"You're staring at me."

"Because you're so beautiful."

He threw his eraser at me and laughed. "I am pretty cute, aren't I?" Then we just went back to our studies.

+++

As the months passed by, Brad and I knew that we had entered unknown territory for both of us. This was part of my downfall with regard to him. I truly believed that I would never find anyone else like Brad. I believed that our connection was unlike any other that existed, and that no one else would understand the nature of our love. No matter the difficulties we inevitably experienced, I thought we had no choice but to stay together. Should we ever part, no one else could fill that void. Leaving each other was not an option.

We were clear that no one else could know about us. If anyone even suspected that we were gay, we'd be ostracized and bullied. And at any rate, I thought, we aren't gay. We're just in love. We bore no resemblance to the depraved examples of homosexuality that Anita Bryant posted all over newspapers. Brad and I were different. I also had a deep fear of being bullied like the few effeminate boys I knew in high school. They were tortured each and every day. I knew that I couldn't live with that reality. Once again, I had no concept of how deeply my internalized homophobia had taken root.

That is what defined our relationship. Being gay was just not something that either of could relate to at 19 years old in 1980. We had been indoctrinated to believe that gay men were depraved and abnormal. All we saw on television were images of men in leather with sadomasochistic tendencies, or effeminate men who swished around. The thought of going to the local gay bar filled me with fear. What if I was attacked? What kind of people would I encounter? I couldn't relate to any of the images we were presented with. Brad was the only man who truly understood what we meant to each other. No matter what, we couldn't lose each other—otherwise, we would forever be alone.

On the other hand, I was still curious. I mentioned it to Brad one day.

"Hey, I heard there's a gay bar in town. Do you want to give it a try, just to see what it's like?"

"No, Luca! What are you thinking? That's crazy," Brad responded vehemently. "We don't need to go to a gay bar. We're not gay. I have a girlfriend back home, and you and I have each other. Let's just keep a level head and not mess with what we've got, OK?"

As the months passed, I became more and more attached to Brad. I was almost obsessed with him, and sought his approval in everything I did. An unhealthy codependence had developed between us and seemed to seep into all our interactions. The playfulness was beginning to be overshadowed by neediness. I couldn't even escape through my social life, because I was fully integrated into his group of friends. If I showed up to someone's room without Brad, they would immediately inquire after him. They simply assumed we would be together.

CHAPTER 12

LUCA

SPRING 1980

Brad and I were on totally different tracks of study. I was an English major and he was in Finance, so we never had classes together. But we were sure to see each other during our free periods and in the evenings. We made the most of our time with each other and were never seen apart while on campus. One Monday at the beginning of the second semester, I closed my book, put my hands on his shoulders and kissed his cheek from behind.

"Hey, I have to go," I said.

"Why? Where are you going?" he asked.

"I have choir rehearsal every Monday at 7 p.m."

"Can't you skip it and just stay? I promise I'm almost done with my homework."

"Sorry. I really can't miss practice. It's only once a week and there's a ton of music to learn. Besides, I'm the new guy. I can't look unreliable."

"That sucks! We hardly saw each other at all today. I miss you."

"Why don't you come with me? You have a pretty voice and we could use another tenor," I suggested.

"I don't know, it seems like a huge commitment and I've already missed a number of rehearsals," Brad said hesitantly.

"Look, you don't have to commit to anything, Brad. Just come and sit by me. You can share my music. If you like it, we can ask if you can audition. Come on, what do you say?"

He broke into a huge grin and said, "How can I say no to you, Luca? Let's do it!"

And with that, we were off to our first rehearsal together. He had a bit of trouble following the sheet music, but had a good ear. I could tell that he was imitating my every sound, and before long, he started to catch on. By the end of the rehearsal, Jeff, the choir president, came over and said, "Hey, who's the new guy?"

"Hi Jeff, this is Brad," I said. "He's got a decent voice. I know that we're short on tenors, so I brought him along. Is it too late for him to audition?"

"Nice to meet you, Brad. It is a little bit late, but we can give you a try. You tenors are in high demand!"

So after everyone left the rehearsal room, the pianist led him in some warm-up exercises. Before long, Brad was singing scales with bravado.

"Nice job, Brad. You have a strong voice, but there

was a lot of music covered during the rehearsals you missed."

"Thanks! Yeah, I was worried about that," he admitted.

"Listen, Jeff—since he's in my voice part, I can teach him all of the music. And given his performance in rehearsal today, it seems that he's a pretty quick study. What do you think?" I asked hopefully.

"Do you think you can catch up, Brad?" Jeff asked.

"Absolutely! Luca is a great teacher," he responded.

He was in. I promised to work with him before each of our rehearsals, and Jeff was more than happy to have another tenor. Brad was in heaven: he loved a challenge, and this seemed to be a big win for him. I didn't realize his other motive until much later in our relationship: singing was one of the talents that distinguished me from him, and he was gaining ground. He was aggressively competitive with me, especially regarding skills that he lacked. In many ways, it was a means by which he diminished my talents. However, those first months together were filled with hope and excitement. Together, we tried to participate in as many clubs and activities as possible. We never seemed to tire of being in each other's company.

On the night of the spring concert, the energy in the green room was electric. When we were given the ten-minute warning, we began to line up and quietly filled in the risers. The curtain opened and the director walked on to energetic applause. The first number was a lengthy medley from "Godspell."

Being a short guy, I was standing front and center in the first row. As the director took to the podium, she looked up and pointed in my direction. I looked behind me, but no one moved. When I turned back, she signaled for me to come forward. "Me?" I mouthed. "Yes," she responded. I was shocked.

The opening solo was a cappella. The accompanist gave the first pitch and Dr. Penforth cued me. There was no time to get nervous. With no prior preparation, I began to sing "Prepare Ye the Way of the Lord." My confidence grew as I could hear my voice fill the hall; by the time the band came in, I was belting it out with the choir backing me up. It was thrilling. I was floating on a cloud for the rest of the concert. During intermission, the president and vice president of the choir, both seniors, came to talk with me.

"Congratulations, Luca! Where the hell did that voice come from? You rocked the house!" Zach said.

"Yeah, you'll have to beat the girls back at the party later. They're all going to want a piece of our new star soloist!" Jeff chimed in.

"Thanks, guys. I was totally taken by surprise. I'm just glad I didn't choke!" I responded.

"Yeah, well you'll have to thank Andy for not showing up. He was too hung over from last night." Jeff snickered. "He just got shown up by a sophomore! That'll teach him."

Zach put his arm over my shoulder and pulled me aside. "Have you given any thought to auditioning for the men's a cappella group? I think you've got a good chance of getting in."

"You know, I hadn't thought much about it." I lied. "That would be awesome!" I had my sights set on the a cappella choir since I had visited the previous year.

"Give it some serious thought, Luca. We need strong voices like yours," Zach replied.

Later, at the post-concert party, I pulled Brad aside and told him about my conversation with Jeff and Zach. He had already been a little jealous at all the attention I was receiving, but this new development was a step too far, and he tried to persuade me against it. "Are you sure you want to do that? You hardly have any free time as it is, Luca."

I was taken aback by Brad's dismissal. "Are you kidding? The a cappella choir is the premier group on campus. How could I turn that down?" Maybe getting him on board will help him be happy for me, I thought. "Brad, you should audition too. Then we could both be in a cappella."

"That's crazy. I just joined this semester." Brad's tone had changed a bit, though—he seemed to be considering it.

"It doesn't matter how long you've been in the choir. The most important issue is whether you can sing."

"Man, that would be so cool. Everyone looks up to those guys. Do you really think I could get in?" he asked.

"It's worth a try. What have you got to lose?"

So, by the end of the semester, we had set our eyes on a new goal. The Squires, the men's a cappella group, was a big deal on campus. Their shows were well-attended, and they had people rolling in the aisles laughing at their antics. They would always pull someone from the audience up onto the stage and mock them during a song. All we wanted to do now was to audition for them. I was determined to improve Brad's musicianship. Since I was never without my guitar, I would play songs from Mass each week. Brad sang the melody and I would harmonize.

"Let's try that again. Don't listen to me, Brad. You'll just get thrown off."

"OK, but don't sing so loud. All I can hear is the

harmony."

I'd strum the first chord and we'd come in on the same note, look at each other and laugh.

"No, that's my note," I'd say.

Brad giggled. "Yeah, but it sounds better when I sing it!"

"Sure, whatever you say."

Hours passed as we sat on his bed singing. We had so much fun just hanging out together. At one point, Mickey opened the door, took a look at us giggling and singing, shook his head and grabbed his books to go to his next class.

Brad turned to me. "Luca, we have to sing this together for Zach and Jeff. We are really good together. They'll definitely let us into the Squires!"

"Well, it doesn't work like that," I explained. "The auditions are pretty challenging. But it doesn't hurt to show them how good we are. Let's try it without the guitar," I suggested.

"No, it sounds so good when you play."

"Brad, we won't have any instrumental accompaniment when we audition, so we had better get used to it now. Come on. We can do it!"

After a few tries, we got it. Our voices blended beautifully, and our confidence grew. Soon after that, we trotted up to Jeff and Zach.

"Hey guys, we've been practicing a great song. Can we sing it for you?" I asked. They looked at each other, rolled their eyes, and said yes.

The first entrance sucked: we both came in on the harmony note. "Wait, wait, let us just try it again," Brad pleaded.

"We haven't got all night. Finals are coming up," Jeff said impatiently.

Our second try was weak, but by the refrain, we had hit our stride and sounded great. When we held the final notes, Zach and Jeff applauded. "So what's the deal? Are you guys hitting the road with a new act?" Zach laughed.

Even though we finished strong, I could tell that they had doubts about Brad. He was the weak link, and I began to worry about him. When audition night came, he was a nervous wreck.

"I shouldn't have let you talk me into this, Luca," he said. "I've never had to hold my harmony alone. You were always beside me singing in my ear."

"Hey Brad, don't worry about it. Just do the best you can. If you don't make it, no big deal. We can still sing in the concert choir." I could hear my buddy John's voice clearly in my head and tried to emulate it. "Besides, I'm still by your side. I've got your back."

As it turned out, I got in and Brad did not. He was crushed, and I felt responsible. I had encouraged him to take the risk and put himself out there. Brad was inconsolable and it was clear that he bore some resentment towards me, both for encouraging him to audition and getting in when he did not. I knew that I had to do something to make things right, so I went to talk with Zach and Jeff.

"Congratulations, Luca! We are so glad to have you in the Squires," Zach said, clapping me on the back.

"That's right, Luca. Out of the whole lot, you were the strongest musician. We are glad to have you!" Jeff added.

"Thanks, guys. I can't wait to start rehearsals. Listen, I just have a question about Brad. What did he do wrong? I thought his audition was pretty good."

"It was OK." Jeff said, "But he doesn't have the experience needed for a cappella singing. He kept losing his harmony."

"Yeah, but that's something that can be learned," I said.

"True, but you know that we all have to learn our parts on our own. We have to sing with confidence at all times. Brad just didn't have that confidence."

"Yeah, but that's because he was nervous. Can you give him another try?" I asked.

"I don't know, Luca," Zach replied. "The list has already gone out. We have a pretty strong ensemble now. I'm not sure we should mess with it."

"Besides," Jeff added, "that would look really bad to the other guys who didn't make it."

I then started pleading. "Listen, you know I have a strong musical background. What if I promise to work on his parts with him before each rehearsal? I'm sure he'd pick it up fast. He's pretty driven toward success."

"If we know one thing about Brad, it's that he's driven," Jeff said sarcastically. "If you are willing to put in the extra time to tutor him, we can let him audition at our first rehearsal. But we can't make any promises that he'll get in."

"You guys are the best! We won't let you down, I promise!"

"Great! We'll have Mutt and Jeff in the Squires. Now that will be a sight!" Zach chuckled.

I ran directly to Brad's room to tell him the good news. He was elated, and moved by my lobbying effort. "I can't believe you did that for me," he said. "What gave you the courage to ask?"

"So, I love you and I want you to be with me when we perform. That gave me all the motivation I needed," I said as I kissed him on the cheek. "Now let's start working on the audition piece."

✝

CHAPTER 13

BISHOP DE SANTO
SUMMER 2015

Bishop De Santo entered Brad's office building with anxious anticipation. It was a brand-new building, made of reflective blue glass and located close to the Connecticut shoreline in Stamford. Long Island Sound glittered in the summer sun. Though he rarely perspired, the Bishop felt drops begin to bead on his forehead, and was relieved that his full head of silver hair covered them.

The entryway was elegant, with leather chairs and paintings of the New England coastline. A huge arrangement of flowers was placed at the center of the expansive hall. The receptionist greeted him effusively, saying, "Oh yes, Bishop De Santo, Mr. Ghenter is expecting you in the executive suite. His assistant will be here shortly to escort you. Please have a seat. Can I get you a cappuccino?"

"Thank you, no. I am fine."

A cappuccino? he thought. He really knows how to impress.

Moments later, he was shown into the suite, and Brad stood up from his desk to greet him. He looked incredibly handsome in his tailored white shirt and slacks. He had good taste and knew how to dress to accentuate his youthful-looking body. When the door closed behind the Bishop, Brad embraced him tightly, and seemed to linger just a moment longer than he should have. Luca felt himself catch his breath. What is happening to me? he thought.

As they began to pull apart, Brad's cheek brushed against his. The electricity between them was unmistakable. Brad continued to hold him close and looked deeply into his eyes. "It's good to see you, old friend," he said. "How could we have lost touch for so long?" Without warning, a rush of emotion washed over Luca. Just moments ago, he envisioned a pleasant reunion and a healing of old wounds. Although he had felt the physical attraction at their last meeting, Luca had not even entertained the fact that there could be an emotional connection after all these years. At least that is what he told himself.

He pulled away reluctantly and spoke with caution. "Life points us toward many unexpected directions, Brad. But we didn't part on very good terms. I don't believe that we would have reconnected if it weren't for our chance encounter at the fundraiser." The energy between them was dangerous, and the knot in the pit of his stomach began to grow. He didn't trust himself or Brad to make good choices. If Brad were feeling a fraction of the sexual tension that Luca felt, there would be little to hold them back. Luca tried to put some emotional distance between them. "To be honest, after all the trauma of our relationship, I'm not quite sure what we are doing here."

"Look, Luca, we were 18 years old—just kids. Whatever conflicts we had were part of growing up. Sure, there was a lot of drama between us, but you can't deny that we were important to each other."

"That's certainly true. I loved you deeply," Luca said as he sighed. "But the scars left by those years took a long time to heal. To me, it wasn't simply teenage drama. I must confess that seeing you now brings up many unexpected emotions."

"Good ones, I hope," Brad replied with a gentle smile. "Please, Luca, let's sit and have lunch. There is so much to catch up on. Let's not put up our defenses before we even get started. Deal?"

Luca felt himself drawn in by Brad's charm, but did not fight it. There was great comfort in being with him at this moment, and he let himself relax. He wanted to be here, and there was nothing wrong with reconnecting on an emotional level. They were not 18 any longer; they were mature men who could certainly manage their behavior.

"Of course," Luca responded. "I'm sorry if I came across as uneasy or guarded. Our chance meeting knocked me a little off balance. But I am glad to see you again."

"Good. Then let's relax and have some fun," Brad replied with enthusiasm. He poured two glasses of wine without asking Luca's preference, and began to serve lunch. It was an extravagant set-up. The table was laid with silver dishes and the view overlooked the Long Island Sound through floor-to-ceiling windows. Long Island seemed close enough to touch. Brad lifted the silver covers to reveal lobster tails and two-inch cuts of filet mignon. They both knew that he was showing off, but he was so nonchalant about it that it didn't feel uncomfortable.

Soon they were telling stories and reminiscing. They laughed easily and their old intimacy returned without either of them noticing. Their legs touched under the table and neither of them pulled away. There was never an awkward pause in the conversation; it was as if time had not passed since the first year they met.

"Come on over to the couch, Luca. I have something to show you," Brad said once they had finished their meal. Out came the photo albums, and the two sat side by side, remarking about how young they looked, and their lack of fashion sense.

"Look how adorable you are, with your guitar and your hair falling into your eyes!" Brad exclaimed. "I was smitten the first time I saw you. You had no idea how beautiful you were, and that made you all the more attractive."

"Yeah, well, I was unsure about a number of things back then," Luca confessed. "I just remember feeling an overwhelming need to be with you all the time. It didn't make sense to me, but I didn't question it. It was like I was drinking you in, watching you laugh and seeing how you entertained your friends. You had me wrapped around your finger."

"I'll never forget watching the sunrise that morning on retreat," Brad said.

"That's when it all changed, Brad. I had no idea I could feel that with another guy."

"I remember how hungry we both were. We couldn't get enough of each other."

"That was the beginning of an enlightening journey for me. It was what opened my eyes to my own sexuality," Luca admitted.

"It was a wonderful ride, Luca, and I wouldn't change it for the world."

"Our lives were transformed after that," the Bishop reflected. "I could never see the world in the same way."

"And here we are now—I'm a millionaire and you're a bishop. Who would have thought?"

"Actually, your life seems to have turned out much the way you planned. Mine, on the other hand…"

Luca's last phrase lingered in the air. There was a lull in the conversation as they continued to leaf through the pages of the album. Luca's awareness of his own body was heightened. He could feel every shortened breath, the pulsing of his blood within his veins, as well as the tightness of his pants. The silence only served to accentuate the sexual tension between them. Luca could feel his heart beat rapidly within his chest and his skin tingled with excitement. He knew that Brad was feeling it too. They leaned into each other as they reminisced at each photo, feeling totally at home with each other. None of the hostility that marked the end of their relationship was present. It was like putting on a comfortable old pair of shoes.

At one point, Brad placed his hand on Luca's thigh and said, "You know, I never stopped loving you. I just didn't do a very good job of it when we were together."

Luca felt the pulse of Brad's warm hand as it moved up his thigh, and he became aroused. "I loved you too, Brad," he confessed. "In many ways, you are the one who taught me that I was capable of loving another person in that way. Our time together taught me so much about myself, about my ability to love and be loved."

"Being with you right now feels as if I have finally come home. You know, I always wondered what our lives would have been like if we had never broken up." Brad paused and looked at Luca. "Would we have gotten married? Would we now be one of those power couples?" Brad looked back at the photo album. "When we were together back then, we were a force to be reckoned with."

"We did create quite a sensation on campus, didn't we? But I fear that it might have ended poorly for me," Luca said with a sad smile.

"Why, what do you mean? I wasn't that bad!" Brad countered defensively.

"I was totally obsessed with you, Brad. I began to completely lose myself in you. You burned so brightly in my life that I was totally eclipsed by you. There were times when all I sought was your approval, and when it didn't come, I doubted everything about myself."

Brad turned and looked squarely at him, placing his hand gently upon Luca's cheek. "Luca, I never meant to hurt you," he said softly.

At the warmth of his touch, Luca felt himself begin to stir. It was like a wash of heat rushing over his body. The warm flush of the wine did not help his self-control. He knew that he should just move away and put some physical distance between them, but Brad's gesture gave him great comfort and he longed for more. He hadn't touched a man since he took the vow of celibacy at his ordination. There were certainly times when it was a significant struggle and, although he had been tempted over his many years of priesthood, he remained firm in his resolve. But here he was now with his college roommate and first love, who was touching his face tenderly, and he had no thoughts of holding back. His entire body was buzzing with excitement mingled with fear.

Brad continued to look into Luca's eyes and moved his face closer. The photo album fell from his lap as Brad's lips touched Luca's for the first time in decades. They were soft and full upon his mouth, and Luca gave into his desire. It was a tender moment as his lips gently melted into Brad's. Their touch was loving and potent with possibility. With the familiarity of their touch and taste, and the sensations they stirred in him, he wondered if Brad was right, that they were returning home.

As their kisses became more confident, Luca felt the flicker of Brad's tongue on his lips and willingly opened his mouth. When their tongues touched, their tentative kisses turned passionate. Luca cupped both of his hands under Brad's face and held him lovingly. How could he have gone without this intimacy for so many years? Luca felt as if a window had been shattered and through that opening came a life-giving breath. He breathed in Brad's loving kisses with insatiable desire.

Just like when they were in college, Luca did not take the time to reflect on what all of this meant for his life. He simply let his heart and his body open up to this new, yet familiar encounter with Brad. He didn't question the morality of his actions in that moment. With one hand, Brad deftly unbuckled Luca's belt and unzipped his pants. Luca was barely aware of the brazen move. Everything felt good and right. But when Luca felt Brad's hand in his pants he snapped out of his trance. What am I doing? This is insane. Luca pulled away abruptly.

"No, stop it, Brad. We can't do this! This is not what I want."

"Oh, but you do want it, Luca. We both know that you do," Brad said as he squeezed Luca's erection tightly. At that, Luca stood, buckled up his pants and ran his fingers through his ruffled hair. He was flustered and didn't know what to say.

"Brad, it was good to see you, but this is not right for either of us. I need to go."

"Come on, Luca. Don't be like that. What harm are we doing to anyone? We are just giving in to our natural desires. You have to admit that we both felt that connection immediately. We were meant to be together."

"Yes, I felt that connection too—obviously. But we made our choices a long time ago. And let's face it, our relationship was incredibly destructive. There was a reason we ended it. We could have reconciled long ago, but we didn't, because there was so much pain." The Bishop sighed. "Or perhaps it was only me who bore the pain."

"Hey, that's not fair, Luca," Brad said. "I was devastated when you walked out on me. You never gave me a chance to apologize or make it up to you. You just cut me off and never spoke a word to me after that. You just disappeared from my life. It was cruel."

"It was survival, Brad. You knew that you had the power to draw me in again, and I knew that if I let that happen, I would lose myself completely. It was a toxic relationship. I did what I needed to make myself whole again."

"Say what you will, Luca, but I loved you. I still do. Don't go—please give this a chance. Let's not leave it like this. Sit down, let's talk about it."

"Brad, we can talk again, but right now I have to get out of here," the Bishop said, taking a step back. "I don't trust either of us at this moment. I should never have let this go so far."

"OK, OK, but promise me that we'll see each other again. We can be friends, can't we?"

"That remains to be seen. Perhaps we can meet on neutral ground next time."

"Absolutely! How is next week? That should give us both some time. I'll have my assistant set it up right now," Brad insisted.

"Brad, I need time to process this. My head is reeling. I am not comfortable setting a date right now. I have to go."

Brad reached out to hug him goodbye, but Luca raised his hand to stop him. "Not a good idea, Brad," he said. "Goodbye."

Luca turned on his heel and made a hasty exit. He tried to be nonchalant as he passed Brad's assistant, and gave him a friendly wave goodbye, but walked as quickly as he possibly could. He was grateful that he wasn't wearing his clerical garb, as he didn't feel very priestly at the moment. He was deeply ashamed. *What was I thinking? Who was that man in that office? It certainly wasn't me. I'm way too old for this crap!* As he opened the door to the street he gasped for air and heard himself say out loud, "What am I going to do now?"

He pulled out his cell phone and immediately began to dial.

CHAPTER 14

LUCA
SPRING 1980

It was the end of our sophomore year. Final exams were swiftly approaching, and everyone was making travel or work plans. Brad and I were talking about what we might do over the summer. Unfortunately, I had missed a few core requirements during my freshman year and had to take care of them during the summer session. A number of my music credits from Hartt didn't apply to my graduation requirements.

"That sucks!" Brad exclaimed. "I was hoping we could travel somewhere on our own little vacation," he added suggestively.

"I don't think that's in the cards for this summer, Brad. I have to take two language classes and either a history or literature class in order to graduate on time."

"Yeah, that makes sense. It's too bad you can't use the opportunity to study abroad, like Paris or someplace cool like that."

"It's funny you should mention that. I've just started looking into a program in Perugia, in Italy. It's known for the Universitá per Stranieri–the university for foreigners. I could brush up my language skills and take a class in Italian Literature."

"Wow! That sounds cool. Do you think you could afford it?" Brad asked. He knew that my dad was out of work.

"Well, I've done some preliminary calculations. If I can earn \$700 before July 1st, I'll have enough in my savings to cover the cost of the program, as well as a little extra for spending money," I responded. I was already excited by the possibilities.

"Luca, that's a lot to earn on minimum wage. How are you possibly going to make that kind of money? Do you plan to work the streets in New York?" he said as he laughed.

"Exactly!" I smirked. "But seriously, my uncle works at the Western Publishing plant in Poughkeepsie. They pay much more than minimum wage. Plus, he said they need people to work the night shift; it pays time and a half. He said that if I want the job, it's mine."

"What do you know about printing?" Brad asked.

"Nothing. My uncle says they'll teach me to do some basic typesetting. It's not my dream job, but if it will get me to Italy, I'm game."

"Luca, you are full of surprises. If it gets you what you want, then why not? But it sounds like it's gonna suck."

"It probably will, but it'll only last seven weeks. I've

had to do plenty of things I hate for longer than seven weeks. I'll be just fine."

I started working immediately after final exams. My initial hours were 3 to 11 p.m.; after I got the hang of it, I worked until midnight for the overtime pay. I was used to keeping late hours, just as most college students did, so the late shift didn't bother me at all. Besides, I still had my weekends free to go out with friends. The job was actually mind-numbing. I was bored to tears, but determined to study in Italy–and making it happen. I had never made so much money before. By the time July came, I had saved over $900. My parents drove me to Kennedy Airport, staying with me until I boarded the plane. They hugged and kissed me as they bid me safe travels and I was on my way.

After an eight-and-a-half hour flight, the three-hour bus ride from Rome to Perugia should have been pure drudgery. But I was so thrilled to be in Italy that I enjoyed every moment, snapping photos at every turn. I caught sight of the medieval city perched high on a hill from miles away. When we reached the bus stop to catch the funicular to the top, I was nearly jumping out of my skin.

The university housing office was in the heart of the medieval town center, at the peak of the hilltop. The cobblestone street glistened in the summer sun as I walked up from the funicular stop, widening into a spacious piazza with a grand medieval fountain where students sat chatting. Cafes dotted the piazza, each filled with people having animated conversations, while tourists roamed about gazing at the sights. I couldn't believe that I would be spending seven weeks in this town.

Once in the housing office, I was given a welcome

packet with maps to each of the university buildings, including la mensa, the dining hall. The receptionist handed me a key and explained that I was assigned to a quad with other guys from the same program. Excited, I lugged my overly-large suitcase up another hill to the dorm. As I reached for my key, the door to my room opened.

"Ciao, I'm Sal. Are you Luca or Tony?"

"Ciao, Sal. I'm Luca. Are the other guys here yet?"

He saw me struggling with my suitcase, backpack, and camera case, so he jumped right in and gave me a hand.

"Did you bring enough stuff with you, Luca? You could fit a body in this bag!" he said in an amusingly sarcastic way.

"Seven weeks is a long time to be away. I have to look good, you know," I said as I winked at him.

"Oh, Luca, I think we're going to be great friends," Sal said. He put his arm around me. "Leave all this right here. It's time for pranzo–lunch–and you don't want to miss the pasta! Let's head to la mensa before the line gets too long."

I dropped my stuff right in the middle of the room and happily followed Sal out the door. I hadn't realized how hungry I was until then.

Sal was right: we hit it off immediately. He was playful and gregarious. During the orientation for our program, he introduced himself to nearly everyone. I was by his side throughout all his mingling, so I did the same. Everyone thought that we had been friends long before traveling with the program. They couldn't believe that we had just met. In many ways, we were a comedy team. There was always some story to tell from our adventures in the city or at a restaurant; our classmates were always in hysterics. Before long, we were known as olio & aceto (oil and vinegar) because we were always seen together.

We had a large corner room that looked out on a little courtyard surrounded by pine trees. By the end of the first week, our roommate, Tony, asked to room with a friend from class, and moved out that weekend. We were still waiting to find out who would be filling the fourth bed in our room. For the immediate future, Sal and I found ourselves alone in a room meant for four people.

We were thrilled to have Tony out of the room. He was a blowhard, loud and boisterous, and he was always making inappropriate sexual comments to the women in our classes. He loved using obscene Italian words that he had just learned. He drove both of us crazy. By contrast, Sal and I had similar personalities and enjoyed hanging out together. He was in a five-year engineering program and, on a whim, decided to study in Italy for the summer. He was two years older than me and took me under his wing.

One night, we went out to a disco with a couple of local Italian guys. They promised us that we would meet lots of nice Italian girls. Sal was like lightning on the dance floor. Disco music was still very much in vogue, and Sal had moves I had never seen before. Not even John Travolta in "Saturday Night Fever" was a match for Sal. I was riveted as I watched him dance. When I got out to the dance floor, I found a girl and copied as many of his moves as I could remember. Sal noticed that I was watching him and maneuvered himself and his partner closer to me. Soon, we were in sync, and a circle began to form around the two couples as the Italians clapped and cheered us on. When the song ended, our new Italian friends huddled around us, clapping us on our backs.

The crowd was so thick that Sal and I were pressed tightly against each other. There was a momentary glance between us before we all went back to our table to drink.

Something had happened to us on the dance floor. I could feel the energy between us change. He and I were more attuned to each other now, and we continued to catch each other's eye throughout the rest of the evening, even when we were trying our best to speak Italian to our new fans. By the end of the night, we were both pretty drunk. I could count the number of times I'd been drunk on one hand, so I was not accustomed to the feeling.

"Let's get you home, caro," Sal said when he saw me rest my head against the wall. I was fading. Arm in arm, Sal and I made our way back to our dorm, staggering and laughing the entire way. Once inside, we fell onto the nearest bed together. Neither of us had any desire to move.

"Oh my God, that was fun!" Sal said.

"So much fun." I replied. "Where did you learn to dance like that? You were amazing."

"I live in New York City. My friends and I go dancing every weekend. You should come sometime. Poughkeepsie isn't that far away."

"No, really, you had every Italian girl drooling over you!" I said.

"Maybe, but I just got into the music. I didn't care who was looking at me."

"Well, I couldn't stop watching you. Man, you can move, Sal."

He took note of what I said and lifted his head to look at me. "You did all right yourself, Luca. Who knew that you could shake that cute little butt of yours like that?"

I laughed. "Just one of my many hidden talents."

"Well, I hope I get to see more of those talents. Tell me, Luca, what else can that butt of yours do?" he said. He moved his face closer to mine and kissed me in one smooth motion.

I closed my eyes, and although I could feel the room spinning, I was completely drawn into his embrace and wanted more. When he lifted his head away, I looked at him with a hint of a smile and said, "Hmm, I don't know, Sal, maybe we'll have to figure that out together."

There was nothing romantic about what happened next. Clothes were clumsily shed as we explored each other's bodies. Each of us giggled at our lack of finesse. When it was over, Sal drew me closer and whispered in my ear. "I told you we were going to be great friends."

"Mmm-hmm," I responded affectionately. Then we quickly drifted off to sleep.

The next morning, I awoke with a huge hangover and could barely lift my head. Not used to drinking, I had no idea that I needed to hydrate. The taste in my mouth was sour, as was the acid burning a hole through my stomach. I moaned slightly and caught Sal's attention. He lifted himself on one elbow, smiled and said, "Poor baby. You look like hell. Do you feel as bad as you look?"

"Worse!"

"Let me get you some water," he offered, standing up and heading to the refrigerator.

"Ughhh!" I moaned, sickened by the slight jostle. "I can't move without my head throbbing."

"Here you go." Sal handed me a full bottle of mineral water. "You should drink one of these every hour."

I gulped down the water with a couple aspirin.

"I think this might be a good day to sleep in. I'll tell la professoressa that you're sick," he said before he left. "I'll check in on you before pranzo."

"Grazie, Sal. You're my savior."

"Well, you can just start addressing me as my lord. By the way, I really enjoyed being with you last night," he said as he kissed my aching forehead.

I smiled weakly and said, "Me too."

As my hangover dissipated, images of our evening together came into focus. I was really drawn to him, especially when he danced. It felt like he and I had danced together rather than with our partners. We never took our eyes off of one another. I hadn't experienced any doubt or fear when we slept together the night before. Everything seemed natural and easy.

I didn't know what implications Sal would have for my relationship with Brad. I felt guilty for having cheated on Brad, but I pushed the thought of him out of my mind. I justified my actions by reasoning that Brad had a girlfriend and that he was with her. Why shouldn't I have fun as well? But now that I was attracted to two different guys, Brad's insistence that we were not gay didn't hold up. I was confused and afraid of what I might discover about myself. I needed to talk with Sal about it. I just had to figure out what it all meant.

After dinner that evening, Sal and I decided to take it easy. We took a leisurely stroll to the piazza, met up with our new Italian friends, and had espresso at a cafe. While the rest of the group went on to the disco again, I declined the invitation. I had had enough the night before. The Italians playfully laughed at me for turning down the offer, joking that Americans couldn't hold their alcohol. With regard to me, they were absolutely right. I just laughed with them and said, "Verró la prossima volta, sens'altro!" (I'll come next time, without a doubt.)

Sal decided to keep me company and we took a long passegiata, or walk, along the city wall. There was so much to talk about.

"So it looks like you've fully recovered, caro Luca," Sal said as he affectionately draped his arm around my shoulders.

"Yeah, I'm a pretty cheap drunk, I guess," I replied. "Sorry I was such a mess."

"Oh, you weren't all that drunk, amore mio. I can tell you that for sure," he said with a wink.

"I should be blushing, but I have to say that it was a nice surprise. I've only done that with one other guy." I conveniently left out the fact that Brad and I were still together.

"Well now, that surprises me. You seemed like an expert," Sal said with a twinkle in his eye.

"Yeah, sure! I was stumbling all through it!" I laughed.

"Luca, you worry too much. We both had fun last night. Nobody stumbled through anything," Sal assured me.

"I meant it, Sal. I am new at this. I didn't even know that there were other guys like us out there," I said.

Sal turned to me with a shocked expression on his face. "Luca, you can't be that innocent," he said. "You've been to New York. There are tons of gay men everywhere."

"But, I'm not gay. I just happen to..." My voice trailed off as my foolishness dawned on me.

"Luca, what do you mean, you're not gay? I don't understand," he said.

"Sal, I don't know what to think anymore. All I know is that I really wanted to be with you last night. It felt like the most natural thing in the world. I never experienced anything like that with girls. It just didn't do anything for me."

"It is natural, Luca. It's just two people who are attracted to each other. Believe me, it's not rocket science. But you have to know that there are tons of guys out there that are just like us."

"Yeah, but all I see on the news are guys in dresses or leather. That's not me, so I'm not sure what I am?" If I allowed myself to use the same argument I got from Brad, I would have stated that I was not gay, but his faulty logic had already begun to break down.

We sat down on the city wall, looking out over the valley. Sal sighed at my last statement, turned to me and took my hands in his. "Luca, gay people come in all shapes, sizes, and preferences. Are all straight people the same? Do they dress and act alike?"

"Of course not. But my friend, Brad, said we weren't like the gay men we see on the news. I know it sounds stupid. I'm obviously attracted to guys, but I just thought we were different. I'm sorry, I feel like an idiot."

"Hey, you come from an Italian Catholic family. I'm sure that everything you heard about gay people was negative. Growing up, the number of anti-gay remarks that came from my father's mouth could fill volumes. And of course, there's all the talk of sin that comes from the Church. How could you not grow up with prejudice? But we're the same as everyone else. We just happen to love other men. Does that make sense?"

"Of course it does. It's so crazy, because it turns out that I was¬—or am–prejudiced against myself. How screwed up is that?"

"Luca, that's called internalized homophobia. We take in all the hatred that we've learned and turn it inward. That's why so many people have trouble coming out of the closet. Hell, I'm not completely out yet, just to my close friends. Definitely not to my Italian Catholic family–not yet, anyway."

"I don't think I can ever tell my family," I said despairingly.

"Luca, first you have to admit it to yourself. You have to get used to seeing yourself through your own lenses, instead of what you've always heard from others. Once you're more comfortable with yourself, then you can think about coming out to people you love. One step at a time, kiddo." At that, he pulled me into a big hug. "What do you say we go back to our room?"

We continued our animated chat along the way to the dorm. I asked scores of questions and Sal patiently answered them. I slowly became less afraid of the word gay. If Sal identified as gay, then certainly I could too. We were so alike: same background and similar personalities. If I was attracted to Sal before that conversation, my desire for him grew tenfold afterward. He seemed so wise and patient with me, and I wanted as much time with him as possible. Thoughts of Brad began to fade far into the background.

When we got to our room, he led me to the bed and gently undressed me. He kissed me tenderly on the lips and said, "Let's take our time tonight. Ask me anything you want at any time, OK? Nothing is off limits and there are no stupid questions—and if anything makes you uncomfortable we'll stop. Got it?"

"Got it. Sal?" I looked at him intently. I needed to tell him what was going on in my heart, but I hesitated.

"What is it, Luca?"

"I just want to say thank you. Thank you for not laughing at me or getting angry at my offensive statements. I know we've only just met, but I feel really safe with you."

"You are safe, Luca." And then he began to kiss me deeply but not urgently. It was passion with compassion.

That night, as I lay in his arms once again, Sal's touch was gentle and confident. It seemed to say, "Don't worry, I'll take care of you." He guided me through new ways of expressing love and passion, and I followed willingly. I never felt uneasy, fearful, or pushed into anything. His first concern was for me and my comfort. We paused often and talked to each other throughout. It was an entirely different experience from what I was accustomed to with Brad, who often seemed selfish in bed. With Brad, it always seemed like our lovemaking was centered on his pleasure, and the focus was always on the finish line. In contrast, my time together with Sal that second night opened my eyes to a whole new perspective of intimacy between two men.

The weeks seemed to fly by after that. Sal and I were by each other's side at every moment, laughing, learning, and eating. The waitstaff at local restaurants knew us by name and greeted us like old friends. We practiced conversational Italian each time we were out, which led to many comical moments with our new Italian friends. In addition, we had many more profound conversations about life, being gay, being in the closet, and coming out. Day by day, my world continued to expand. By the end of the study tour, my perspective was transformed. I began to accept myself as a gay man. In the meantime, we were exploring Italy with trips to Florence and Rome. Sal and I often joked that it was as if we were on our honeymoon.

I was so immersed in my Italian experience and my relationship with Sal that I rarely thought about home. On my occasional phone calls with my parents, I spoke almost entirely in Italian without even thinking. I remember my mother stopping me at one point to say, "Luca, speak in English so your sisters can understand too. They are on the extension." I hadn't even realized that I was speaking in Italian, which meant that I had begun to think in a foreign language. I was on the road to fluency.

Five weeks had gone by; there was only one more week left in the program. I had planned to take the train up to Venice to spend some time with my Italian cousins. Sal had readily agreed to come for part of the time, since he'd never been to Venice. We were both looking forward to concluding our program with a week of touring by ourselves.

One afternoon, he and I were lounging in our room, doing a bit of homework, when reception rang and indicated that I had a call from the U.S. I thought that was strange, since I had spoken to my parents the night before. When the call connected, I heard Brad's voice for the first time in over a month.

"Buona sera Luca! Did you forget about me already?"

"Brad! What a wonderful surprise," I said uneasily.

Sal looked over at me with a quizzical look.

"So, my Italian stallion, why haven't you called me?" Brad asked.

"I'm sorry, Brad, but you know how expensive these calls are. I haven't even called my parents. How are you?" I tried to change the subject.

"I'm fine. I've been spending a lot of time at the beach, hanging out with some of the St. Robert's crew. But I miss you, Luca."

"I miss you too, Brad." At that, Sal lifted his head from his books. I turned my head away in embarrassment.

"It's just torture, not being able to hold you and kiss you every day," he said.

"I know, yeah, me too," I responded vaguely, trying not to reveal too much of our conversation to Sal.

"I love you, Luca."

Now I had to respond in kind, otherwise Brad would suspect that something was up. I mumbled, "I love you too."

Out of the corner of my eye, I could see Sal stiffen. He was not happy.

"When are you coming home?" Brad asked.

"I'll be home near the end of August. I'll call you when I get in. If you want the specific details you can call my parents. You've got their number, right?"

"Of course I do. I need to see you as soon as you get home, Luca. I'll make a plan."

"That sounds great, Brad. It will be good to see you."

"I love you, Luca."

"Me too. Ciao."

I hung up and knew I was in trouble. Sal sat up straight and closed his books. "What was that all about? Isn't Brad your ex-boyfriend?"

"Yeah, well, he's not exactly my ex. We're still together. He and I never had any discussion about seeing other guys. I'm sorry, Sal, I just didn't know how to tell you."

"Luca, how could you lie to me this entire time? I thought we really had something together." Sal was angry.

"We do, Sal. I wasn't lying, I just didn't tell you because I didn't want it to interfere with us. You have changed me; I was so ignorant about all of this before you. I thought that we were meant to be together. To be honest, I haven't really thought about Brad since I met you. I am so sorry. I don't know what the rules are in gay relationships."

"Seriously, Luca? The rules are the same for gay and straight relationships. You don't cheat and you don't lie!"

I was beside myself. Everything he said was making perfect sense. Why hadn't I thought of any of this before? I just didn't think before I acted. I had to fix this. I didn't want to completely ruin my relationship with Sal.

"Please, Sal, don't be angry with me. I really love you. Please try to understand. I was just being stupid," I pleaded.

"I definitely agree with you there. Listen—say I forgive you, Luca. What happens when you go back to school? Are you going to break up with Brad to be with me?"

"I, I don't know. We're going to be roommates in September. How can I break up with him? That would make the entire year miserable."

"This is what I'm talking about. You go back to your comfortable old life with Brad and forget all about me. What am I supposed to do with all the feelings I have for you, Luca? Have you ever thought about anyone else but yourself through all this?"

"I'm sorry, honestly, Sal. I don't know what to do."

"Well, when you figure it out, let me know!" Sal walked out of our room and slammed the door.

I really screwed this whole thing up, I thought. Although it felt like I was cheating on Brad, I continued to rationalize my behavior. He has a girlfriend and I'm sure he's been with her all summer. We never talked about other guys. I couldn't believe how angry Sal was. But the worst part was the fact that I had hurt him. How could I have done that to him after he'd been nothing but kind and loving to me? Everything changed with one stupid phone call. But how could Sal and I be together when we get back? He goes to NYU in the city, and I'm in Poughkeepsie. Plus, this will be his last year there. Who knows what he'll do after graduation. I sat on my bed and began to cry. I love Sal but I'm still in love with Brad. Why is life so complicated? What am I going to do?

Later that night, Sal slipped into our room long after I had gone to sleep. The following day, he seemed to have calmed down. I tried not to make eye contact for fear of another outburst. I was tiptoeing around him as if not to disturb a sleeping bear.

Finally, he said, "Luca, come here." He patted his bed. "Let's talk about what happened yesterday."

I ambled over sheepishly and sat across from him.

"I am sorry for getting so angry with you, Luca. I shouldn't have stormed out of here like that."

"No, I understand, Sal. I should have told you about Brad. I was just so into you and I really didn't know how to make sense of the whole situation. I really love both of you."

"Look, I know you are new to this and I am quite aware that I have taught you more than you imagined about being with another guy. Maybe I expected too much from our relationship. Maybe this is just a summer fling and we just need to let it end," he said, taking my hand.

I was not expecting such a final ending to our relationship. I didn't want it to be over, but couldn't figure out how to keep it going in New York. I stared at him with a look of disbelief on my face, so he continued. "But I have to confess that I started to fall in love with you, Luca." He let out a heavy sigh. "Realizing that you are still in love with Brad was like a punch in the gut. I was completely blindsided."

"Sal, I am so sorry. I didn't mean to hurt you," I replied.

"Well, it was good while it lasted," he said with bitterness.

"Sal, don't say that. I really do love you too. I just didn't look to the future and what would happen when we left Italy. I feel like such a fool. There's got to be a way for us to be together. We have to find another solution."

"Well it seems pretty clear to me, Luca. You either break up with me or with Brad."

I bowed my head and squeezed my eyes shut. I didn't like what I was hearing.

"Luca, I'm not blind. Your feelings for Brad run pretty deep. I honestly don't think I can compete with that."

"I am so sorry, Sal. You have to believe me, I never meant to deceive you."

"Yeah, well." There was a long pause, and then he said, "All right then. Obviously, I shouldn't travel with you to Venice."

"But why? You've never been there and I know you'd love my cousins. Please come."

"No, Luca. We'd be delaying the inevitable. That would be torture for me. We need to stop being a couple now. I don't want to prolong the pain."

With tears streaming down both our faces, Sal pulled me in for a hug. When he let go I began to cry in earnest.

The week I spent with my cousins was filled with family dinners and visits. I never had a free moment, but there was a shadow darkening all that I did. I was clearly mourning the loss of my relationship with Sal. Over such a short period of time, he had had a greater impact upon me than Brad. And yet, with my return to New York only days away, I began to feel even more guilty about betraying Brad. How could I have done that to him?

One day, I asked my uncle to bring me to a jeweler. "Zio, I want to by a gift for a friend. Would you come with me?"

"*Certo, caro.* What do you want to buy?"

"Since Italy is known for its gold, I thought I'd buy a chain and cross."

"Oh, no, Luca. That is not good for a girl. Perhaps a medal of the Blessed Virgin Mary."

"Zio, it's not for a girl."

He was taken aback. Why would I spend so much money on a boy? "I don't understand. He must be a buon'amico, a dear friend," he said.

I seized upon that phrase, though I had never heard it used before. "Yes, yes, Zio. He is my most important friend."

That seemed to quell his concerns, and with his help, I chose a beautiful image of Christ on the cross with an 18-karat chain. It was more than I could afford, but I just had to buy it. Without knowing it, I had just made my first guilt purchase.

When I got back to New York several weeks later, Brad was waiting at the airport for me. I was completely surprised. He had brought a bouquet of flowers and a sign in Italian, saying Welcome home, Luca!

He drove me home to my parent's house and stayed for a number of days. That first night was full of so many intense emotions. Being with him again made me realize how much I had missed him, and I couldn't wait to give him the chain and cross that I had bought for him in Italy. We were sitting on the floor in my childhood bedroom and I pulled out the little jewelry box from my backpack.

"Hey Brad, I got you a little something from Venice." I handed him the finely wrapped box. He fidgeted with the tie and gently pulled at the paper. When he opened the lid, he gasped. As the gold cross glittered in the low light of my room, he looked up at me in disbelief. His eyes welled up and he pulled me into a hug.

"Luca, I, I don't know what to say. It's gorgeous. This must have cost a fortune!"

"I love you Brad, and I wanted you to have something special to remind you of that." He bowed his head as I fastened the golden chain around his neck and I said, "Promise me that you'll never take this off."

"I promise, Luca. I love you, too."

The next day I gathered my courage and I told him about my relationship with Sal, and all that I learned about being gay. However, I didn't tell him that I had begun to fall in love. I couldn't bear losing both of them. He listened intently, but didn't seem angry.

"Wow, I wasn't expecting that. So, how do you feel

about us?" he asked.

"I love you, Brad. I hope that we can continue to be together."

"Me too. Hell, I was with Theresa all summer. If you're not upset about that, I suppose I can't be angry about Sal." He paused, then added, "Of course, you won't see him again, will you?" It seemed more like a command. He made it clear that I was never to see Sal again.

"Not as boyfriends. We had a long talk about it after your phone call. He was very good to me and I hope we'll remain friends."

"Well, I don't ever want to meet him. He almost took you away from me," Brad said.

"Don't say that. No one could take me away from you. You know that. Sal's a great guy and I think you would love each other."

"Don't count on that. I don't like competition."

I could tell that Brad was more upset about my affair with Sal then he let on.

CHAPTER 15

IRENE
SUMMER 2015

Irene was one of Luca's oldest and dearest friends. They had met through the campus ministry department at St. Robert's College. They were volunteering at a local soup kitchen and stood beside each other while serving dinner. Her sense of humor and love of life drew him in immediately. She visited Luca on several occasions during her year abroad in Paris, when he was in seminary in Rome, and Luca had escaped to Paris to visit her whenever he could. As a result, Irene was one of the few people who witnessed the complicated dynamics of the Roman seminary and the impact they had on him. At that time, she was the only friend with whom he had discussed his sexuality, and she certainly got an earful whenever they were together. With

Irene by his side, Luca felt safe and at home. There was never any judgment or posturing; they were always their true selves with each other. They shared some of their darkest moments and insecurities, as well as their greatest joys.

Luca's face flashed on Irene's phone. Well this is a surprise. She thought. In the middle of the work day? She answered the phone as she closed the door to her office.

"Hey, Irene, it's Luca."

"Is it really?" she said sarcastically. "You know your face shows up on my phone when you call, right? What's up, honey? Aren't you working today?"

"Irene, I did something stupid, something really stupid!"

She could hear the tension in his voice. "OK, take a breath. Tell me what happened."

"I had lunch with Brad today. It didn't go as I expected."

"Wait, Brad? Brad from St. Robert's? What the hell? How did that happen? I didn't even know you were in touch with him."

"I ran into him at a fundraiser a few weeks ago and we exchanged numbers. Look, Irene, I know it's last minute, but can we have dinner tonight? I need to talk to you in person."

"Seriously? You're going to drive all the way up to Boston for dinner?"

"Yes, I can be there by 6:30. Does that work for you?"

"Sure, Luca. Maybe we can go have a drink first and then eat at home. That way we can have a little privacy."

"Perfect. I can't tell you how much I appreciate this. I'm a complete mess right now, and you're the only person

I can talk to about this. See you in a couple of hours. Love you."

"Love you too, honey. Drive safely, OK?"

Irene was worried. She knew Luca inside and out. Their brief phone conversation spoke volumes. Luca was in trouble and he needed his friend. Where the hell did Brad come from and why are he and Luca back in touch in the first place? she wondered. Irene had never liked Brad, and she certainly didn't trust him. After what he did to Luca in college, she would never forgive him. She watched the clock for the entire afternoon. Her rendezvous with Luca couldn't come quickly enough.

After he hung up with Irene, Luca dialed again. "Fr. George, this is Bishop De Santo. Something unexpected came up. Can you clear my schedule this afternoon? What is my day like tomorrow?"

"Hello Bishop. Of course! You only have a staff meeting today at 4:00. I am sure everyone will be disappointed that you cancelled," Fr. George chuckled. He always got a kick out of his own jokes. "I will get someone to cover your 9:00 Mass tomorrow morning and I can easily reschedule the rest of your appointments. What time do you expect to return?"

"I should be back in the office before noon tomorrow. Thanks George, I'll see you then."

Luca swung by the rectory to pack an overnight bag and got on the road. He knew he was driving too fast, but his adrenaline was pumping. He just hoped that he wouldn't get caught in a speed trap along the way. It was less than three hours from Bridgeport to Boston, but it seemed to take forever. He put Handel's Messiah on at full blast and sung along to every chorus and solo. Messiah is about three hours long; he hoped that it would keep him distracted throughout the drive.

Meanwhile, Irene had selected a private wine bar in the South End and texted Luca the address. Thankfully, it had valet parking. As his car pulled up, she crossed her arms and pointed to her watch. Irene stood there in one of her usual flowing bohemian outfits smoking a cigarette and tapping her foot.

"It's about time, buddy. I was just about to leave."

"What do you mean? It's only 6:20, I'm early!"

"Wow, you are tense. Just kidding, honey. Come give me a hug." She wrapped Luca in the tightest, most wonderful hug. It was just what he needed.

"If I wasn't an infamous lesbian in these parts, people would think we were having an affair!" she joked as she released him from her grasp.

"Yeah, not funny right now. Not funny at all," Luca retorted.

Irene's jaw dropped. It had been a long time since she was speechless.

"Come on, you catatonic beauty. I'll tell you more inside," he said as they linked arms to enter the bar. They found a quiet table in the corner and after they ordered, Luca told Irene of his lunch encounter with Brad.

"So there we were on his couch, making out like teenagers. Things were getting pretty heated. Everything was so familiar and comfortable. It was like the most natural thing in the world."

"This is not what I was expecting to hear, Luca! So, what happened next?" Irene asked.

"Then he became more insistent. He caressed me through my pants; his touch felt so good, and it has been so long. I kept kissing him, and it got more intense. Then he began to unzip my pants, and I just let him do it. I wanted him so much, Irene."

"This is crazy! I can't wrap my head around this, Luca."

"I don't know what was going on in my head. When I felt him pull my zipper down, something snapped. I just stood up with my zipper down and pants unbuckled. I got out of there as fast as I could."

"Holy shit, Luca!"

"Yeah, I know. This is a nightmare. I can't believe I let this happen."

"You can't believe it? That guy is a snake! You remember that, don't you?"

"Irene, I don't know what I was thinking. As soon as he pressed his leg against mine I should have pulled away. Better yet, I should have gotten up to leave. I could have made up any excuse so as not to offend him. Now it's a big mess."

Irene knew that they needed more privacy to continue this discussion. This was the worst news he could have possibly shared with her. She was worried about him. They left the bar and walked to her apartment. As the two of them prepared dinner, they continued their conversation.

"So, how did you leave it with him, Luca? Will you see him again?"

"He pleaded with me, asked me not to leave, then made me promise to be in touch. Hell, I don't know what to say to him."

"Why not? You're a bishop, for God's sake! That should be reason enough not to pursue anything with him. That is, unless you have feelings for him. Do you… have feelings for him?"

"No. Well, yes… maybe… I don't know, Irene."

"Spill it! You still love him, don't you?" she prodded, "After all that you went through with him?"

"Hell, it was just so intoxicating. I didn't even feel like I was in control of my own body."

"Luca, you've been alone for a very long time. I don't know how you do it, honey. That fact that you were physically and emotionally drawn to him isn't that surprising."

"That's the thing. I felt this overwhelming urge to touch him, to kiss him. I just couldn't hold back."

"You have a significant history with him. In spite of the fact that he's an asshole, isn't it natural for you to fall back into your familiar patterns?" she asked.

"I guess you're right, but I'm so confused. Our relationship was so destructive in college. I bore the scars, literally, for years. But somehow he has a hold on me once again. I don't understand it."

Irene was exasperated. She didn't want Luca to be entangled with Brad again, but she knew he needed a compassionate ear right now. "Well, my dear, he was your first love—your only love." She thought for a moment. "Hmm, that's not really true, now is it?"

"Listen, this is no time to rehash the soap opera of my seminary love life," Luca chuckled. "But, you have a point. In many ways, it's because of Brad that I began to understand my sexuality. My relationship with him paved the way to my coming out, however privately."

"You obviously have unresolved feelings for him, Luca. You can't just ignore them and hope that they'll go away." Fighting her own disdain for Brad, she said, "The two of you need to talk this through. But first, you have to figure out what it is that you're feeling for him."

"That's the difficult part. When we kissed today, I wanted nothing more than to be with him, to hold him and love him. But I hated him for so long. I just don't understand how I could feel any tenderness for Brad."

In Irene's mind, there would be nothing worse than Luca getting back together with him. She wanted to tell Luca stay the hell away from him—that he was dangerous—but instead she said, "Honey, you were 18 years old. Now you are in your mid 50s. Getting older gives us perspective. Things that devastated us back then have become just bumps in the road of our lives—they gave us character and made us who we are today." She reached out and put her hands around his. "But you already know that, and I'm sure it isn't bringing you much comfort right now."

"Irene, I love my life. I love being a bishop. I feel like I make an impact on the lives of real people, and I am so fulfilled by the work I do. But, God, at night I am so damn lonely. Sometimes I just ache for someone to hold me."

"Goddamned celibacy! It's such an antiquated notion. You should become an Anglican like Beth. Even though she grew up Catholic, she loves the Episcopal Church. At least you'd be able to marry—even marry another man. I hear they're looking for bishops in Boston," she joked.

"Hmm, something to seriously consider," he joked. "But as for now, I am stuck. This is my Church and my tradition. As crazy as it sounds, I still believe in it. Catholicism is so deeply ingrained in me that I don't think I could ever leave the Church. Even so, at this moment, I can't seem to reconcile its teachings with what I am feeling. This is so damned difficult."

"But that doesn't make sense to me, Luca. You know I love you, but the Catholic Church is still in the Dark Ages. Why do you still cling to it?"

"Irene, I understand what you are saying. It has caused us so much pain. But I can't explain it. I just can't seem to let it go. It's so deeply a part of who I am."

"Luca, honey, I was mostly kidding about the Anglican Church. But it's virtually the same faith without the cruelty and judgment."

"Point taken, Irene. But I just don't feel at home there. As similar as it is to the Catholic Church, its traditions are very different."

"OK, OK, I get that it's not that easy–although I wish for you that it were!"

"In the meantime, my little rendezvous with Brad has turned my otherwise comfortable life inside out."

"All right, then. What do you want to do, Luca? What is your heart telling you?" Irene asked.

"Honestly, Irene, I am inexplicably drawn to him," Luca admitted.

Irene sighed heavily. That was not the answer she hoped for. "So, Luca, do you love him still?" She paused and then asked, "Do you want to have sex with him?"

With only a moment's hesitation he said, "Yeah, I think I do. And yes, I would love to sleep with him. Damn it." He buried his face in his hands and let out an exasperated cry. "Fuck!"

Irene and Luca talked late into the night. The morning light came much too soon, but he knew that he had to get back to his office by midday. After a quick coffee, he gave Irene a huge hug and said, "What would I do without you?"

After he left, Irene was plagued with worry. How could this be happening again? After that final semester together at St. Robert's, she was sure that Brad would be out of Luca's life forever. She hated the fact that he still had a hold over him. And what is Luca thinking? she thought. He is crazy to think that this could end any other way but badly. Irene felt a strong sense of foreboding, but could do nothing about it.

CHAPTER 16

BISHOP DE SANTO
SUMMER 2015

The morning after he saw Irene, Bishop De Santo awoke with a clear head. The jumble of thoughts competing for attention seemed more orderly. Spending time with Irene always helped him put things into perspective. She never let him get away with anything, and her questions were direct and challenging. His own answers made him realize how deeply he was affected by this thing happening with Brad; he could see that there was a great deal left unresolved. Luca had to confront his feelings for Brad. They had to meet again to sort everything out. Before that, however, Luca needed more time to process his many conflicting emotions.

When he arrived at his office, Fr. George had several messages and a list of calls for him to return.

"Mgsr. O'Doherty would like to see you about the finances at St. Leo's. Can you see him tomorrow? Fr. Ferrero called about his new parish assignment. Well, anyway, here is the stack of messages. Oh, and this package arrived for you this morning. Shall I open it?"

Bishop De Santo glanced at the box. "No, don't bother. Leave it on my desk and I'll get to it later. Please close my door. I need to get to these phone calls. Thanks, George."

As soon as he heard his door click, he began opening the box. In it was a vintage port from 1979, the year he and Brad met. He opened the card.

"Dear Luca, I am so very sorry about yesterday. I do hope that you can forgive me. You are very important to me. Let's reschedule lunch very soon. B."

His feelings and fears from the previous day resurfaced immediately. He had to resolve this soon, but how? Before he could have a reasonable conversation with Brad, he had to understand what his heart was telling him. What happened with Brad was not simply a matter of breaking his vow of celibacy. Priests have always fallen; some go on to live holy and celibate lives after that. But Luca knew what he was feeling was not only about sex. This was about his life and his loneliness. It called into question his entire vocation. One heart-to-heart conversation with Irene would not suffice; it had only served to reveal the depth of his crisis. Luca was truly worried. He need serious spiritual direction, so he picked up his office phone and dialed.

"Yes, of course Bishop De Santo, the retreat house has rooms available next week. How long would you like to stay?"

"I'd like to do the eight-day silent retreat. Is it possible for me to check in on Saturday, the end of this week?" the Bishop asked.

"Why, yes. We have a beautiful room available with a view of the water. Would you like a directed retreat, or would you like to do it at your own pace?"

"I will be self-directed. Will Fr. Garcia be available for spiritual direction?"

"Yes, he will be here that entire time. I will let him know that you are coming."

"Thank you so much, Sister Ann. See you in a few days." Bishop De Santo hung up the phone and sighed with relief. It's Wednesday, he thought. I can make it until Saturday. I just need to remain busy, and that shouldn't be a problem given the pile on my desk.

For the next two days, he buried himself in his work. He filled his schedule with budget meetings, appointments with clergy, and parish visitations. There were always personnel issues to contend with, and he was sure they would occupy his mind, as well as using much of his emotional energy.

But Brad was relentless. He had a gift basket delivered to the rectory on Thursday, and a bottle of fine wine arrived on Friday. He left voicemails and sent emails to Luca each day. No matter how packed Luca's schedule was, he couldn't avoid Brad's insistent intrusions. Damn it! Luca thought. Why can't he give me a little space? He was even more frustrated by how unnerved he was by Brad's persistence. Luca chose not to respond to any of Brad's overtures. He simply wasn't in the right state of mind yet.

On Saturday morning, Luca wrote an automatic reply and voice recording that informed anyone trying to contact him that he would be on an eight-day silent retreat and that he would not be checking his mail during that time. At least Brad would get the message that he was incommunicado for the next eight days. He was in his car around 8 a.m. and drove 40 minutes to the retreat house, which was directly on Long Island Sound in Madison, Connecticut. It was so close, and yet he felt as if he were in another country.

Before he entered the retreat house to register, Bishop De Santo walked out to the beach. Just seeing the calm waters lapping on the shore brought his blood pressure down. Now the hard work would begin.

After he checked in, Luca took off his shoes and socks and walked along the shore. Being near the water always calmed him when the chaos of life swirled around in his head. Images of himself and Brad flashed in his mind. Their first encounter on the beach while on their college retreat brought memories of innocence and self-discovery. They were so young and so filled with wonder. The first kiss they shared was like being born into a new world. He could feel the exhilaration even now. He had loved Brad with his whole heart, but he knew that there were many unresolved emotions regarding their relationship. The struggle and pain were less acute with the passage of time, but they were there nonetheless.

Given how he was feeling now, it seemed almost impossible that he hadn't thought about Brad in 30 years. I don't remember feeling any regret over the end of my relationship with him, he reflected. When I went on to seminary, I rarely if ever thought of him. Although, he had run into Brad a few years later. One summer, Luca and several other seminarians thought it would be crazy and daring to go out to a bar. They chose a gay bar in New York City that catered to businessmen. They reasoned that it was the most benign of gay establishments where they could gather. Luca was standing with his friends when he spotted Brad leaning against the bar alone. Luca made his way over to him and they exchanged small talk, but nothing more. Luca thought it odd that Brad was there since he was still dating Wendy. But who was Luca to judge, he was a seminarian at a gay bar.

After their tumultuous relationship, Luca had moved on and was happy. "So, why is his re-emergence in my life so disturbing now? It doesn't make any sense," he said aloud to himself.

Bishop De Santo had faithfully kept a prayer journal since his years at St. Robert's. During his first few days in silence, he filled many pages with his conflicting thoughts and emotions. On the fourth day, Luca decided to set an appointment with Fr. Garcia. Garcia had been De Santo's spiritual director during his years in Rome. He needed to talk to his beloved old mentor about his reflections. For Luca, sorting it out as he spoke always put his dilemmas into a more coherent argument. It gave him perspective.

"So, how have your first few days been, Luca?" Fr. Garcia asked as he reached out to give Luca a hug. He was well known among the seminarians in Rome for his comforting bear hugs.

"Ricardo, you have no idea how glad I am to see you," Luca replied.

"You look troubled. Tell me what weighs so heavily on your heart," Fr. Garcia instructed.

"We have known each other for a very long time, Ricardo. Haven't we?"

"I'd say that being your first spiritual advisor in Rome cemented our friendship over the years," he said with a compassionate smile.

"So then, you must remember all the emotional attachments I shared with you during that time, drama after drama," Luca began.

"Those attachments, as you call them, helped teach you how to love and be loved, Luca. Never chide yourself for what your heart leads you to. Tell me, where has it led you today?" Ricardo asked.

"How is it that you are always so perceptive, Ricardo? You are two steps ahead of me at every turn." Luca was delaying as much as he could. He was so ashamed of himself right now. How could he tell Ricardo what had happened? Nonetheless, he knew it was time to spill his heart to his trusted advisor.

"I am in crisis, Ricardo. I am seriously questioning my vow of celibacy for the first time since ordination. My heart is heavy and it pulls me in two directions at once."

"The heart doesn't address life in black and white. You know all too well that it isn't always rational. It is often more complicated than we would like. Tell me what you mean. What are the two directions, Luca?" Ricardo asked.

"Last week I had lunch with a college roommate."

"I assume 'roommate' is a euphemism?" Ricardo asked knowingly.

"I can never get anything past you. Yes, Brad was my first love. It was not a healthy relationship. In fact, it was the most toxic relationship I have ever had. But seeing him after so many years rekindled so many emotions that I was not expecting."

"Did anything physical occur between the two of you?"

"Yes." Luca bowed his head in shame. "We kissed and caressed each other. It was on the way to much more when I stopped it and ran out the door. He begged me not to go, but I couldn't get out of there fast enough."

"Have you spoken with him since?"

"No. He has made numerous attempts to contact me, but I just don't feel strong enough to respond."

"And what have your days of silence led you to? Have you sorted out your feelings for him, Luca?"

"Let me just say that I love being a priest and bishop. My vocation is stronger than ever and…"

Ricardo held his hand up to halt Luca's rambling. "No need to tell me what I already know. What do you feel for Brad?"

Luca let out a heavy sigh and with his head hanging low once again, said, "I want to be with him. I long to hold him and make love to him."

"So much shame for such a human desire, Luca. You should know better from all your years of spiritual counseling. I am sure that you have ushered many struggling souls through similar circumstances. More than likely, you have guided some of your own priests through crises regarding celibacy. We both know that you have little control over what your heart leads you to feel. The only thing you do have control over is how you choose to act with regard to those feelings."

"Yes, I know you're right. But I thought I was beyond such feelings. I'm 55 years old, for God's sake!"

"Careful, Luca, you're sounding awfully ageist. Do

you think that men of my age have lost the desire for love?" Ricardo gently chided. "So, what do you want to do about Brad?"

"I want to see him again. I want to explore the resurgence of this emotion, to see if there is anything to it, or if perhaps it was simply a nostalgic urge for my youth and innocence."

"And you are worried that you might have to give up your ministry," Ricardo said bluntly.

"Yes, and that would devastate me," Luca replied.

"Well, it's clear to me that you cannot simply ignore your encounter with Brad. It won't simply go away. You must confront him face to face. Repressing sentiments of such depth will eat away at you and your ministry. There is no easy answer to this, Luca, but you must follow your heart to see where it leads you. The rest are only trappings. The details of your life will work themselves out, perhaps not as you would have expected, but you will certainly be able to cope."

"Ricardo, the idea of leaving the priesthood to be with him fills me with dread. I can't imagine what I would do for work. There is nothing I've ever wanted to do other than be a priest," De Santo shared.

"Luca, remember your passion for teaching? You still have that. I am certainly not encouraging you to throw away your life's work as a priest and bishop. But if you worry so much about what might happen if you carry on with Brad, you may never discover what it is that your heart truly wants. The heart will not be ignored. You cannot repress these resurfacing emotions. You must talk to him."

"Sage advice as usual, Ricardo. This situation has

caught me completely off guard. I have no desire to turn my life upside down. But I know I have to see this through in order to resolve it. Pray for me."

"I always do, my friend, and please return the favor."

CHAPTER 17

LUCA
AUTUMN 1980

By our junior year, Brad and I were roommates at last. It was a major move for me to stop commuting and apply for campus housing. The comfort of living on campus didn't really offset the added cost to my tuition. However, I received a scholarship from the concert choir so my parents relented. There were two new dorms down by the riverfront that were usually filled by seniors, but Brad and I hit the jackpot in the room lottery and got a room in the dorm closest to the river. We were in a suite of two rooms connected by a bathroom. We didn't know the guys in the other room, but they seemed nice enough. It was going to be great.

After I returned from Italy, we had gotten together to plan what we would each bring. By moving day, we each had carloads of stuff to fill our tiny room. It was hectic and exciting.

"I can't believe that we are actually living together, Brad!" I exclaimed as we continued to unpack and put our room in order.

"Yeah, we really lucked out. No more late nights with you and me in my tiny bed."

"And no more commuting. That really sucked," I replied.

"And no more waiting for Mickey to fall asleep to have sex. We can do whatever we want, when we want." Brad said as he pulled me towards him and kissed me deeply. "Like, right now. I want to taste you all over, Luca."

"Seriously, now? We have so much to set up yet," I protested weakly. He laid me down on the bed and whispered in my ear, "So how about you show me what you learned in Italy this summer?"

"Are you sure? You won't get angry with me?" I asked hesitantly. Sal was still a sensitive subject. But Brad nodded and let me take the lead for the first time. That afternoon, we embarked on a new phase in our relationship. We were able to make love in our own room without interruptions or having to hide from anyone.

When we were setting up our room, I felt like a married couple moving into our first apartment. During the final days of summer we went shopping for a coffee maker, hot plate, and glasses. We even searched for artwork that we both liked. My uncle worked on a construction site and offered us a big wooden spool that was used for coiled electrical wire. If laid on its side, it could make a cool table. I set it up in my parent's basement and sanded the top until it was smooth. Then I used a walnut colored stain and shellac to make it shine. When Brad saw the transformation, he went crazy.

"Oh my God, Luca, this is beautiful. You did this yourself? Where did you learn that?"

"I had a woodworking class in high school. I wasn't very good at it, but I really had fun," I responded.

"Well, you obviously learned a lot because this is great. It's going to be perfect between our two beds."

Of course, living together brought its own set of problems. As the months passed, we discovered that our rhythms were totally different and we had to navigate differing preferences. However, it seemed that I was the only one compromising when our desires conflicted. Minor arguments began to erupt and I was always the peacemaker. I reasoned that our relationship was more important than any of our minor scuffles. We were still very much in love.

Both of us had stopped dating girls on campus, but Brad would mention his girlfriend, Theresa, from back home every now and again. In fact, on his desk, he displayed a photo of the two of them from her senior prom. I didn't think much of it until one weekend, when Brad suggested that a group of us head to his house in Connecticut to celebrate his birthday.

Five of us packed into my car and drove to Hartford. His parents could not have been more welcoming. They had a huge dinner waiting for us on Friday night, and the wine and beer flowed freely. I stood directly behind Brad as his birthday cake was placed in front of him. Since all of us were in the St. Robert's Choir, we broke into four-part harmony as we sang Happy Birthday to him. Brad was giddy with excitement and blew out the candles. He cut the first piece of cake and stuck his finger in the creamy frosting. The next thing I knew, he had smeared it all over my face. Soon cake was being smashed into all our faces as we pressed our gooey cheeks against one another. We were as silly as could be and having a great time.

After a raucous evening, we all slept in the basement and laughed late into the night. There was a pile of bodies strewn all over the floor. My sleeping bag was right next to Brad's and, although we were tempted, we knew that it was way too risky for us to attempt anything more than a cuddle or a stolen kiss here and there.

Early Saturday morning the doorbell rang and I heard Brad's mom squeal in surprise. "Theresa! I thought you were away at school. What are you doing here?"

"Well I certainly couldn't miss Brad's birthday weekend, could I?" she responded.

Theresa, the infamous girlfriend, had arrived unexpectedly. To be honest, I thought she was just a cover. I had seen photos of her, but I assumed that their relationship ended after high school. She descended the basement stairs and bounded onto the pile of sleeping bodies where Brad and I lay. Straddling him with her knee grinding into my ribs, she sang an off-key wake up call.

"Good morning birthday boy! Wakie, wakie, my love."

"Theresa! I thought you couldn't make it home, I can't believe you're here." Brad exclaimed. With that, he pulled her to the floor and kissed her passionately.

My entire body tightened with anger. What was going on here? When they came up for air, Brad sat up and said, "Hey everybody, this is my one and only Theresa. Say hi."

Sleepily, everyone moaned a weak chorus of hellos through their hazy hangovers. Everyone but me. I was seething with jealousy.

For the remainder of the weekend, Theresa and Brad were joined at the hip. He couldn't keep his hands off of her and she hung on his every word. Their cutesy talk was nauseating.

"Come here my sexy candy corn. Give your pookie a little kiss."

"Anything you want, honey bunch. I missed those sweet lips so much."

Our friend, Scott, made eye contact with me as he snickered and I feigned an amused smile. The rest of our friends playfully mocked them behind their backs, but I was too angry to do even that. Brad barely spoke to me while she was there. The constant making out and groping was over the top. I kept thinking, Who is he trying to fool? Is he putting on a show for our benefit or his own?

Later that day, we went out to see a movie. Brad sat between Theresa and me. They were kissing throughout the entire film. And yet, I was startled to feel his hand on my thigh halfway through the movie. He hadn't even broken for air with Theresa, and he was groping me at the same time. I moved my leg away as far as I could; I was furious. When the lights came up at the end of the movie, he gave me a questioning look. I turned away and walked out with Scott.

In the car on the way back to school, I didn't say a word. Everyone was as animated as usual, but no one seemed to notice my reserve. Even Brad didn't take note of my somber mood. I dropped everyone off near their dorms and turned toward the river. Brad placed his hand on my thigh and said to me, "I can't wait to get back to our room. With all our friends around, we didn't get one moment together. I miss you."

"You didn't seem to miss me much while Theresa was around."

"What do you mean? We hadn't seen each other in months. Of course we spent most of our time together. What's the big deal, Luca? She's my girlfriend."

"Yeah, no big deal. I felt right at home as you made out with her while feeling me up in the theater. Seriously, Brad. What was up with that?" The simmering anger within me started boiling over. "I've got studying to do. I'm going to the library. Don't wait up."

"Hey, don't be like that. Come here."

"No, Brad, I'm not in the mood to argue or hear your excuses."

"Look, don't be such a baby. You can't be jealous. You knew I had a girlfriend."

"Yeah, so what does that make me? Just a convenient body to fool around with?" I spit out.

"Come on, Luca. You know you mean more to me than that. Teresa is my girlfriend, but we hardly ever see each other. You're way more important to me. Come on, let's go inside."

"Sorry, not tonight. See you tomorrow. I'll be at the library." I left him standing outside our dorm as I peeled out of the parking lot and drove into town. In my rearview mirror I could see Brad with his mouth hanging open. He didn't get it. He just didn't understand that I felt left out, abandoned the minute Theresa came on the scene. What made me feel worse was that he acceded to the description of me being just a convenient body to have sex with. How could he think that? I thought we were in love.

Memories of my time with Sal in Italy came rushing back. He would have never treated me like this. I was beginning to believe that I had made a significantly bad decision by choosing Brad.

CHAPTER 18

BISHOP DE SANTO
SUMMER 2015

By the time Bishop De Santo began the eighth and final day of his retreat, he had resolved to meet with Brad. He didn't know where their discussion would lead, but he had to find out if his feelings were simply longing for a lost love and paths not taken, or if there was a deeper meaning to their mutual attraction. After several sessions with Fr. Garcia, he was certain of his decision, and hoped he had the inner strength to address the consequences of any action he might take.

On his drive back to the rectory in Bridgeport, Bishop De Santo reluctantly dialed into his voicemail. There were 16 messages from Brad, each one pleading for a response. It was now or never. He hit the call back button after listening to his final voicemail and took a deep breath. Brad picked up on the second ring.

"Luca, I thought you'd given up on me again. I am so glad you called," Brad said with relief in his voice.

"Brad, you knew I was on retreat. Why so many messages? I just got them moments ago."

"I hoped you were lying and that you'd check your voicemail. I guess you're much more disciplined than I am."

"Perhaps, but I certainly don't cheat while on retreat. What would be the point?"

"So, was our little encounter the reason for going on retreat, Luca?"

"As a matter of fact, it was. I needed time away to process everything. I had a lot of time to reflect on it."

"And?"

"And it is clear that we have some unresolved feelings to deal with. I agree that we should get together to talk it through."

"That's great news, Luca," Brad cried out. "When can I see you?"

"Soon. But I have to warn you that I am really ambivalent about my feelings for you," Luca said honestly.

"That's fair. I have a great deal on the line as well."

"I know you do, and we can't jump into anything without thinking about the consequences," Luca said.

"You're absolutely right. I'm not ready to upend my life either. But, Luca, I am clear on one thing." He paused.

"Don't keep me in suspense," Luca said impatiently.

"My feelings for you are not fleeting. I've thought of you many times over the years."

Luca felt a knot in his stomach. He thought, It's not

that simple, Brad, but in response, he only said, "We left indelible marks on each other's lives. We just have to figure out what that means to us today."

"We should do this right away, don't you agree? What do you say we head to my cottage on Candlewood Lake? It's a short drive and it's very private."

"Brad, I've been away from the diocese for eight days now. It will have to wait until my next day off."

"Ughh! When is that?" Brad asked with frustration.

"A week from Monday. I have Masses all weekend long and plenty to catch up on. As a businessman you can certainly understand that."

"Of course. I'm just anxious to see you as soon as possible. Can we plan to meet at the cottage next Monday, then?"

"That sounds fine, as long as you understand that this is not a commitment to do anything more than talk," Luca clarified.

"Of course not, Luca. You have my word."

Brad promised to send him the address and they made arrangements to meet there the following week. Although he was nervous about seeing Brad alone, Luca knew that this was something he needed to do.

His first week back after the retreat was more hectic than usual. Although it was still summer, plans and arrangements had to be confirmed for numerous autumn and winter fundraisers. Due to new clerical assignments, personnel troubles were already bubbling up. By Monday morning, he realized that he hadn't had a moment to reflect on his impending meeting with Brad. Whenever he came to mind, De Santo busied himself with another task. He was still unsure of his feelings, but hoped that they would become clear as he talked them through when they met.

Luca thought through every possible scenario on the way up to the lake. As he drove up the long, tree-lined driveway in the woods, he could see that the cottage was completely obscured. It felt like he was in the middle of nowhere. When he got out of his car, he could see Brad standing on the porch waving him in. Luca felt butterflies in his stomach. Brad was in a t-shirt and shorts that showed off his golden tan, and he flipped his blond hair out of his eyes. *How can he possibly look younger than at our last meeting?* Luca thought.

"Hey there, Luca," Brad said as he embraced him warmly. "I'm so glad to see you again. Let's go out back so you can check out the view of the lake. It's a sight to see." Brad's carefree demeanor put him at ease. When Luca passed through the glass doors to the deck, his face brightened at the natural beauty before him. The surface of the water was like glass. The sun sparkled on the lake and there were soaring pine trees framing the view.

"This is absolutely stunning!" Luca exclaimed.

"Yeah, it's not bad," Brad said as he offered him a drink.

They made themselves comfortable on luxurious lounge chairs that looked out over the lake. Luca was the first to break the silence.

"Brad, I…"

"No, Luca, please. Let me say what I have to say first. I feel responsible for how things went the last time we met. I am so sorry to have assumed that we wanted the same thing. It was incredibly disrespectful of me to think that you would simply break your vows just for an afternoon of fun. I was foolish and I apologize."

"Apology accepted, Brad. But I have to acknowledge my own actions as well. I didn't give you any reason to stop. I was frightened by how easily I was swept under your spell. I wanted it as much as you did."

"My spell? What do you mean by that?" Brad asked. "You make it sound as if I'm an evil spirit."

"Well, you did tempt me," Luca responded honestly.

"I suppose I did, but it was never my intention to force you into anything you didn't agree to."

"No, Brad, it goes way back to when we were kids— and that's what we were back then. I knew nothing about love and relationships. You could have suggested anything and I would have gone along with you. Your presence consumed me and I had no will resist you. That's why I had to put distance between us back then. I knew that if I let you back into my life, I would lose myself. So when we found ourselves on your couch with your hands on me, I feared it was happening again." Luca paused to sigh. "I obviously have unresolved feelings toward you."

"What can I say, Luca? I've always been irresistible," Brad joked. Luca chose to ignore it. This was heavy stuff and he didn't want to minimize its importance.

"Can I ask you, what was going on in your head, Brad? Was it just a tryst? Or was there something more?"

"Honestly, Luca, I have had my share of infidelities over the years. I am not proud of my actions, but I don't beat myself up about them."

"So was I simply going to be another infidelity?" Luca pushed.

"No. That's a hard no, Luca. When we were sitting so close to each other on the couch, I was overwhelmed with feelings. It wasn't the usual sexual tension, though that was certainly a part of it. When I was with you that day, my heart ached. I felt something different, like I was returning home to something that had been missing in my life for many years. Being with you again just seemed right."

"I had the same reaction. That's another reason that I had to get away from you. Being with you calls my entire vocation into question. My entire life would be blasted apart. Perhaps yours would be too, but you would still have your career and your wealth. I would be left with nothing. Not even my priesthood."

"Understood. We would both face risks, but yours would be foundational. I get it. But let me ask you a question: Do you want to be with me?" There was a long pause. "Do you?" he repeated.

Luca let out a deep sigh and looked out over the calm ripples in the lake.

"Brad, when we touched there was nothing more in the world that I wanted. But I am not clear that we fully know our feelings for each other. Is it lust? Or nostalgia? Or is it something more?"

"Luca, if we don't pursue it, how will we know? Do we deny ourselves a second chance in our adulthood because it's messy? That doesn't seem fair either. Isn't it worth the risk?"

"Then let me ask you an obvious question. Are you willing to give up your marriage to Wendy?" Luca asked.

"To be honest, no. She is my best friend."

"And how will your son and daughter react? Then

there's your reputation; it would certainly take a hit," he pushed further.

"To be honest, I'm not ready to give all that up right now," Brad said candidly, "not until we know what this is between us. Can't we just give it a try? If it's truly love, we can sort out the details of our lives then."

They were both silent again, looking out over the lake. Luca could hear the birds chirping as a warm breeze rustled through the trees. Then Brad turned to him.

"I know that we would be able to get through all of the painful consequences if we did it together. What do you say, Luca? Can we give it a try?" he asked as he placed one hand on Luca's knee and the other at the base of his neck. It was a very intimate touch. Luca could feel Brad's warmth radiating up his thigh. He closed his eyes and took a deep breath. What should I do? Could he be right? Why throw our lives into chaos before we know what's really going on between us? I know that I want to, but–

Luca turned his head back to the lake and said, "Brad, let's slow down before we dive into something we can't control." He paused and then looked directly at Brad. "I want to talk about what happened all those years ago. About why it all fell apart back then. Our time together was fraught with conflict and pain."

"Of course we hurt each other, but don't forget, Luca, there were also many wonderful times. Remember the first time we kissed? We were on the beach during the retreat."

Luca smiled as he pictured Brad's head leaning against his own, wrapped in a blanket and watching the sunrise. "Perhaps I have let the struggles overshadow the good times," he admitted.

"Luca, no matter what our conflicts were, you must know that I truly loved you."

"And I loved you. You were my first love. I learned that I could actually fall in love because of you. You had a profound effect on my life, Brad."

"It was a miracle that we found each other. There were no same-sex couples on campus that I can recall. In fact, I don't remember anyone even acknowledging gay students at all," Brad added.

"We were a safe harbor for each other," Luca acknowledged.

"It's crazy to think that we never left each other's sides. We did everything together," Brad said with a chuckle.

"Mutt and Jeff," Luca laughed. There was an expectant pause, then Luca mustered the courage to say, "But, Brad. Do you remember our final night together? That was the most violent fight I have ever had. After that night, I was afraid to get close to you."

"Afraid of me? Really?" Brad looked away from Luca. How could that be? He thought. "We were only 19 years old. I was foolish. I drank too much. I know I got physical, but it wasn't that dramatic. We have both grown up since then. You can't hold that against me, please."

"It's hard to forget it happened, but I don't hold it against you. I forgave you many years ago. But, Brad, it wasn't just a drunken fight. For me, it was much worse; its impact affected me for years to come. It was a nightmare." Luca stood and walked over to the rail and out gazed over the lake. The pain of that memory came rushing back.

"I am so sorry, Luca. I honestly didn't know that. You must know that I would have never tried to hurt you like that if I was sober," he said as he joined him at the rail.

Luca turned to look directly at Brad. "But that's the point, Brad. You weren't sober and you did attack me. A line was crossed and we could never go back to where we were before."

"Again, I am so very sorry. But Luca, there was so much more to the two years we spent together. Surely you can see that now. Our hearts were intertwined; we truly loved each other," Brad replied, trying to make Luca understand the depth of his feelings.

"They were two incredible years, and yes, my heart ached for you whenever we were apart," Luca said, as memories of their self-discovery unfolded in his mind. "But I can't forget how toxic our relationship was for me. Our fight on that final night together seemed to be the manifestation of all that was wrong with us. And yet, here I am feeling drawn to you after decades. My intellect tells me to run, while my heart wants nothing more than to say yes to you."

"So let me ask you again," Brad interjected. "Can we give this thing between us a try?" He placed his hand on Luca's shoulder and gently turned him so that they were facing each other. Luca lifted his head and looked into Brad's pleading eyes. As their lips touched, time seemed to stand still.

What am I doing? Luca thought as he gave in to the moment. Brad broke the kiss and leaned his forehead against Luca's. "Let's go inside," he said softly.

Luca followed willingly as Brad silently led him to the bedroom. They undressed each other slowly and gazed at their 55-year-old bodies. Time had softened them both, yet they knew they were still fit and attractive men. They shrugged their shoulders and laughed.

"I think we look pretty good, especially compared to our contemporaries!" Brad joked. "Have you seen Bill? He's huge!" They laughed again, and that broke the tension.

There was no frantic need to consume each other. They lay on the bed and tenderly reacquainted themselves. Luca was transported to a time when he was allowed to love, to touch another man and be touched. He let his fingers trace the outlines of Brad's biceps and chest. He explored his still flat abdomen and followed the trail of hair leading down. He was filled with a slow-burning desire so similar to that of his 18-year-old self. However, in contrast to his younger self, Luca's need was much greater. His emptiness more profound, and after so many years of celibacy, ached to be filled. It was a languorous afternoon of re-awakened passion–but more importantly it revealed Luca's desperate need for love.

Afterward, Luca was roused from his dozing and watched as Brad got out of bed. He returned from the kitchen with two glasses of Pellegrino. He would never have been this kind 35 years ago, Luca thought.

"How do you feel? Are you OK?" Brad asked, worried that Luca would be filled with regret.

"My thoughts are so scrambled, and I'm not sure what this means for me, but I feel good. I never dreamed it could be like this between us."

"Yeah, this has been the most intimacy I've had in many years." To lighten the mood, he said, "It was like a religious experience."

"Well, I am a bishop," Luca joked weakly.

"Perhaps not for too much longer, Luca. It's going to

be tough for me to let you go this time around."

CHAPTER 19

LUCA 1980-81

Brad and I were pretty popular at St. Robert's. We were involved in some of the most visible activities on campus, including the choir and a cappella group. We were actively involved in campus ministry: both of us were Eucharistic ministers, and I was a leader of the folk group that led the singing at Sunday Masses. I knew many of the faculty and staff had a great deal of respect for us. Plus, we were very good students and held leadership roles in numerous of clubs.

But our unusually close relationship didn't go unnoticed. Rumors made the rounds at times. "Why are they always together?" "They always seem to be hanging all over each other. Are they gay?" Although people might have suspected that there was something more to our relationship, most chose not to entertain the idea. However, there were a number of exceptions that made our lives difficult.

I vividly recall the conflicts we had with the guys in our suite. Although we were not friends, we seemed to have a cordial relationship with them. But as the first semester wore on, tension grew between the four of us. Since our bathroom connected our rooms, it was impossible to avoid them. It also made privacy a challenge. One could easily hear what was going on in either room when in the bathroom. We overheard them talking about us and calling us faggots and queers. That freaked us out and we began to feel uncomfortable in our shared suite.

One day, I entered the bathroom. I had a white terrycloth bathrobe hanging on the back of the door. My mother had made it for me and I loved it. When I went to put it on, something smelled off. I held it away from me and saw that someone had used it to wipe himself. There were brown stains all over it. I was disgusted and furious.

I knocked on our neighbor's door immediately. Griffin answered and belligerently asked, "What do you want?"

"What happened to my bathrobe?"

"I don't know. Looks like you got shit all over it," Griffin mocked.

"No, it looks like one of you used it to wipe yourself. What the hell?"

"You can't prove that. Besides, isn't that what happens when queers mess around?" he sneered.

"What did you say?" I asked threateningly.

"You heard me, faggot. Why don't you go back to your butt buddy and leave us alone. It's bad enough that we have to share a bathroom with a couple of queers!"

Then he slammed the door in my face. I was shaken

to the core and was afraid for my safety in my own room. I sat on my bed in disbelief. I couldn't move, but I could feel my body shaking. Later that day, I told Brad about my interaction with Griffin and he was furious.

"See, this is what I'm talking about, Luca. We can never tell anyone about us. Our lives would be hell!"

"So what do we do now?" I asked fearfully. "If they know, I'm sure they've spread the word already."

"You're right. We have to make it look like we're not a couple. We have to date girls," Brad declared.

"That's stupid, Brad. I don't want to date anyone else but you."

"We have no choice. We can't take any chances," he said with finality.

Brad's solution was to make a show of his relationships with girls. From then on, things between us took a turn for the worse. Brad was always pursuing girls at dances and social gatherings. It was at keg parties that Brad really let loose. He would drink to excess every weekend and his sharp humor edged out. He was very handsy with some of the friends, and they would call him on it. He would laugh it off and say, "Sorry, you're just so irresistible," or "I couldn't keep my hands off of you." He was so well liked that he got away with much more than he should have. Brad's drunken escapades became more and more frequent as the year went on.

I hated when Brad would get so drunk and I was embarrassed by his behavior. Often, I would find myself trailing after him to apologize when he said or did something offensive.

"Sorry, Gail. He's just so drunk. He shouldn't have been that forward." At times they would become angry and say, "That's not cool, Luca. You need to make him stop. Can't you get him out of here? He's being such an asshole." But more often, they would nod their heads and say, "Don't worry. It's not your fault. You shouldn't be apologizing for his rudeness." Regardless of the reaction of his victims, his behavior was inappropriate and it made everyone uncomfortable.

When Brad would get to that point, I would try my best to convince him to leave the dance or party. But Brad would fight me off. "It's still early, Luca! We can't leave now, I'm just starting to have fun."

"You've already had too much to drink, Brad. You're slurring your words and Tina almost slugged you. You went a little too far with her."

"Aw, she loved it! Besides, I was only playing. She knows that. And I'm not slurring my words."

"Seriously, Brad, let's go. I'm tired and I just want to go back to our room."

"Lighten up, Luca. Try to have some fun for a change. You're always such a stick in the mud. Go have a drink."

I didn't realize at the time that his overdrinking was likely due to his internal struggle with his sexuality. The worst part was when we got back to our room. Brad would argue with me all the way to the dorm. It was simply a rehashing of what had transpired while at the keg party. I tried to reason with him, but then I would end up as the target of Brad's drunken anger. It was my fault that we had to leave early. Our friends were pissed at me because I was so lame. When he started on that path, I just got quiet and let him rant. At the end of the night, the routine was always the same: I led Brad to the bathroom so he could pee and brush his teeth. I'd undress him and lay him down on his bed. All the while,

Brad would be cursing and belittling me for interfering with his good time.

But once in bed, Brad would become needy and amorous. He would begin to caress me. "I love you, Luca. Do you love me?"

"Yes, of course Brad, I love you."

"Lay down with me for a little while—just until I fall asleep."

"Brad, just close your eyes now. It's late and you need rest."

"I will, after you get in bed with me. I promise," he begged.

Most times I would relent because it was the only way to keep Brad quiet and get him off to sleep. However, it would rarely end up with Brad passing out. He would kiss me roughly and tear at my clothes. He persisted until we had sex. When he was that drunk, Brad was aggressive, pushing my head down on him or worse. He was so rough that there were times when he physically hurt me during sex. It was so degrading, so I tried to get it over with as quickly as possible. It was the only way to get Brad to pass out and leave me alone.

Afterward, I would go back to my bed and try to fall asleep. I always felt dirty and abused after nights like that. Sadly, they seemed to happen almost every weekend. I was so confused. How did our relationship end up like this? It would turn hot to cold in the blink of an eye. I never seemed to know which Brad I would find. When he would wake the next morning with his usual hangover, he'd call out to me in his sweet, but needy voice, "Hey there buddy, can you get me a glass of water and a couple of aspirin? My head is killing me."

"Sure, Brad. Here you go. Why don't you stay in and sleep some more? I'm going to head to the campus center to get some breakfast."

"No, Luca, no. Stay with me for a while. Let's just cuddle. I always feel better when you're with me."

"OK, but just for a few minutes. I'm starving and you know how I am without my coffee." I gave in more often than not. It was easier than arguing with him.

"You're so good to me, Luca. What would I do without you?"

"You'd be in a pile of vomit beside the keg. You were a mess last night," I said pointedly.

"You know I love you, right?"

"You have a hell of a way of showing it, Brad."

"Yeah, I can be a real dick."

"That is so true." I sighed.

That scenario played itself out over and over again. Brad and I seemed to be at each other's throats constantly, and the continual bickering was getting to me. I was tired of giving in just to keep the peace, and I found myself staying away from our dorm as much as possible. During the day, I searched for a quiet corner in the humanities building to study. I knew that I wouldn't run into Brad there since he had completed all of his core academic requirements. He had most of his classes at the business school.

I also found a great deal of comfort in hanging out with Irene or my high school friend John. He and I had lost touch in the months that Brad and I were together. We never seemed to have the time to socialize, and the dynamic between us was drastically different when Brad was around.

The two of them just didn't get along. I never knew whether he suspected that Brad and I were a couple, but it was clear that John could see through Brad's bullshit. They would often lock horns when we were together.

Another great diversion for me was working on the college newspaper. Joining as a staff writer was exciting, and it introduced me to an entirely different group of friends. I frequently found myself working in the newsroom during the evenings.

I still loved Brad, and my feelings for him were still strong, but our relationship had changed. I found more comfort with other people, and realized that I needed my own group of friends. I needed a space where I wasn't being criticized for my "useless" major or for being such a bleeding heart. Brad just didn't respect my dreams and passions.

Although my brief relationship with Sal the previous summer in Italy should have taught me otherwise, I still believed I would never find anyone like Brad. I thought our bond was one of a kind, however flawed it was. Still, I could hear Sal's voice in my head when I went down this rabbit hole: "There are tons of wonderful guys just like us out there, Luca. You deserve better."

CHAPTER 20

BRAD
SUMMER TO
AUTUMN 2015

B rad Ghenter was like a new man when he returned from the cottage. He began to look at his life with a new lens. To anyone who knew him, it seemed that he led a charmed life: he had wonderful wife, two beautiful children and was quite wealthy. But that was not all that he wanted. Following his latest encounter with Luca, he realized that he no longer needed to prove himself to anyone.

Being in love with another man was never a part of his business plan. There was his reputation to consider. He had always been concerned with how his peers viewed him. Even so, he thought dreamily about his day with Luca. Maybe they could start a life together; maybe that would actually be possible. He had never loved anyone as much as he loved Luca. No one had ever come close to measuring up to him. He couldn't wait until the next time they would be together again.

However, Brad's old fears began to surface as mulled over that cataclysmic effects their relationship would have on his life. He wondered if, perhaps, there was no need to change anything in their lives. Maybe he could convince Luca that they should continue their relationship in secret. That would be a tough sell. Luca was the most ethical man he had ever known and he took their vows quite seriously. But Brad knew that he had a hold on Luca's heart once again. If he chipped away at him slowly, he was confident that he could prevail. Hopefully their renewed love for each other would supplant Luca's ethical concerns. Then they could have the best of both worlds. There would be no need for all the drama that divorce would bring, not to mention Luca's fall from his post as bishop.

In the meantime, he would carry on with his marriage as if nothing occurred. Wendy was his wife and he loved her. They had celebrated their 30th wedding anniversary this past year with a lavish cruise on the French Riviera. But after so many years together, they rarely made love. Their passion for each other was long gone. Even so, they were good friends and enjoyed each other's company. It was difficult to imagine his life without her. There was no need to upset a perfectly good arrangement.

Brad and Luca met every Monday for the rest of the summer. Luca went through this period in a haze. His heart ached for Brad when they were not together, and he was grateful for their weekly rendezvous at the cottage. However, when he acted in his official capacity as a bishop, he felt tortured, and continued to feel a great deal of guilt over his affair. He knew couldn't sustain their deception for much longer.

During that very same time, his work in the Church began to heat up. He had recently been elected to a leadership position on the National Council of Catholic Bishops. He would be chairing the committee on marriage, family life, and youth. It was an influential and powerful chairmanship that he had wrestled away from one of the most conservative bishops in the country. It was important because it could be a real step forward for the American Catholic Church. He believed that he could affect significant change in the practical application of Church teaching. The idea of leaving his position as bishop at this point was unthinkable. His two loves were in direct conflict, and neither would loosen their hold on Luca's heart.

Brad, however, couldn't be happier. He had his full life with Wendy and his two children, his beautiful home on Long Island Sound in Greenwich and, for the last several months, he had Luca. The true love of his life had returned, and Brad's heart was bursting with love. The unfortunate mistakes they made in their late adolescence stood as reminders of how far they had come as adults. He believed that their relationship was honest and true.

But as summer turned to fall, Luca would often miss his weekly meetings with Brad. His travel schedule was getting more and more busy. Whenever he was away, his administrative work piled up and required his full attention upon his return to the chancery. He spent much of his time there trying to catch up. During the last two months, he had only been able to see Brad twice. Although he missed Brad's touch, the distance made him more confident about his vocation. Weeks would go by without talking to Brad, but the time away from each other seemed to put his mind at ease. During those times, he wasn't constantly confronted by the fact that he was breaking of his vow of celibacy. The distance from each other gave Luca perspective.

For Brad, however, it was torture. He had no sooner gotten Luca back than their weekly meetings began to wane. It was already the week before Thanksgiving when Brad called Luca to schedule some time together at the cottage.

"Hey stranger, where have you been? Don't you love me anymore?" Brad joked.

"Hi there, Brad. It's good to hear your voice," Luca responded with a neediness that surprised him.

"I have to see you. It's been too long. Can you meet this week?"

"It's going to be tough, Brad. I'll try, OK? But I can't make any promises; I am drowning in my piles of work. I'll let you know as soon as I can."

"You're getting way too important, Luca. I'm afraid the Church will take you away from me," Brad said, only half-jokingly. He was truly worried that he was losing Luca.

"It's not that, Brad. I hope you know how much you mean to me. It just seems I can never take a breath here. Things are moving so quickly."

"Hey, don't get yourself worked up, my love. If nothing else, you could certainly use a day off. When was the last time you took one, Luca?"

"It's been well over a month, and you couldn't be more right. I have to make time to take care of myself. Let's set a date," he said with determination.

When they finally met at the cottage, it had been nearly two months since they had seen each other. When Brad opened the door to let him in, Luca felt the warm glow of the fire and heard the comforting sound of the crackling wood. They fell into each other's arms with their familiar ease and kissed hungrily. Brad felt the reassurance he needed. Their meetings were a touchstone for him. They buoyed his heart and helped him believe that his relationship with Luca was real.

With haste, they made their way to the bedroom. After so much time apart, their lovemaking was more urgent. They couldn't get enough of each other and their passion burned fiercely. Although they were accustomed to their usual sexual routine, today's encounter was met with renewed energy and vigor. Afterward, they lay together under the comforter, dozing to the sound of the fire nearby and the cold wind blowing off the lake.

Brad was trying to bolster his courage to speak with Luca about keeping their relationship as it was, without having to alter both their lives. He knew it would be met with resistance, but he had to try. He turned to see Luca staring at the fire pensively. He broke the spell and said, "So, I was thinking. You've been very busy with your Church work, Luca, and you seem so content."

"In many ways that's true. I'm at the center of a whirlwind of change, positive change. I finally feel like I'm making a difference on the institutional level. I am very happy with my work. So, what's your point? What are you thinking, Brad?"

Brad had the opening he hoped for. "Perhaps

we've been looking at our relationship the wrong way?" he suggested.

"What do you mean?" Luca asked as he propped himself up on his elbow. He became more alert, even a bit wary.

"Why should you give up what you love doing most just so that we can be together? Why can't we have it both ways?"

"You know we can't we have it both ways, Brad? It's just not possible," Luca insisted.

"Hear me out, my love. We can just carry on the way we have over the last six months. It's working out really well, except for the lack of frequency, don't you think?"

Luca paused and took a deep breath. Brad didn't get it. He could not understand the concept of commitment. It was a matter of integrity. Whereas this affair was eating away at Luca, Brad rested in his deception. The only reason Luca acceded to their affair was to better understand what they meant to each other, and whether they should break their commitments to the Church and to Brad's marriage. For Luca, it was one or the other. He could never sustain this lie.

"Brad, you know I can't do that," Luca said emphatically.

"Why not? It's nobody's business but our own. We love each other, Luca. No one else has to know."

"Brad, ordained ministry and married life are mutually exclusive. I have to choose one or the other. It's the only way."

"There's always another way. Look how wonderful it has been to be together after all these years. And the best part is that neither of us had to give anything else up. It's working, Luca. Don't you see?"

"No, Brad, this is not the solution. It was never meant to be. I think it's time for us to make a decision. Where are we going with this relationship?"

"What do you mean, Luca? We love each other. Don't you think that we've discovered that? It's not simply physical attraction. We need and care deeply about each other. Don't we?"

"If that's true, then we both have to make that choice. I have to leave the priesthood and you have to get a divorce. There's no other way."

"I don't understand why you can't just let it be. Our relationship is working just the way it is. This way no one gets hurt and no lives are shattered, Luca. It's as simple as that."

"No," Luca said, sitting up now. "What is simple is that we both took vows. You to Wendy, and me to the Church. Right now, we are both breaking them. I can't continue like this. It's tearing me apart."

"You have always been so dogmatic, Luca. Life is not black and white. Don't give up on this idea. Just sit with it for a while, will you?"

"I would have never agreed to starting this if it were going to be a permanent arrangement. You can understand that, can't you?"

"Look, Luca, I just don't think it's necessary to turn our lives upside down to be with each other. If I get a divorce, Wendy would be crushed–plus, she would get half of everything I have."

At that statement, Luca could taste the bitterness rising in his throat. "It always comes down to money, doesn't it Brad? I should have known. In that regard, you haven't changed a bit." He got out of bed and put on his shirt and pants.

"Hey, that's not fair. It's not about the money. I have a business and a reputation. How would it look if I divorce my wife to shack up with an ex-bishop? And what about all my Catholic clients? I could just kiss them goodbye."

"Come on, Brad, you told me that you've made enough money to stop working altogether. Why are you so concerned about that now?"

"Well, if I get a divorce, I won't have all that money anymore, will I?

"Seriously, half of 50 million isn't enough? What is this really all about, Brad?"

"Look, it's simple. I like the arrangement we have now and I'm not ready to tell the world I'm gay. It simply isn't what I want for my life," Brad finally admitted.

Luca stared at Brad in disbelief. This has always been his issue, he thought. The big plan for his life could never include self-identifying as gay. Perhaps it was his deep-rooted self-hatred that prompted his violence so many years ago. That took the wind out of Luca's sails. There was no use in discussing this any further. If Brad could not accept that he was gay, or at least bi, then there was no relationship to fight for.

"I am sorry, Brad. I'm sorry we started this whole thing again. I really thought I could love you. I do love you. But I can't be with someone who is not true to himself. It's over. I can't see you again."

"Please, Luca, I really thought I could do it—leave everything behind and start my life again with you. I tried, really tried, but I just can't. Maybe I'm not strong enough. I don't know. But let me be clear: I did not go into this trying to deceive you. Having you back in my life has transformed me. I haven't been this happy in a very long time. I know I can make this work. Please don't give up on us, Luca–please?"

Luca looked at Brad with sympathy. He believed him; he could feel his genuine affection and love. But that was not enough. Brad's inner demons fought for control and won. No matter what Luca did now, they were both going to suffer. He could feel tears building behind his eyes. "Brad, I love you too, but I cannot live a duplicitous life," he said. "You've got to understand that. And although it pains me to say it, this has to end. I am sorry for both of us."

With tears streaming down both of their faces, they embraced as lovers for one last time. "I don't think I'll ever get over you, Luca," Brad said. "I do love you, more than you understand."

"I love you too. Let's just be thankful for what we had," Luca said, his heart broken once again. He still bore some resentment, believing that he was indeed deceived into this affair by Brad. Even still, his heart ached at the finality of their decision. Then Brad leaned in and tenderly kissed him for the last time.

Brad could not believe that it was over. For the second time in their lives, they had failed–he had failed. Luca was the most significant love of his life. Why couldn't he do as Luca wished? Why was it so difficult for him to leave the comfort of his marriage to be with the only man he had ever loved? During the last hour with Luca, his heart was torn in two. He stared out the window as he watched the taillights of Luca's car fade away. How could I have lost him again?

During his drive home, Luca could not stop the tears from flowing as he beat himself up for being drawn into this mess. For all of his hurt feelings, he was sure of one thing: he loved the Church and could not leave his post as bishop. He had a mission and was only beginning to make a difference in this institution. He knew that he had to drive to Madison later this week to see Fr. Garcia. If there was ever a time for the sacrament of reconciliation, this was it. Going to confession would help him to wash himself clean of this stain, and his penance would have to fit the gravity of his sin. Through his tears, he was thankful for his sense of clarity. He was a priest and he needed to recommit himself to his vocation.

CHAPTER 21

LUCA
SPRING 1981

It was spring, just a few weeks before exams, and everyone was trying to finish final papers and projects. You could sense the tension as you walked around campus. I was holed up in the newspaper office, seeking inspiration for my final American Lit paper. I'd been poring over my books in vain, trying to find two authors to compare, contrast, and analyze. But I just couldn't concentrate. Brad was getting more and more unbearable. It was so bad that I couldn't hang out with him anymore. I kept ruminating about the argument he and I had earlier that day.

"Luca, you just have to relax more. You never stop worrying about this paper or that test." Then he said with snicker, "You really shouldn't bother, it won't matter that much when you can't find a job after graduation." I could see he knew he shouldn't have said that, but he couldn't help himself.

"Seriously, Brad? Is this your way of making me feel better? Of relieving my stress? You're doing a great job so far," I snapped.

"Dude, calm down. I'm just busting your balls. You used to know how to laugh."

"It's not funny when you're constantly putting me down, Brad. You should know what bothers me by now—or is it that you don't give a damn?"

"Lighten up, Luca. I've got to get to class. I'll see you this afternoon." With that, Brad slammed the door behind him. I could hear him whistling down the hall. He could be so aggravating.

By that evening, our argument was behind us. It was Friday night on the last weekend before finals, and the campus was abuzz. There was a huge keg party and bonfire on the east end of campus, right on the shore of the Hudson River. It was a beautiful spot at the water's edge where events were often held. Our crew of friends was all hyped up for the bonfire, so we had a pre-party gathering in our room.

Brad was in his element, entertaining and flirting. I let go of my worries about my finals and dove into the fun with everyone else. Brad and I were back to our old selves, bouncing off the walls and joking around. We were all pretty buzzed when we left the dorm and made our way to the end-of-year bash. There were around 15 of us singing and laughing all through campus. We made quite a boisterous entrance to the party and received an amused round of applause from the crowd that had already gathered. Brad and

I had our arms draped around each other's necks as we all sang the St. Robert's Alma Mater in harmony. There were a few flubbed words and notes, but we finished with a flourish.

The band started to play cover songs and people were dancing and singing along. It was a beautiful clear night. The moon was close to full and its beams bathed the exuberant crowd with silver light. Soon, Brad and I were immersed in our different groups of friends and mingling as usual. Irene came over to me and gave me a vice-grip hug. "Luuuucaaaa! Where have you been all my life?"

"Waiting for you, gorgeous." I replied.

"What's going on? You mean to tell me you're not joined at the hip with Brad? Is there something brewing in paradise?" She needled me.

"Nothing is brewing, at least not that I know of. He's probably off flirting with some of the freshmen girls," I replied, trying to not to dwell on our recent conflicts.

"Well, we are a few hours into the party. I'm sure he's plastered by now. It's a good bet that you're right," she quipped.

"Let's not ruin a perfectly good celebration by dwelling on him," I said.

"Dwelling on who?" There was Brad right by my side. I hadn't even seen him approach.

"Who? What are you talking about, Brad? Give me a kiss, honey," Irene reached out to him.

"I heard you talking about me, Luca. What did I do now?" Brad was agitated and brushed Irene off.

"Nothing. We were just kidding around. Have you seen Chris? He was looking for you earlier." I tried to distract him because he could be really volatile when he was drunk.

"Never mind. I need a refill. You coming?" he asked.

"Nah, Irene and I haven't seen each other all week. I'll catch up with you later, OK?"

"Suit yourself. Why don't you go find your boyfriend, Irene? I'm sure he misses you." Brad sniped.

"Oh, no worries, Brad. Bill is over by the keg. Why don't you go over and give him a big wet kiss for me." Irene blew Brad a kiss and put her arm around me.

Brad stormed off. He hated being teased, especially when he was drunk. Irene let out a wicked, playful laugh. Meanwhile, I knew that this was a bad omen. It was much too early for him to be acting up. When Brad got like this, he was impossible to handle, and the one person he would take out all his frustrations on was me.

"Well, I might as well enjoy the evening while I can. He's going to be a sloppy mess by the end of the night," I said as I turned to Irene.

"You know, you're not his mother, and he's not the only friend you have, Luca. Why do feel the need to take care of him all the time? Let's wander over to the bonfire, there's a whole crew of choir nerds there!"

"Hey, there's John and Carol." I kissed Carol hello and hugged her, and then turned to John. "What's up, old friend?" I asked, punching his shoulder as hard I could.

"Ow, you asshole," John said, but he was smiling. "I guess you got me back, but you're next." Our routine of shoulder punches had carried over from our high school days. "How the hell are you?"

"Pretty good. I can't believe how many people came out for this tonight," I said.

"Yeah, it's a huge crowd! So what's been happening

with you? I haven't seen you since our concert!"

"Wow! That's way too long," I acknowledged. "We really should spend more time together."

The four of us hung out for the rest of the night and had a really great time. But by 2 a.m., I was wiped out. I had been up late the night before working on my American Lit paper, and I just wanted to go to bed. Most normal people would have simply made a quiet exit, but I knew I had to tell Brad I was leaving. If I didn't, there'd be hell to pay. I found him draped over a freshman girl from the choir. He was indeed sloppy.

"Hey Brad. How's it going?" I asked guardedly.

"Juss great. How's you?" He was slurring his speech and could barely stand.

"Hey Meg, let me have him, I'll take him off your hands," I said, removing his arm from her shoulders and putting it around mine. "Hey buddy, what do you say we head back to the dorm?"

"Hell no! I'm just starting to have a good time. Come on, let's go get a refill," he suggested.

"That's not a good idea, Brad. You can hardly stand up on your own. Let's just head home."

"You're always ruining my fun, Lucy. Juss leave me alone. I can get home on my own."

I hated when he called me Lucy and Brad knew it. As usual he was trying to get me angry. I just ignored the jab and said, "OK, I don't want to stand in the way of your fun. I'll see you at the dorm. Enjoy!"

"What? Wait, are you leaving already?"

"Yes, Brad. I told you I was heading home. I've had enough—and so have you, apparently." I regretted that as soon as it came out of my mouth. I knew it would just set him off.

"What do you mean? I'm fine. Juss leave me alone and go the hell home. I may stay out all night." He then stumbled toward the keg, nearly tripping into a trashcan. Everyone turned and laughed, as did I. Brad turned and scowled at me. I was going to pay for that later.

When I got back to our room, I was relieved to be alone and in a quiet place. I had never experienced drunken behavior before college. At home, there was always a jug of wine at my father's feet during our big Italian dinners, but drinking was simply something to accompany a meal. It was never taboo at our house. I recalled my grandfather mixing a drop or two of wine in my ginger ale. "Eh, Luca, taste, you like," he'd say. I did like it, but when I tried the wine from his glass, without the soda, I pursed my lips in disgust.

As I grew older, drinking held little allure. I never really took to it during my high school years, and was pretty moderate now that I was in college. That's not to say that I didn't overdo it at times, but I never went out with the goal of getting drunk. Dealing with Brad's constant drunkenness was wearing me down. I just didn't want to be around him when he got sloppy, or around anyone who was drinking to excess. I always worried about what kind of outbursts were coming, or if I'd have to wipe up vomit from all over our bathroom. I began to shut down anytime people started to get out of control.

I slipped into my bed, far from all the crazy drunkenness, and made myself comfortable. I hoped that Brad would just pass out as soon as he hit the bed. I wasn't up for a huge argument with him in his inebriated state.

Maybe I'd get lucky and he would stay out all night. I could only hope.

It didn't take long for me to drift off to sleep and leave my worries behind. Then, at about 4 a.m., Brad burst into the room and turned on the overhead light. I lifted my head and squinted at its brightness.

"You missed a great party, Luca. It was the best."

"Yeah, it was really a fun night," I replied groggily.

"No, I mean it got really crazy after you left. You should have stayed. You missed it."

"Sorry, I was too tired."

Brad shed his clothes in a blink and sat back on his bed.

"What's wrong with you, Luca? You never want to party anymore. You're always leaving early and ruining my fun," he began.

My muscles tightened. I was on high alert once again and I could feel one of his tirades coming on. Where did he find the energy? He must have drunk a whole case of beer. He should have been passed out a long time ago.

"I wasn't ruining your fun, Brad. I was just tired."

"No, you always do that and I could feel your judging eyes on me all night. Mr. Goody-Goody watching me every time I filled my cup at the keg. Then you talk about me to Irene and John." He was on a roll.

"I wasn't judging you, and I wasn't talking about you. Let's just go to sleep. It's late."

"You're supposed to be my best friend. We're supposed to party together and have a good time. But you don't even want to be with me when we go out. What's wrong with you, Luca?"

"Nothing is wrong with me. You just woke me from a sound sleep. Please, just go to bed," I pleaded.

I had to stop engaging him in conversation. It only got him more wound up and there was no way I would come out on top. I had learned if I just let him get it out of his system, he would eventually calm down or pass out. But his ranting tonight was turning out to be particularly bad. Brad would not let up. He began blaming me for ruining his life and taking all his friends. Where was all this anger coming from?

"I don't know what to do anymore, Luca. I don't even know why I love you. Do you hear me? Say something!" He shouted.

I kept silent. He was getting me nervous now.

"I mean it, you've ruined everything. I was happy before we got together. Now I just hate my life. The problem is, I can't stop thinking about you. You are the only guy I mess around with, you know that?"

Silence.

"What the hell? Not talking to me? This is exactly what I mean. You make me so mad that I can't breathe. The only way out of this mess you've gotten me into is to stop loving you, and I don't know how to do that."

Silence.

I was on high alert. I could feel Brad spinning out of control and I braced myself for his inevitable eruption. I prayed that his own silence would help disarm the ticking bomb that seemed to live within Brad. But tonight, it didn't seem to be working. Where is he going with this? I thought. He's spinning out of control.

"I guess the only way to stop loving you is to hate

you, and I do hate you Luca!" he yelled.

I kept my eyes closed and my mouth shut fearing what he might say or do next.

"Did you hear me, Luca? I hate you!" he shouted again.

Then, with a burst of anger, he jumped on top of me and began punching me ruthlessly. I shot up in bed and put up my forearms to block each blow. I couldn't comprehend what was happening. No one had ever struck me like this before. Adrenaline was pumping through my veins and my heart was beating rapidly. Where was he getting all this energy? He was relentless, and when he finally got tired of punching, he tried to wrestle me to the floor. We rolled over, back and forth. I was grateful for his uncoordinated state because he wasn't able to do much damage, but then I felt a searing pain in my right arm, just above my bicep. What the hell? He was biting me! I knocked his head away with all my might.

"Get the hell off of me, you animal! What the fuck is wrong with you, Brad?" I was fuming.

He seemed startled, almost as if he had woken up from a bad dream. Then he started crying uncontrollably and rocking forward and back. "Look at my hands, look. They're all swollen and they hurt. What's wrong with them?"

"They're swollen because you've been punching me for the last 15 minutes, you maniac." He tried to come over to me for comfort, and although I pushed him away, he continued to reach out to me.

"Please, Luca, come here. Don't pull away from me. I need you to hold me," he pleaded pathetically.

"You're crazy. You know that? Crazy. Get the hell

away from me. NOW!" I shouted, shoving him down onto his bed.

"Please, just hold me, Luca. I'm sorry, I'm sorry," he said as he continued to cry.

My anger continued to build. I threw on my pants and shoes as quickly as I could, turned to him and said, "I'm out of here, Brad. You're completely out of your mind. I can't be in the same room with you after that." He tried to pull at me as I moved to the door.

"Get away from me, Brad. I'm warning you."

He backed off with a look of shock on his face. I slammed the door and walked out into the night.

The campus was finally quiet. Not a soul was awake. What just happened? I thought. What kind of animal is he? I began to shiver as if I was cold, but it was a warm May night. The shivers grew into full-on shaking as the reality of his physical abuse set in. What is wrong with me? How could I have let this happen? An overwhelming sense of shame washed over me as I wandered the campus aimlessly.

Eventually, I made my way to the campus ministry office, knowing that it would be closed. By then, it was nearly 6 a.m. No one would be awake for hours. Although the office was closed, the chapel remained open at all times. Opening the heavy wooden doors, I could barely see the vigil candles near the altar. The usual spicy scent of incense filled me with comfort while the darkness enveloped me like a cocoon. I quietly slipped into a pew near the flickering candles and started to cry.

I was still in the chapel when Fr. Murphy walked in to set up for the 7 a.m. Mass. Few, if any students attended Mass so early in the morning. But the neighborhood community enjoyed coming to the campus chapel because the homilies were more interesting and progressive than at their local parishes. Fr. Murphy was startled to see me. Kneeling with my head resting on the pew in front of me, I looked up when I heard the noise. Relief washed over me and I quickly went to him.

"Luca, what are you doing here so early? What's this? You've been crying. Are you OK?"

"It's Brad. We had a fight. A really bad fight," I said as the tears began to flow uncontrollably.

"OK, OK, let's go to my office so we can talk in private," Fr. Murphy suggested.

Once there, I began to cry in earnest. For the first time, I let down my guard and explained what the last few months with Brad had been like. I told him everything–everything except that we had been sleeping together. I just couldn't admit that to anyone yet. But then, Fr. Murphy asked me point blank.

"Are you two a couple? Are you having sex?"

"What? No, no, just friends," I blurted out. My denial was a bit too forceful. I knew he didn't believe me, but he didn't press any further.

"Let me see your arm, Luca. What happened here?"

My arm was red and swollen, and was already turning black and blue. You could clearly see marks where Brad's teeth had sunk into me: each puncture was caked with dried blood.

"Did Brad do this to you? Did he bite you?" Fr. Murphy asked in disbelief.

"Yeah, after he was unsuccessful in his punching frenzy, we wrestled to the floor. I think the bite was what snapped me out of it. I freaked out and pushed him off me with all my strength and ran out of there."

"We need to get you to a doctor, Luca. This could easily get infected."

"OK, but I don't want to report him. I don't want to get him in trouble, Father."

"That is not your concern, Luca. You need to let us take care of you for a change. You are always trying to save the world, but you often leave yourself behind. Just lie back on the couch and get some rest. As soon as Mass is over, I will make a few phone calls."

"Thank you, Father. I don't know what I'd do without you." He gave me a sad smile as he turned to leave.

"Father Murphy? I can't go back there. I just can't."

"Don't worry about that now, Luca. No one will ever let that happen to you again," he assured me.

CHAPTER 22

BISHOP DE SANTO
WINTER TO SPRING 2016

After his reunion with Brad and the ensuing emotional crisis, Bishop De Santo was even more determined to reach out to gays and lesbians in his diocese. In part, he believed that as part of his penance, he needed to take the risk of fighting for the LGBTQ community, regardless of the consequences. Fairfield County, Connecticut was not a backwater place. It had a wealthy and highly educated population. Its proximity to New York City exposed its citizens to a great deal of diversity. It was time he took a chance and actively open his doors to a community that bore so much pain at the hands of the Church, a community that he himself was part of. There was a great deal of education to be done as well. If Brad could have such a narrow view on the issue, so could many others.

So much had changed since 1980. Being gay no longer carried a stigma in many places. More young LGBTQ people were open about their sexuality, and with the legalization of same-sex marriage, there was much more exposure all over the country. There were many positive role models for questioning youth to look up to. But the Church maintained its fear of homosexuality, and had done nothing to amend its destructive policies. Bishop De Santo believed that the Church was severely lacking in its ministry to the LGBTQ community. He had to do something bold, something to show that he was an advocate. Although he knew he knew that he might jeopardize his career, he was determined to make a difference.

Although there were many Pride celebrations in New York and Boston during Gay Pride month in June, Bishop De Santo felt the need to organize something in Connecticut. He took his cue from Pope Francis and two of the newly appointed U.S. Cardinals. Just as the Cardinal in Chicago had done, De Santo organized a series of liturgical celebrations throughout the Diocese of Bridgeport to welcome and embrace LGBTQ Catholics. "This is your church too!" he wanted to say. He put together a panel of LGBTQ Catholics of all ages and set up a lecture series, with a question and answer period to follow. He would hold these events at three major churches in the diocese. De Santo hoped to create a culminating event to welcome all LGBTQ Catholics and their allies. His goal was to spare the younger generation of gay youth the pain and struggle that he himself had endured. Although Bishop De Santo had not publicly come out as gay, he knew that he had to make more of an effort to care for those who were struggling with their faith and sexuality.

The program was launched in May and was to culminate in June, and while it received rave reviews in many circles, it also garnered a considerable amount of protest. Conservative Catholic groups organized picket lines and spread hateful messages on social media. However, there was always a packed auditorium at each lecture. On the third Sunday in June, a week before the annual Pride celebration in New York City, Bishop De Santo would say a Mass of thanksgiving to conclude the Pride Month outreach. He had chosen to hold it at St. Catherine's in Greenwich, rather than at the Cathedral in Bridgeport. Because of its proximity to New York, there were a greater number of LGBTQ people in this part of his diocese.

When the day arrived, the church was at capacity. Bishop Luca had wanted this to be a grand celebration of welcome and acceptance. He used his creative energy and deep well of resources to pull together the best the diocese had to offer. The choir at St. Catherine's was excellent, and he augmented it with the finest singers from each church in the diocese. He authorized the hiring of brass, strings, and timpani to augment the grand organ. And of course, he had a heavy hand in planning the music. It was majestic: the congregation filled St. Catherine's with exuberant song and prayer. Luca fed off of the incredible positive energy and felt empowered to do more. After the closing blessing, Bishop De Santo looked out on the many smiling faces, hungry for a community of love.

"Here you are, one family gathered in the house of God. This," he said with a sweeping gesture indicating the church building, "this is your home, and no one will ever close these doors to you!" His declaration prompted the congregation to rise as they broke out in thunderous applause. The great organ and brass echoed that great call of love as the final hymn began. Then Bishop De Santo processed down the main aisle of the church. Pew by pew, hands reached out to touch him. He paused at every hand and greeted this family, his family, whom he invited into his church. This is why he had become a priest. There was no doubt in his mind that he was meant to lead this flock. They needed him, and he needed them.

He stood outside the doors of the church for over an hour greeting people and pulling them into his strong embrace. He was moved to tears with each new face and each plea for more celebrations such as this. Bishop De Santo assured them that this was only the beginning. When the line of people dwindled, he entered the church and made his way to the sacristy to change out of his vestments. He was exhausted, but filled with happiness.

CHAPTER 23

MICHAEL
SPRING 2016

Michael was desperate to talk to the Bishop. If anyone could help him right now, it was Bishop De Santo. Michael's internal struggle was ripping him apart and he knew that he needed guidance. At Mass that day, he felt that he was finally at home. He looked around to see people younger and older than him, holding hands, and kissing during the sign of peace. Why couldn't he do the same? Why couldn't his father accept him as he was? As the celebration progressed, Michael began to feel emboldened. He decided that he would introduce himself to Bishop De Santo as soon as possible. However, the crowd engulfed the Bishop after Mass, and Michael didn't want to speak to him in front of other people. Instead, he waited in the church until the line of people dissipated. The Bishop would have to come back inside eventually.

In hopeful anticipation as he waited at the sacristy door, Michael drew in an anxious breath as he watched De Santo walk up the aisle of the church. It's now or never, he thought. When he and the Bishop made eye contact, Michael broke into a shy smile and stuck out his hand.

"Hello Bishop De Santo. My name is Michael, Michael Ghenter. I believe you know my father."

Luca's heart skipped a beat. Could this really be happening? This strikingly handsome young man with blond hair and deep blue eyes was Brad's son. Luca had had broken it off with Brad over six months ago. He had made his peace with their brief affair, but they hadn't been in touch since. What was this all about? A bit on edge, Luca offered his hand.

"Nice to meet you, Michael. Of course I know Brad, we were college roommates, after all. How are your parents doing?" Luca couldn't help but suspect that something was brewing. But what?

"They are fine, Bishop. Thank you for asking. I am sorry to bother you. I know that you have been inundated with people this afternoon, and I'm sure that you want to go home and rest," Michael said. "I just wanted to connect before you left today."

"Yes, I am a bit weary. But, I've been energized by such an incredible celebration. What can I do for you, Michael?"

After a moment's hesitation, Michael gathered the courage to say, "I wondered if I could talk with you about my personal journey. I am really struggling right now and I don't have anyone I can confide in. Can I make an appointment with you to chat?" As he asked, a tear trickled down his cheek. Michael didn't expect to be overwhelmed with emotion. His desperate need lingered just below the surface.

Luca was moved. "Of course you can, Michael," he said, reaching out his hand and resting it comfortingly on Michael's shoulder. He felt compassion for this young man who was clearly in pain. "Listen, have you eaten? I was just going to get a bite to eat. Perhaps we can go to dinner and chat then. What do you say?"

"Oh, no, I couldn't ask you to do that. I know that you have had a full day. I can wait until later this week. Really, Bishop," Michael responded unconvincingly. He hoped that the Bishop would ignore his protest. Now that they had met, Michael wanted nothing more than to pour out his heart to Bishop De Santo. There was no way he could wait for another week.

"I insist. There is a great little Italian restaurant not too far from here, Positano. Do you know it?"

Michael nodded. "Yes, it's right on the water."

"That's right. Besides, Michael, I hate to dine alone. Please join me."

"Sure, I would love to. Are you sure you are not just being kind?" Michael asked.

"Yes, I am being kind, but I am taking care of myself as well. I'd rather not dine alone and I would love to have your company," the Bishop responded. "I will meet you there in 20 minutes. I just have to get out of this outfit!" he joked.

Once at the restaurant, Luca felt more relaxed. He was a regular at Positano. It always felt like he was back in Rome or with his Uncle Pete during their many dinners together. The maitre d' greeted him with a warm smile.

"Buona sera, Bishop De Santo. It's good to see you again. Your usual table?"

"Buona sera, Giuseppe. Si. But there will be two of us this evening. Grazie."

"Di niente, not a problem. Right this way."

Michael appeared a few minutes later and took a seat. The table was over by the window, looking out over Long Island Sound—a peaceful vista. It was also very private, and would be perfect for him to share his dilemma with the Bishop. Michael was quite nervous. He had never had dinner with a priest, let alone a bishop. Although he grew up Catholic, his parents didn't attend Mass regularly. But Catholic traditions were a major part of his upbringing. His parents made sure that he had received his first Communion and Confirmation, and they always attended Mass for Christmas and Easter.

After the waiter came to take their orders, Bishop De Santo began to ask Michael about his life. Michael was grateful that their conversation was benign. He shared that he had just gotten his MBA at Fordham University and had started with an investment firm on Wall Street. His father had landed him the job, and he was grateful for the help. Michael confessed that his father had always been a controlling force in his life. His influence loomed large at every crossroad. He never felt that he could voice his own opinion, especially if it differed from his father's.

By the time the pasta was served and the wine poured, Michael knew that he had stalled long enough. It was now or never. "Bishop, as you probably figured out by my attendance at that Mass, I am gay."

"Yes, I suspected that might be the case. Is that what has you so troubled, Michael?"

"Well, actually, it's my father. I know that you were friends in college, so I am sure you know how he is. He's quite driven toward success, and I feel like everything I do is part of his drive. He's very concerned about how things appear. What's making it complicated right now is that he is pushing me to get married–to a woman. I don't know how to tell him I'm gay. He is going to freak out on me."

"Michael, your father knows many gay and lesbian people. He's got gay friends. What makes you think that he'll freak out? His love for you will never change."

"Pardon my bluntness, Bishop, but you don't understand. It's fine with him if other people are gay, as long as it's not one of his kids. He's actually said so on many occasions. Maryann and I have had little say with regard to our futures. He's always had our lives all planned out. Plus, I am the only son. I have to carry on the family name, so I am told."

"I see. I am sorry, Michael. I know that your father is a force to be reckoned with. He always has been, but this is your journey. You have to find some way to assert your independence, otherwise you are going to be miserable for the rest of your life."

"But Bishop De Santo, he wouldn't even entertain the idea of me majoring in anything else but business. There is no way he will accept a gay son."

"Come on now, Michael. I'm sure your father knows a number of gay people. It's just part of life these days, especially in the tri-state area. How do you know he'll react so poorly?" the Bishop asked.

Michael shook his head. "I was dating a guy about a year ago. Jim and I were spending a lot of time together and I used to bring him to many family functions. Although I wasn't out yet, I suggested bringing him to my cousin's wedding. You should have seen my father's face."

"What did he say?"

"He was pretty blunt," Michael continued. "He said that I had better be careful about how much time I spent with Jim, because people would get the wrong idea. When I asked him what the big deal was, he said that it could ruin my job prospects. Then he told me I should be out there trying to meet a nice girl."

Luca was quite surprised by Michael's description of Brad. It wasn't 1980 any longer. For the most part, being gay did not carry the stigma it had so many years ago. Times had indeed changed for the better. "Well, that's not promising," he began, "but if he has no idea that you are gay–did you ever tell him you were dating Jim? He may just be assuming that you are straight and will marry a woman someday and settle down. That doesn't mean he's homophobic."

"No, I didn't tell him, but it was all about his tone. He was incredibly condescending and dismissive. Besides, he'd have to be stupid not to pick up on the nature of our relationship. He made me feel as if I were doing something disreputable by hanging out with Jim. Without naming it, he was telling me that I couldn't be gay. I was totally demoralized," Michael explained.

"Well, I do remember him mocking me for my major, my liberal attitudes, and wanting to become a teacher. He said I would be poor and unhappy. His tone said it all," De Santo replied. "But I had to find a way to assert myself and follow my heart. Granted, I am not his son. But we were very connected back then. His influence on me was quite strong."

"Yeah, that's what I gathered by the way he talks about you. He still admires you a great deal."

That last remark took Bishop De Santo off guard. Admires me? What does that mean? he thought. What could Brad really want from me? Is it only because I am a bishop now and he sees me as powerful? After all this time, his insecurity regarding Brad surprised him. Luca was also disheartened by Brad's homophobia, especially after all they shared just a few months ago. Though he himself couldn't identify as gay, certainly he could relate to his son. This was too much to process at the moment. He turned his attention back to Michael.

"So let me ask you a question, Michael. What do you fear most from telling your father that you are gay? What's the worst that could happen?"

"Other than being belittled and shamed?" Michael asked wryly. "I suppose he would cut me off–financially, I mean. Maybe he wouldn't want to see me anymore. I just don't know how far he'd go. He has a temper, as you know."

"All right–so can you handle that? Can you manage without his financial help? More importantly, could you put up with his anger and disapproval until he cools off?" De Santo asked.

"Yes, I think I can. I pay my own bills and am self-sufficient. I don't live at home anymore and, though it would be painful, I think I can manage the distance."

De Santo went on. "So then, what is worse, the self-loathing and fear that you carry around with you now, or the fear of rejection?"

Michael was silent and bowed his head. Bishop De Santo continued, "Each time you withhold what you are feeling or what you dream for your future, you distance yourself from your father. What are your conversations about? Do you ever share your thoughts and dreams, or do you remain in safe, superficial territory?"

"It's always surface stuff and it's always the same. We talk about the market, business prospects, and real estate. I can't remember the last time I shared any feelings with him. When I was a kid we used to spend so much time together. He was always concerned with my happiness. It all changed when I got into high school. He became a helicopter dad, hovering over every choice I made. It was–is–suffocating."

"So, Michael, it sounds like you have already lost a significant part of your relationship by keeping your secret. It seems to me that you know what you have to do."

"I do, Bishop. But I am so afraid. I am 26 years old and I feel like a bad little boy who is afraid to disappoint his father. I am so ashamed of myself."

"Please, Michael, don't do that to yourself. That's not fair. There is so much you have to be proud of. Don't let your fear drag you down. You have nothing to be ashamed of. Being gay is perfectly normal. You must believe that."

Michael bowed his head once again as his index finger played with the condensation on his water glass. *He has no idea what he's asking me to do,* Michael thought. *Dad can be such an ogre.* "Can you help me tell him, Bishop? Can you tell him for me?" Michael pleaded.

What have I gotten myself into now? Luca asked himself. *I just can't see Brad again; it's too risky. This* wonderful young man has no idea what he's asking me to do. There are so many layers to this story. He had to give Michael the confidence he needed to tell Brad on his own.

"Look, Michael, you can do this. Try to tell him yourself. That show of strength is the first step to claiming your independence. If I were to do it, you would find yourself in a weakened position. If you let me know when you are going to tell him, I can be available to chat with him or you, if need be. How does that sound? Do you think you can do that?"

Michael smiled weakly. "It'd be way easier if you told him for me."

On his way home, Michael ruminated over their dinner conversation. He was amazed at how comfortable he was with Bishop De Santo. He had never had as frank a conversation about his sexuality with anyone else. That evening, he felt safe and secure. There was so much more that he wanted to share with the Bishop, and he hoped that he'd be willing to see him more often. Why can't my father be more like him? Michael thought. Shouldn't a father be someone who you could confide in? Shouldn't he be there to guide and love me no matter what?

Michael dreaded telling his father that he was gay. In his heart, he knew that he would disapprove. But as the Bishop said, this was his life, and he needed to take charge of it himself.

CHAPTER 24

LUCA
SPRING 1981

The student health center sent me to St. Francis Hospital to get a tetanus shot. Brad's bite had broken skin, and apparently, the human mouth contains a whole host of bacteria that could easily lead to infection. The shot hurt like hell–just another reason to hate Brad, as if I needed one. After that, I felt like a wounded puppy in need of comfort. Without a moment's hesitation, I drove directly home.

"Ciao Mom, Dad, I'm home," I announced as I walked into the house.

"Luca!" Mom said as she wrapped me in her arms. "What a wonderful surprise. Are you hungry? Have you eaten?"

"That's how I know I'm home, Mom. The first

question is always about food. I'm starving. Do you have any sauce? I miss your pasta."

"Of course, I was just about to cook. Here," she said, handing me a bowl, "why don't you make the salad while I get everything else started?"

Dad sat at the kitchen table while Mom and I were busy preparing supper. She put the water on and began making a fresh marinara sauce. The smell of garlic sautéed in olive oil brought me back to my childhood. I always said that it was the smell of Sunday morning. I would wake to the sounds and smells of her preparing the Sunday sauce and frying meatballs. There was nothing that could comfort me more than being safe at home with Mom and Dad.

"So, Luca, what brings you home today? Don't you have finals? Where's Brad? He usually comes for my pasta."

"Finals start this week. I have so much studying to do, Mom, and the dorm is too noisy. I just figured I could concentrate more easily here," I lied. "I may commute for the last week of the semester."

"Oh, it will be wonderful to have you at home. What about Brad?" She wasn't going to let me glaze over that question.

"He's fine. He has some study group to go to tonight. He couldn't get away, but he sends his love." I realized that I'd eventually have to come up with some explanation about why we wouldn't be rooming together during senior year. But that could wait.

A meal at Mom and Dad's table was just what I needed that night. They filled me in on what each of my siblings was doing and on all the family news. Dad complained about his bossy brother and Uncle Gino's drinking. Then Mom took me by the hand and the three of us went out to the back yard. They were just starting to plant the vegetable garden, and had to show me each and every seedling. It was a perfectly ordinary evening at home.

After we washed and dried the dishes, I walked down the hall to my childhood bedroom. I knew that I had to tell my other friends that I wouldn't be on campus for a few days. I wasn't sure the excuse I fabricated for my parents would hold up to their scrutiny, and I feared that Brad might make up a story about me. The first person I dialed was Irene.

"Hey there gorgeous. Are you deep into your books tonight?" I asked.

"Puh-leeeease, me? It's way too early for that. I'll start around midnight. I'm about to go out with the girls on the floor. We're heading out to the pub for a bit. Want to join us?"

"Thanks, but no. I have a final on Monday."

"Well, then you have all day Sunday to study. Let's meet in 20 minutes. That should be plenty of time to get yourself together."

"I'm actually not on campus. I drove home to spend some time with Mom and Dad."

"And you didn't bring me home for pasta? You suck."

"Yeah, I do," I said with a snicker. "But that's another story."

Irene laughed out loud. "Pig!"

"Actually, I'm thinking about staying home for the week. It's been pretty tense in my room."

"Did you have another one of your blowouts with Brad?"

"Yeah, it was a blowout to end all blowouts," I

replied.

"That bad, eh? It seemed inevitable after his drunken display Friday night. He was in the worst shape I've ever seen, and I've seen a lot."

"Yeah, it got pretty ugly. I just needed to get out of there for a while. But I'll tell you about it when I see you," I said.

"Have you thought about getting a new roommate for next year?" she asked perceptively.

"Yeah, I have. Can we talk about it later, though? I don't feel like thinking about it tonight."

"Of course, honey. Let's meet after your final, OK?"

+++

On Monday morning, I drove to campus earlier than planned. Fr. Murphy had made an appointment for me with student services, and met me outside the office. "How are you feeling this morning, Luca?" he asked. "Did you sleep?"

"Better. I drove home after the hospital. Mom took good care of me."

"Good. Now let's take care of your rooming situation," he said as he walked me to the office. Changing rooms was complicated, and the first answer a student received was always a hard "No." Fr. Murphy's presence meant that the change had to happen.

Mrs. Jensen greeted us with a look of annoyance; she could tell something was up.

"You know that we don't make room changes this late in the semester," she said. "The room lottery has already taken place for September. If there is anything available at all, you will simply be assigned there. You will have no choice in the matter."

"Mrs. Jensen, if this were not absolutely necessary, I would not be here with Luca, would I? I am sure that he will be happy with whatever you can give him. This room change must happen. I hope that you understand the gravity of his situation," Fr. Murphy said with authority.

Mrs. Jensen gave an audible grunt of displeasure. She was such a nasty woman, and seemed to hate her job. Every interaction I had ever had with her had been unpleasant.

"The senior dorm rooms are all spoken for, but there is a room in Gonzaga Hall. That's all I can offer."

"That's perfect, Mrs. Jensen. Thank you," I replied. I was willing to take anything.

Gonzaga was a dorm on the quad, which was where most of the underclassmen were housed. I had never met the guy who was already in the room, but I didn't care. I would be free from Brad. As we left the office, I let out an audible sigh of relief. Fr. Murphy put his arm around me as we walked.

"OK, that is done. Now, have you spoken to Brad since Friday night, Luca?"

"No. I guess I need to tell him about the room change."

"Luca, you have to confront him about what he did to you. You need to get that off your chest. I know you—if you don't, it will be much more difficult to move on," Fr. Murphy advised.

I couldn't believe what I was hearing. How could I possibly be in the same room with Brad after what he had done? How do I know he won't attack me again? I thought.

But instead of voicing any of my fears I just agreed and said, "I know you're right. I just have to gather up my courage, Father."

"If there is anything you have in droves, Luca, it's courage."

"I don't know about that, Fr. Murphy, but thanks for the vote of confidence," I replied.

"Luca, when this is all settled, come by my office. I think we should talk a bit more about your relationship with Brad."

He knows, I thought. How can I talk to him about that?

"Oh, OK, Father," I replied tentatively.

With an encounter with Brad looming over my head, I resolved to go back to my room to pack up my stuff. I knew that I could plan to move almost all of it out when Brad was taking his finals, without ever seeing him. However, I had to tell him the news before he got a call from student services informing him that he had to find a new roommate. Who knows what kind of scene that would prompt? No, I had to tell him in person.

As I walked across campus, my resolve strengthened. What he had done to me on Friday night was unacceptable. Never in my life had I experienced anything so violently demeaning. I had been with Brad for nearly two years, during which time he steadily chipped away at my self-worth. His constant bullying became so much a part of my everyday life that it seemed commonplace. I began to feel that I didn't measure up to his standards and that somehow it was my fault. I believed that I was lucky to have Brad in my life, and I was entirely consumed by him. Whenever it would get really bad, I would remind myself that I would never find another guy who would love me the way he did. Although I knew better, the misguided script he imprinted on me would play over and over in my mind: We're not like the gays on TV or in bars. We are simply in love with each other, and there are no other guys like us. As a result, I felt trapped and gave into the idea that this was just the way it had to be.

But that faulty logic had long since fallen apart. Something in me snapped on Friday night. The moment his first punch landed on me, I knew his behavior was bizarre. There was something foundationally wrong with our relationship. As I thought back on it, I became progressively angrier; in fact, I was outraged. How could he have done that to me? Who hits someone they love? It took his violent attack for me to realize that I was in an abusive relationship. Although his verbal assaults did not produce scars like the one on my arm, they were just as destructive and violent. It dawned on me that I had lost a sense of who I really was. It was as if I was under his spell, following him blindly regardless of how much he hurt me. No, I thought, there can be no reconciliation between Brad and me. I have to make this a clean break. If I even entertained the idea of working it out, I could find myself trapped within his poisonous charm once again. I didn't trust myself to be strong enough to fight that.

I took a deep breath when I arrived at our door. The hall was quiet and I paused in order to gather my strength. Although I had a key, I knocked and he opened the door immediately.

"There you are. Where have you been for the last three days?" Brad asked with a worried look on his face.

"I went home. I'll be staying there throughout final exams."

"Why? Why wouldn't you just stay on campus until exams are over?" Brad asked.

"I need time to think," I said evasively.

"Why? Are you OK? It's been two days, why didn't you call me?"

"I didn't know what to say, Brad."

"What do you mean? Come in, don't just stand in the hall." He reached out to hug me and I pulled away. "What's wrong? I'm not going to hurt you. Come here." He reached out a second time and I held up my hand.

"No, Brad. I can't. After what you did Friday night, I can't be near you."

His jaw dropped in disbelief. It took him completely by surprise.

"What do you mean, you can't be near me? I love you and you love me. I was drunk on Friday. It didn't mean anything. Come on in and let's talk about it," he pleaded.

I was tempted. Even after all the violence on Friday, and my firm resolve as I walked over, I still felt drawn to him. But who knew what could happen if I allowed him to rationalize it all away? I couldn't let him touch me because I knew I didn't have the strength to say no. How could I still love him after all he had done to me? It didn't make any sense. I just wanted to fall into his arms and go back to the way it was months ago.

All of this internal struggle was going through my mind as I stood outside our room in the dorm hallway. Then he glanced at my arm. The teeth marks had been healing, and I had taken the bandage off, but my arm was still spectacularly black and blue.

"What happened to your arm? It's all swollen. Did I do that?" he asked with dread.

"Yeah, when you couldn't land a punch on my face, you bit me and wouldn't let go."

"Holy shit! I don't even remember that. Oh my God, Luca, I'm so sorry," he said as he pulled me in for a hug. It was an automatic response. We both fell into our normal interaction. I could smell him and feel his soft skin against mine. It felt so natural. But as soon as our faces were close enough to touch, I came to my senses.

"No, Brad, please. We can't do this. I can't do this."

"It was only a hug, Luca, nothing more. I just want you to know how sorry I am. Please come in so we can talk. I know we can work this out. I promise that I will change. Please, Luca."

"There's nothing left to work out, Brad."

"What does that mean?" he asked with fear in his eyes.

"It means that I'm moving out. You will need to find a new roommate next year."

"You've got to be kidding. After one little fight, it's over?"

"Get real, Brad. You attacked me and you bit me. That's not little and that's not normal. It's over between us," I said firmly.

"Come on, Luca. You can't just throw away two years together. Please." he pleaded. "I am so sorry. I know we can work this out."

I had never seen him like this. He was always the aggressor, the strong one in each encounter. His supplication made me realize how weak he truly was. I looked at him with sympathy and said, "I have to go. I'll come back later to get my stuff. I just can't be here with you right now."

I turned and marched down the hall with determination. As I exited the dorm, the sun shone brightly on that warm spring day. I can't believe that I almost got myself back into that abusive relationship, I thought. How could I be so weak? What is it about him that makes me want to give in? I knew that I had to make a clean break. There could be no contact other than what was necessary for our shared activities. I needed to be completely free of his influence.

I managed to move out of our room while Brad was taking a final exam. I found it so hard to concentrate on my finals, but I couldn't worry about that. I would make it through, and life would go on. I couldn't face seeing Brad during those last few days, so I made sure to change my routine. Sadly, I had to distance myself from our group of mutual friends. I still didn't know what I would say to them. Neither of us was out to our friends, and so it couldn't be explained away as a break-up, although that's exactly what it was. My moving out would make little sense to them. I just needed to be away from all of them, and the summer break would provide that respite.

As I made my plans, I thought to myself, I don't need a boyfriend to be happy. I have always known I was meant to become a priest; I just got diverted by this thing with Brad. I need to trust that I was always on the right path. Now I am more certain than ever.

CHAPTER 25

BRAD
SUMMER 2016

Brad lived in an exclusive neighborhood in Greenwich, Connecticut. It was an easy commute into his offices in Manhattan and Stamford, but far enough away to provide a beautiful green lawn and a grand house on Long Island Sound. After a stressful day at the office, he sat in his parlor with a glass of scotch in his hand, waiting for Luca. The phone call he had received from him surprised him. Luca said that he wanted to speak to him about his son, Michael. How in the world does he know about Michael? he thought. And why does he want to talk to me about him?

Brad was shocked when Michael came out to him, although he should have suspected something was going on back when his son was always with his friend Jim. His first response was to dismiss it, not even acknowledge the statement. But Michael was assertive. He told Brad that he was gay and that he hoped to find the right guy to marry someday. Michael said that he hoped his parents would welcome his future husband into the family, just as they would a wife. It was nonsense. Michael's life would be miserable. Why couldn't he keep it to himself? There was nothing wrong with having trysts with handsome young men during his youth, but as a mature man, he would have to give that up and settle down—or at least be incredibly discreet.

He needs to marry a woman who can support him in his career and give him children, Brad thought as he waited. Surely that is a more attractive option than living a gay lifestyle. It doesn't matter how far our country has come with regard to gay rights and general acceptance. The business world still harbors deep-seated prejudice. He had witnessed it many times throughout his career. Michael should not subject himself to that kind of denigration. He wouldn't allow it.

The doorbell rang and Wendy answered the door. "How good to see you again, Bishop De Santo. Please come in." Brad turned to see Luca lean in and give her a kiss on the cheek. "Stop addressing me so formally, Wendy," Luca smiled. "It makes me uncomfortable."

"Sorry, Luca. I just can't wrap my head around the fact that you're actually a bishop. I love saying it."

"Wendy, you're as delightful as ever," he responded as she showed him into the parlor.

"The Bishop has arrived, my dear," Wendy announced, putting her arms around Brad and kissing him.

"Well, boys, I will leave you to your visit. I am sure that you have a lot to catch up on. Brad, I'll be in the exercise room. Let me know if you need anything."

"Thanks, my dear," Brad responded.

Two leather wing chairs were angled toward the empty fireplace. Photos of Brad and Wendy's life decorated the mantel: their wedding portrait, a family shot that included Michael and his sister Maryann, and many others. Luca took his place across from Brad. He wasn't exactly sure what he was going to say, but he figured that he'd be inspired during their discussion. That's how he often approached difficult conversations.

"You look good, Brad. It's good to see you again," he said sincerely.

"Is it, Luca?" Brad said staring into the fireplace with a hint of bitterness in his tone. Then he looked directly at him. "You always look good. I am glad to see you as well." His tone softened immediately as he stood and poured himself another scotch. "So, how is it that you want to talk to me about Michael? I didn't even know you had met."

"I met Michael after the Mass in celebration of the LGBTQ community last month. He introduced himself to me after Mass."

"Yes, I heard about that. What possessed you to do something so controversial, Luca? I'm sure that you've always had to play it safe within the Church, otherwise you wouldn't have been raised to bishop."

"Since Pope Francis's more welcoming tone, things have begun to change. It was Pride Month, and I believe that outreach to the gay community is long overdue. The Catholic Church has caused a significant amount of pain to so many people in our community."

"Your community, Luca, not mine," Brad said, his bitterness returning. Luca could sense that anger was simmering just below the surface.

"Look, Brad, I didn't come here to argue. Michael reached out to me after he came out to you. He was distraught. He asked me to help, so here I am. Frankly, I was surprised by your negative reaction to his news," he said honestly.

"Why in the world would I be happy about it? Everything will be more difficult for him. He will have to fight for rights that straight people already have. People will call him queer and faggot."

Luca could tell that Brad had had a couple of drinks already. He wasn't his usual affable self.

"Brad, you know as well as I that being gay, bi, or whatever is not something one chooses for themselves. It's just who we are. Michael is hurting right now. It took a great deal of courage for him to come out to you. He needs your acceptance."

"Oh, I see now. You told him to come out to me, didn't you?"

"Well, I guess in a way I did. I told him that hiding his true self from you would ruin your relationship. He was already distancing himself from you, Brad. Both of you deserve more than a superficial father and son relationship. He's your only son. He's not that much older than we were when we were in love in college. I should think that you of all people could understand him. Can't you simply accept him the way he is, as a gay man?"

"That's what you want, isn't it? It's payback for what

I wouldn't give you. You wanted me to give up my life and run away with you. You just wanted to rub this in my face, you bastard!"

Luca physically recoiled from Brad's angry words. Just then, Michael burst into the parlor. "Are you kidding me, Dad? All those homophobic comments I had to endure for the last ten years, and now I find out that you've been sleeping with the Bishop?"

"Hold on. We are not sleeping together, Michael!" Bishop De Santo tried to clarify.

"Watch your tone, son!" Brad warned him. "This conversation is about you, not the Bishop and me. How dare you burst in here making absurd accusations?"

"Accusations? I heard everything, Dad. You're in love with him. Well, at least you were. So why is it OK for you but not me? You're such a hypocrite, Dad. I can't even look at you!" Michael screamed.

Wendy came running into the parlor. "What's going on in here? Why is everyone yelling? Calm down," she cried.

"Hey Mom, did you know that Dad slept with the Bishop when they were in college? What a self-loathing homophobe!"

Wendy's face hardened and her eyes grew narrow. "What nonsense are you spouting, Michael? What your father did in college is none of your business. That's ancient history."

"It's not ancient history when he calls me a faggot and tells me how disappointed in me he is." Michael spat out.

"I didn't call you a faggot! Now you're making things up. Of course I'm disappointed in you. Your life is going to be a constant struggle and it will be much harder for me to use my connections to advance your career." Brad seemed determined to continue escalating the argument.

"Are you kidding me? What is it, Dad? Are you afraid that I'll embarrass you in front of all your rich friends? Will they shun you because you have a gay son? Or is it too close to home? Are you afraid of your own sexual desires? To think I feared you, longed for your approval–all while you were hiding from who you really are. You're pathetic."

Bishop De Santo stood there with his mouth agape. He was in the midst of a huge family argument, and there was no sign of it abating. He tried desperately to think of something that would calm Michael down, but his mind was reeling. Michael was saying many of the same things that he himself felt about Brad. Luca didn't want to be the second hypocrite in the room by contradicting Michael, so he just remained quiet and let the scene unfold.

"I'm warning you, Michael," Brad said in a low, measured tone. "Don't push me any further."

"Or what, Dad, you'll disown me? Go ahead, who wants a father who is ashamed of him, who calls him a dirty queer? He sneered. "I'm out of here!"

Michael stormed out of the parlor. Wendy ran after him and stood at the open front door watching him fly down the driveway in anger.

"Michael, please don't go. Listen to reason," Wendy pleaded through her tears. "Come back so we can talk this through. You know we love you, Michael. Don't leave." She let out a sob and leaned her forehead against the doorjamb as she watched his car peel out of the driveway with a squeal.

Brad and Luca stared at each other in disbelief. Brad

was visibly shaking. He never meant it to get so out of hand. He really didn't believe most of what he said to his son. It was just that Brad never backed down from an argument; he always had to have the last word. For the first time, he realized that Michael was like him in more ways than one.

Wendy marched back into the parlor. She was fuming and sobbing at the same time. "It's your fault my son is leaving! How could you say those things to him, Brad? You know, you can be such a bastard at times."

"Wendy, please, this is not my fault. He overheard Luca and I discussing our time as roommates in college. There was nothing nefarious about it," Brad pleaded.

At that, she turned to Luca. "Why are you here? Haven't you done enough? You have been a shadow over our marriage since the beginning. Why can't you just leave us alone?"

"I'm sorry, Wendy," Luca replied. "I was just trying to help."

"Help? Help? Why would we need your help? After all these years, you think you can just insert yourself into our family? What gives you the right to interfere?"

Luca stared at her in shock. She had this all wrong. He knew that she didn't understand, but clearly, she was expressing years of repressed anger. He couldn't respond. There were no words to quell her fears or defend his intentions.

"That is not fair, Wendy!" Brad interjected. "Luca came to speak with me because Michael asked him to. He was just trying to talk some sense into me when Michael overheard us. This is not his fault. It's mine, goddamn it."

"I don't give a damn!" Wendy burst out. "I knew it

was bad news when you two met at that fundraiser last year. I could feel the energy pass between you. How could you do this to us, Brad? Don't our 30 years of marriage mean anything to you?" Then Wendy turned on her heel and flew up the stairs to her bedroom.

Interminable silence filled the vacuum left by her departure. Brad and Luca looked shell-shocked. "Well, we certainly made a mess out of this," Brad said to Luca as he wiped the sweat off of his brow.

"Look, Brad, I am so sorry for this. I never meant to interfere. If Michael hadn't come to me, I…"

"Just stop it, Luca. This is not your fault, and I'm sorry I accused you of trying to get back at me. After our last encounter, I didn't think I would ever see you again. I know how difficult it was for you to come see me tonight. Once again, your compassion for people who are hurting supersedes your fears. I'm sorry that you were in Wendy's crosshairs."

"She obviously resents me for what you and I shared so many years ago. I never imagined it would be so intense," Luca said. "I was totally taken off guard. But I suppose given our relationship this past year, I deserved it."

"I'm not so sure about that. But Wendy is intensely protective of her children. She's like a mother bear. God help anyone who gets between her and them, especially me," Brad replied.

Luca ran his hand through his hair and let out an exasperated sigh. "So what are you going to do now, Brad?"

"I honestly don't know," he said with agitation. "I need to find Michael and apologize. I don't know why I had such a visceral reaction to him being gay. I could hear all this judgment flowing from my lips, but I couldn't stop it."

"Perhaps it's because it hits too close to home, Brad. Regardless of the choices you made regarding your family, you realize that you are still attracted to men. You can't repress that. You just need to make peace with it."

"Make peace with it? And how do I do that?" Brad asked sarcastically.

"I really don't know. Only you can determine what's best for you, but it might help to talk to someone neutral about it," Luca offered.

"What, like a psychiatrist? No thanks. That's more your line of work. I'll work this out on my own."

"Do you want me to give Michael a call?" Luca asked hesitantly.

"No, no, I think we have to sort this out as a family. I am sorry you were dragged into this, Luca. Listen, you'd better go now. I need to get upstairs to Wendy."

"Oh, yes, of course. Good luck, Brad. I'm really sorry about all of this."

"No, I'm sorry." Brad placed his hand on Luca's shoulder and squeezed. "It was really kind of you to try to help."

Luca nodded and walked out to his car. He sat in the driver's seat and rested his head on the steering wheel. Why is everything concerning Brad so damn complicated? he thought. He had assumed that by ending their relationship, he would be free of him. He didn't need this drama in his life.

☩

CHAPTER 26

WENDY

1981 TO 2016

Wendy had always been on the periphery of Brad and Luca's circle of friends. Although she was not a member of the St. Robert's choir, she faithfully attended all of the concerts. To say that she was infatuated with Brad was an understatement. She noted his every move from afar, and made every attempt to float within his orbit. However, it was nearly impossible to get a moment alone with him. When he wasn't in the midst of an admiring crowd, he was with Luca. They came in a pair. You never saw one without the other.

She had heard the rumors about them, but she didn't believe a word. It disturbed her when she heard some of the guys calling them a couple of queers. She noticed that they were taunted any time they walked by the recreational complex, but neither of them ever acknowledged the insults. Other than the fact that they were always together, there was nothing to convince her that Brad was gay. He was an incessant flirt who was constantly pursuing girls—unfortunately, they were always underclassmen. Wendy wondered why Brad never dated juniors or seniors.

In their senior year at St. Robert's, Wendy noticed a major shift. Brad was no longer rooming with Luca. In fact, she never saw them together anymore. "I wonder what happened between the two of them," she said to her best friend.

"I don't get it either. For two years they were hanging all over each other and now they don't even talk," Diane responded.

"Maybe they had a fight or something," Wendy wondered.

"Guys don't fight like that," Diane offered. "It seems more like a break-up."

"So you think they really are gay, Diane?"

"It seemed so obvious, Wendy. You mean to tell me you never suspected anything?"

"I did, yes. But then I'd see Brad with a different girl every weekend," Wendy defended herself.

"That was probably just for cover. You know Griffin, don't you?" Diane asked.

"Yeah, your roommate's boyfriend. Isn't he on the rugby team?"

"Yeah, he and Tony were in the same suite as Brad and Luca."

"So, what about him?" Wendy asked impatiently.

"Well, Griffin said he could hear them having sex

through the bathroom door!"

"Get out! That can't be true. Griffin's kind of a Neanderthal. He's always putting someone down. You can't trust a word he says," Wendy said, defending Brad vehemently.

"Maybe so, but the rumors came from somewhere. I mean, I don't really care one way or another, but I heard the whole rugby team was pretty cruel to them last year."

"Like I said, they're a bunch of Neanderthals." Wendy exclaimed.

Wendy could not accept that Brad might be gay, and she made it a point to be nearby whenever he came out of class or was heading to the cafeteria. One day, she fell in step with him as they entered the dining hall. He looked over at her and smiled, and she made her move.

"Hi Brad, I'm Wendy. Don't we have accounting together?"

"Hey Wendy. Yes, we do, and I know I've seen you at our choir concerts."

"I'm a big fan. A lot of my friends sing, so I can't escape," she said as she did a hair flip and giggle.

"Are you meeting anyone for lunch? Why not come sit with me?" Brad suggested.

That began their friendship, and by the end of the year, they were dating. Wendy could not be happier. She had finally gotten Brad.

+++

Looking back at the diocesan fundraiser and their first encounter, Wendy realized that her sense of foreboding was justified. Wendy could feel her muscles tighten as she witnessed Brad and Luca's reunion. Initially, when Brad suggested going, she thought it would be fine. Luca was now a bishop, and she and Brad had been happily married for 30 years. But she was no fool. She could clearly feel the energy that passed between the two of them; it was palpable. Their eyes were locked on each other and it seemed that no one else existed but the two of them. It was like watching two lions circling each other waiting for the right moment to pounce. The only difference was that they weren't looking to kill one another. No, they were completely entranced. She could feel the sexual energy between them, and knew there could be nothing but trouble ahead.

Now, as she buried her face in her pillow, Wendy wailed in pain. What just happened down there? How could Brad have treated Michael with such cruelty? He was their only son and he was the most wonderful child a parent could ask for. What did it matter if he was gay? The cruelty that Brad experienced was commonplace in the late 70s and 80s, but the world had changed. LGBTQ people were out in the media, politics, and everyday life. No one cared anymore. It wasn't like it was back when they were in college. Wendy just wanted Michael to be happy, to find a person he could love with all his heart. Who cared whether it was another man?

It was an ugly fight. How in the world did Michael find out about Brad and Luca? For that matter, why was Luca involved in this at all? She had hoped that they could have an appropriate relationship after 35 years, but now she doubted that. That sexual tension was there again today. Somehow, Brad and Luca still shared an intimacy that went beyond friendship. Wendy didn't want to see it, but today it slapped her right in the face. Is something going on between them? she wondered. Could they be sleeping together again? Then a truly frightening thought occurred to her. Could he have slept with other men since we've been married? The very thought of it turned her stomach. What would she do if she lost Brad after all these years?

Wendy thought back to the night they got engaged. Brad was a perfect gentleman and got down on one knee as he proposed. It was traditionally romantic.

"Wendy, you are the love of my life. Will you marry me?"

"Oh Brad, yes, of course I will marry you!"

However, as she gazed at the sparkling diamond on her finger, Wendy's fears welled up within her. She thought of the rumors from their college years. She knew that the romance of the moment would be completely ruined, but she had to be sure about Brad before she made this commitment. She had to say something. It was now or never. After they had toasted to their engagement, she reached across the table and placed her hands upon his.

"Brad? You know I love you with all my heart."

"Of course, Wendy. What's wrong?" Brad asked.

"Don't get mad at me, please," Wendy said as she watched Brad's whole body tighten. "I have to ask you a question and I need you to be completely honest with me."

"Anything, Wendy, ask me anything. I want you to be my wife," he replied, wondering what she could possibly ask.

"I need to know about you and Luca. Were you guys in love? Were you sleeping together?" Wendy blurted it out before she lost her courage. Brad physically moved back from her. He hesitated; he seemed to be having trouble forming his thoughts. There seemed to be no way to get out of answering the question. He had to be honest.

"Wendy, you know I love you, right? Before I answer, let me just say that what happened between Luca and me is in the past."

"So, you were having sex with him," she stated emphatically.

"It was complicated. Luca and I were best friends, and after a while it became physical. Honestly, Wendy, we were just experimenting. I have never had sex with any other guy, and I promise you, it will never happen again. It was just a phase."

So much for honesty, Wendy thought, remembering that moment vividly.

"How can you be sure you won't be attracted to other men? How can I be sure that you're not gay?" She dared to ask.

"Wendy, honey. I love you, not Luca or any other man. Please believe me when I tell you that I only want you," Brad pleaded.

That was over 30 years ago. And here we are now, Wendy thought. Luca in the middle of a family crisis. What right does he have to interfere? Why would they even discuss their college relationship at this point, unless there is more to the story? Wendy felt as if her comfortable life was falling apart all around her. Is Brad still in love with Luca? Is he going to leave me? She wasn't sure of anything, and began to sob with greater intensity. Moments later there was a light knock on the door, and Brad came in.

"Wendy, my love, are you all right? Please stop

crying, I'm here," Brad said as he rubbed her back.

Wendy had no more words. She lay with her face buried in her pillow.

"Honey, please talk to me. I am so sorry. I will talk to Michael and I will make this right, I promise."

And what about Luca? What about us? Will we ever be free from that shadow? Wendy remained silent as all these thoughts swirled in her mind.

CHAPTER 27

LUCA
SPRING 1981

It was May of my junior year in college. I had just completed final exams and was sitting in the campus pub waiting for Irene. I had to tell someone what had happened, and there was no one I could trust more than Irene. I ordered some fries for us to share and waited, lost in my thoughts and feeling drained. Although my body ached for rest, I hadn't slept for days.

It was more than lack of sleep that was exhausting me, however. During the last few months, I had been on high alert every day. I knew that Brad could flip into an abusive rant at the drop of a hat. I began to realize how much I had been holding in. Just three days ago, I was running after Brad in his drunken state while fearfully waiting for the next eruption. But now it was over. I was finally free.

I put my head down in my hands and sighed.

"Come on, honey!" cried out a familiar voice. Irene had arrived. "It can't be all that bad. You just finished finals, for God's sake," she said as she settled in the booth across from me.

"It's not bad at all now that you're here," I said as I kissed her hello.

"All right then–spill it. You've obviously got something on your mind. Get it out in the open so we can go drink," Irene joked.

"Ok, so you know how close Brad and I are?"

"Seriously? That's your opening line? The two of you hang off each other like your lives depend on it."

"Well, there's more to that story." I took a deep breath. It's either now or never, I thought. "We've been sleeping together for the last two years," my words rushing out before I could lose my courage.

"So that's the big news? Tell me something I don't know. You guys were so obvious!"

"Seriously, Irene?" I started to panic. "Does everyone know?"

"No, honey, not everyone. But I know you inside and out. You could never hide your feelings from me. You've been gushing about him since you met. When you have a fight, you come to me and complain. It was a typical romantic relationship." She laughed. "And to top it off, you started to wear those white painter's pants bond matching rainbow suspenders. If that doesn't scream gay, nothing does!"

"Yeah, that was pretty gay, wasn't it? So why didn't you ever say anything to me about it?" I asked.

"Luca, honey–because that's not my story to tell. I figured that you would tell me when you were ready. I mean, honestly, wouldn't you have denied it if I asked you?"

"Well, you have a point. I denied it to Fr. Murphy just few days ago. I suppose he saw right through me as well."

"Yes, my dear, he's pretty perceptive. And don't you think he's gay too?"

"You know, now that you mention it, yes," I replied. "He wants to talk to me about my relationship with Brad after all the dust settles. I guess it's time to come clean with him too."

"Long past time, Luca," Irene gently chided.

Little did I know that Irene herself was struggling with her own identity. But it would be years before she would come out to me.

"Irene, there's so more to tell you, and this is the hard part." I paused as I gathered my strength. "It got really ugly on Friday night."

"What do you mean, ugly? What did he do, Luca?" she asked with protective concern.

"Well, you saw how drunk and belligerent he was at the keg party. He reached a fever pitch by the time he got back to our room. That's when all hell broke loose."

I launched into the whole saga about Brad's drinking and the night he attacked me. For the first time ever, Irene sat speechless with her mouth agape. She reached out to hold my hand when I began to tell her about Brad jumping on my bed and punching me. "Oh, honey," she whispered with tears in her eyes.

When I finished there was a moment of heavy silence. Then she said, "I love you, Luca. You know that, right? So, don't you ever let anyone treat you like that again. You are too good for that."

"I love you too, Irene. I don't know what I would do without you."

"Well, you don't have to worry about that, do you?"

"I just needed to tell you about all of this. I couldn't bear going through this alone," I confessed.

"Look, Luca, you have to promise me." She pulled my hands across the table close to her as she leaned in. "You can never keep something like this from me again. Do you understand? I will always be there for you, always!"

Tears spilled from my eyes and I nodded my head.

"I never knew he was hurting you so bad," she said.

"You have no idea. As it turns out, his savage animal bite was the least of it."

"Wait—he bit you? Get out! How could you leave that detail out of the story? Where did he bite you? Show me." I lifted my sleeve and she could see the scabs healing over. "That bastard!" she cried.

Our fries came and we decided to order a couple of beers to wash them down. We were both in need of a drink after such a heavy conversation. By the time we left, we were both feeling good and closer than ever. My big secret was finally out. I had just come out to someone for the first time, and I survived.

After that, I felt that I had a whole new lease on life. I felt like I was back in control and that I was the one calling the shots again. As a result, I decided to place a call to the diocesan vocations office the very next day. It was time to take concrete steps toward my ultimate goal.

+++

"Hello, this is Luca De Santo. I'd like to speak to someone about applying to the seminary program." My heart was beating so quickly that I could hear it.

"Good morning, Luca," the voice at the other end of the line said. "I will connect you to the vocations office. They will be able to explain the process to you."

The following week I was in the chancery office speaking with Msgr. Ryan, the vocation director. "It's great to meet you, Mr. De Santo," he said. "I know your Uncle Pete very well. He is one of our finest priests."

"Yes, and he's a pretty good uncle as well," I said in a weak attempt at humor.

"I have no doubt that he is. I see that you are at St. Robert's, going into your senior year in September. You came to me just in time. I assume that you have your core credits in philosophy and religious studies taken care of, yes?"

"Yes, Monsignor. I have 12 credits in each. I will be taking mostly electives next year."

"Well, that's good news, Luca, because in order to go directly to the theologate, the graduate program in theology, you must have a minor in philosophy. That means a minimum of 18 credits. Do you think you can take two more philosophy courses next year?"

"Absolutely, That will be no problem at all. I will also be taking two more Religious Studies courses."

"All right then. You will need to complete the application and make an appointment to get a psychological evaluation. That's standard procedure, nothing to be worried about. Have St. Robert's send us your official transcript as soon as you can. In the meantime, you should select a priest to be your spiritual director. It should be someone you trust, with whom you can be completely candid about your journey. If you don't have anyone in mind, I can give you several recommendations."

"Thanks, Monsignor. I do have someone in mind. He's the head of campus ministry at St. Robert's–Fr. Murphy."

"Very well then. Let's set up an appointment in two weeks and we can discuss your progress."

"Absolutely, Monsignor."

"In the meantime, there is a diocesan gathering of seminarians next Friday evening. If you are free, it would be a great time to chat with some of the other men in the program."

"Yes, I'm free on Friday. I would love to meet the other seminarians. I have lots of questions," I responded eagerly.

"I'm sure you do, Luca. I'm looking forward to having you aboard. The priesthood is an important calling."

"Thank you, Monsignor. I will see you soon."

I left his office walking on air. I was finally following the path I had dreamed of since I was a child. If all goes according to plan, five years from now I will be Fr. De Santo. That's not that far in the future, I thought. I'm finally doing it.

However, I didn't feel comfortable making my decision public. I knew that my parents would be thrilled, but if something were to change, I didn't want to disappoint them. I needed to get further into the process before I could tell them. And there was no way I wanted anyone at school to know that I was entering the seminary. I couldn't imagine having to endure endless questions about celibacy. Besides, I didn't want anybody to treat me differently. This was my journey—and at this point, it was nobody's business but my own.

CHAPTER 28

MICHAEL
SUMMER TO AUTUMN
2016

Michael needed time to process the new information he learned about his father and Bishop Luca on that fateful evening. At first, he was angry with both of them—his father for obvious reasons, but also Bishop De Santo. He felt deceived. How could the Bishop have kept that from him? However, with the passage of time, Michael had come to realize that De Santo was under no obligation to share his story with him. In fact, it would have been a breach of his father's trust.

Michael missed his new friend. Bishop De Santo had been nothing but good to him. There were countless Italian dinners over which Michael had poured his heart out to the Bishop. His support throughout Michael's coming out process was unwavering, and he seemed to genuinely care for Michael. He knew that he couldn't leave things as they were. He had said some hurtful things to the Bishop and needed to apologize.

Bishop Luca hadn't heard from Brad or Michael in nearly two months. He was more than little curious about whether Brad would reconcile with Michael, and he had to admit that he feared that Michael, in his anger, would publicly reveal the affair he had had with Brad. That would have destroyed both their careers and their lives. However, in the brief time he had known him, he could sense that Michael was a good and caring young man. He didn't believe that Michael could be that vindictive. At least, that was what he hoped.

When Michael called to make an appointment, Luca breathed a sigh of relief. He asked if they could meet as soon as possible and if it could be in private. Michael was relieved when the bishop suggested they meet at his rectory in Bridgeport.

"Michael, I didn't expect to hear from you again," Luca said as the young man arrived. "I am so glad you came by. Please come in. Can I get you something to drink?"

"Do you have any scotch?"

"Just like your father. He loves his scotch." As soon as that came out of his mouth, he regretted it.

"I guess I'm like him in more ways than I knew," Michael retorted.

"I'm sorry, Michael. I didn't mean to imply anything. Please sit–here you go," he said, handing him the scotch and sitting down nearby.

"Look, Bishop De Santo," Michael began. "I came here to apologize. I was a complete ass when I barged into the parlor that day. I was incredibly disrespectful toward you. You didn't deserve that."

"Thank you, Michael. You were rightfully angry, and I am sorry you had to overhear our conversation. What happened between your father and me should have been discussed with you personally. But I hope you understand that it wasn't my place to tell you. It should have come from your father."

"Well, that would never have happened. You can see that now, can't you?" Michael asked. It was a rhetorical question.

"Yes, I can. But Michael, you have to know that he wasn't trying to hurt you, and neither was I. I brought it up with him in order to help you, and to help him understand that he went through something similar."

"I understand that now, Bishop, although, at the time it was such a shock—you and my father, lovers. I still can't wrap my head around it," Michael said, shaking his head.

Bishop De Santo hesitated at that last statement. He really didn't know what to say.

"You know, Michael, people are not born parents, or bishops, for that matter. Each of us followed our own paths as we grew up. Your father and I fell in love back in college, but it was not a healthy relationship. We both moved on with our lives. He fell in love with your mother and raised a family, and I went on to the seminary. Who's to know what direction a life may take? But, I'll say this: we are both better for having known one another, even though our relationship caused us both so much pain."

There was a brief moment of silence. Michael looked up at Bishop Luca.

"Do you have any regrets, Bishop? Did you ever wonder what life would have been like had you stayed together?" he asked.

"No, no regrets. As I said, it was a very destructive relationship. It had to end, especially for my sake. But celibacy can be terribly lonely. I have to admit that there have been times when I've wondered what it would have been like to have a partner in life–to have someone to share my fears and my dreams with."

Michael released a deep sigh and looked at the Bishop with sadness. "All that history between the two of you, and all I did was scream at you both. I had pleaded with you talk to him because I was too weak. You were there trying to help me and I turned on you. I am so ashamed of myself, Bishop. Please accept my apology," he said with tears in his eyes. He knew that he had caused the Bishop more pain. What kind of man attacks a person trying to help him? he thought. How do I make up for that?

"Of course I accept your apology, Michael. I greatly value our new-found friendship and I feared that we had lost it. I am just sorry that coming out to your father has caused you so much pain."

They both rose and Michael fell into Luca's comforting embrace. He could no longer control his tears as he openly cried. He hadn't realized how much he needed to be comforted. In the Bishop's fatherly embrace, Michael finally felt safe and loved.

"It's OK, Michael. It's OK," Luca said, holding him

as one would hold a distraught child. It was a tender moment that seemed to seal their friendship.

They sat back down in their chairs and the Bishop asked him, "Tell me, how is it going with your father? Have you come to a detente?"

"He's actually starting to come around. We've been talking pretty regularly," Michael said.

"And how is that? Do you think he is beginning to accept you and your wish to be open with your sexuality?" the Bishop asked.

"He still doesn't like the fact that I publicly identify as gay, but he is not fighting me on it anymore. He's even asked me about potential boyfriends," Michael added with a wry smile.

"Well, that is progress. I am so happy for you, Michael. How are your mother and sister dealing with your revealed identity?"

"Maryann has known for years, and Mom probably knew as well. I think all three of us are relieved that we can chat about our lives openly. It's really quite sweet."

"Bravo, Michael. It sounds as if you are in a good place."

"I am, Bishop De Santo, but I could still use someone to talk to. Would you mind being that person for me? I know it's a lot to ask, especially given your history with Dad. But I feel so comfortable with you, and you have already played an important part in my life."

Bishop De Santo smiled inwardly. Who could have imagined such an outcome—my former lover's son seeking spiritual direction from me? he thought. The unpredictability of life never ceases to amaze me.

"Michael, you and I have a relationship that's independent from your father. My history with your Dad only serves to give insight and color to what you are struggling with. To be quite honest with you, I have found getting to know you quite refreshing. I would be happy to be an ear for you."

They agreed to meet every two weeks, and were faithful to their commitment. More importantly, though, they were becoming real friends. Luca felt that he had a surrogate son, and that filled a very important place in his heart. For Michael, Bishop De Santo was everything he wished his father to be.

☩

CHAPTER 29

BISHOP DE SANTO
SPRING 2018

The call from the Vatican was a huge surprise. I had been getting lots of press for my advocacy work with the LGBTQ community–both negative and positive. There was a great deal of pushback from conservative Catholic organizations. In fact, protesters were common at many of my speaking engagements, some of which were canceled due to all the negative press. I was not sure if I would continue to get hierarchical support for my work. But some of my fellow bishops were trying to make their dioceses more hospitable as well, and they encouraged me to continue.

I began to deliver my message of welcome at churches within my diocese, and continued the tradition of an annual lecture series and a celebration Mass each June during Pride

Month. But that was not enough. Our community needs love and support all year long. I opened several Catholic community houses for LGBTQ youth throughout the diocese, where they could get counseling and be part of a loving family. We provided numerous social events and activities, as well as spiritual guidance. It was an entirely new approach for any Catholic organization–and it was working. Our houses were becoming known as cool places to hang out. Families of the young people we served began to visit as well, and provided much needed financial support for our services–and of course, the diocese held fundraisers that specifically targeted these programs.

I couldn't have done any of this without the approval of some of the more powerful bishops and cardinals in the U.S. I sought counsel from the cardinals in Chicago and Newark. They had taken bold steps to support the LGBTQ community, and I made it clear that my aim was to follow suit. As a result, invitations to speak at conferences or diocesan gatherings came in at an alarming rate. I found it difficult to keep up.

During a recent conference for the National Council of Catholic Bishops, a number of my colleagues were anxious to discuss my work, as well as to find out what reactions and feedback I was getting from other bishops and cardinals. A classmate of mine from Rome, also a bishop, pulled me aside. "Luca, what you are doing is groundbreaking. You need to publish a book. You could transform so many more minds and hearts if you published," he said.

"Patrick, what would I publish?" I asked. "Besides, I don't have the time to sit and write. I am away from my diocese so much these days that I can't even keep up with all the administrative work I have."

"Luca, you've already done the work. You have given that talk hundreds of times at this point. Cardinals McGovern and Daly are big fans of yours. Get them to sign off on it. That would act as an official church endorsement of your work–an imprimatur, if you will."

"I don't know, Patrick. It just seems so overwhelming to write a book."

"Well, you have so many guys here at this conference who have already done that. Come with me. Have you spoken with Bishop Cortona from Oregon? He has written numerous books on prayer. Honestly, Luca, how hard can it be? You've always had a lot to say. Now you just have to put it to paper."

"Are you saying I'm a blowhard?"

"If the shoe fits, Your Eminence." he joked.

That was just the beginning. Now that the book has been published, my public persona has been somewhat of a lightning rod. Controversy has followed me throughout this journey. The protesters became more numerous and mounted an organized campaign against me and my message. Last week, when I received a call from the papal nuncio informing me that I was summoned to Rome, I immediately panicked. This is it: I've done something terribly wrong. Did I go too far at one of my speaking engagements? Are they concerned about all the conservative Catholic campaigns against me? Then a deeper fear reared its ugly head. What if someone found out about Brad and me? That would be the end of my work as a priest. That thought had me spinning. This can't be happening now, not after all I've accomplished. How could this be?

With fear and trepidation, I returned the call. The nuncio informed me that the Council of Cardinal Advisors was aware of my work and writings regarding the Church teaching on homosexuality. My book had reached their desk with the endorsement of two U.S. Cardinals. I was asked to come to Rome to discuss not only my book, but also the efficacy of the current Church document regarding the pastoral care for homosexuals, which was written in 1986. That document was so outdated and caused so much pain throughout the last three decades. Its very language was pejorative and was difficult to understand for people without a deep understanding of philosophy. One of the most damaging lines from the document states that homosexuals are oriented toward moral evil.

As a gay bishop, I had a great deal of difficulty with that statement. The nuncio informed me that the council would like me to advise them as they reexamined the 1986 document. I prayed that it would be completely overhauled, but I had no illusions. Though the environment in the Church had become more welcoming, the basic doctrine had not changed. It would likely continue to teach that homosexual acts are sinful.

Nevertheless, it was not lost on me that one of my first feelings in response to this call was that of dread. I bore a deep sense of shame for my transgressions with Brad, and although I confessed my sins and toiled with my penance, I found it difficult to let go. When I felt ashamed, though, I could hear Fr. Garcia's voice in my head: "You are human, Luca. Never forget that, and never fault yourself for your human errors."

+++

The following week, as I began to prepare for my travel to Rome, I was sifting through old notebooks from my seminary days. I was trying to find a paper I had written that challenged the common understanding of the Biblical passage in Leviticus. The common language used since the King James version from the 17th century referred to men lying with men as an abomination. However, the actual Hebrew translation simply states that this act would require ritual cleansing—not that it was a sin punishable by death. At that time, I had done a great deal of research on ancient interpretation and translation errors of Biblical texts. I knew this work would be perfect to use when I presented to the Vatican.

In the back corner of one cabinet, I found a pile of my old journals. There were 20 or more notebooks filled with my daily musings, beginning in my senior year of high school. During my seminary years, they became prayer journals and sources of meditation, but most were simply filled with my emotional crises along the way. I pulled out the piles of journals and put them in chronological order, then I began to read. As I leafed through the pages, I let my mind take me on a journey.

A flood of images washed over me. I am 18 years old and full of youthful exuberance. There I am on the beach with Brad. It is there that I am drawn into that first forbidden kiss and my life is changed forever. There was so much about myself that I never imagined, so very much that was revealed to me from that first kiss. My relationship with Brad taught me that I could love another person with my entire being. It was the first time that I felt that I could not live without this other person, that I was incomplete without him. Before that kiss, a life of celibacy seemed easy. For the first time, my body and mind responded viscerally to those intensely beautiful moments, and they were made so much more profound by my youthful inexperience.

During those two years with Brad, I also learned how destructive or poisonous a relationship could be. I witnessed the steady erosion of my self-confidence. I learned how easy it is for someone to be manipulative—even someone you love. I also learned of my inner strength and will to survive. When I began to pull away from Brad emotionally, I began to rebuild my sense of self. But it was when our relationship ultimately turned violent that I pulled away completely and stopped being a victim.

The moment Brad laid his hands on me in his drunken attack, something snapped. It was as if a spotlight was shined on our relationship. The emotional abuse had been easier to dismiss, although it was just as damaging. But with each punch, I became clearer about the need to remove myself from such a destructive person. I learned that love is much more than need or emotional attachment. I did fall in love again in the following years, and it was then that I learned to be an equal partner, someone who is better in what they do and who they are because of that relationship. I felt supported, challenged, and worthy of love. Those loves made me more confident and successful in everything else I did. But I have to admit that the romantic encounters during my seminary years posed their own unique challenges, not the least of which was the eventual vow of celibacy that was required for ordination. There always seemed to be a struggle between body and soul, and neither would loosen their hold on me. Ultimately, I could not let go of my dream of becoming a priest. Still, I had no regrets. Each of those relationships helped to form the man I am today, the bishop I am today.

Several years had passed since I reconnected with Brad at the diocesan fundraiser. The drama that ensued still haunted me. Our brief affair upended my life once again. But what struck me most about my relationship with Brad, when we were 18 and at 55, is that neither of us changed all that much. Yes, we grew up, matured and learned many life lessons. However, I saw that Brad's motivating force never changed. He always looked out for number one. If you were in his circle and added benefit to his reputation or his drive to be a millionaire, you would be graciously welcomed into his fold. But the minute you were no longer of any use to him, you were immediately let loose.

Looking back on my journal entries, I realized that there was an essential attribute that was lacking in his treatment of me: kindness. Brad was never a kind man. He didn't put anyone else before himself. With me, it was a matter of how I fit into his world and how I fulfilled his needs.

Kindness is one of the most important qualities for me—not just as a bishop, but as a human being. I am never more unnerved or angry than when I witness someone taunting or bullying others, or anyone who treats others with a lack of kindness. Even when Brad and I reconnected, I quickly saw that he thought only of himself and his reputation. He never considered what I was risking to enter into our affair. He didn't even comprehend the concept of a vow or commitment. No matter how much I tried to explain how I valued living a life of integrity, he would always return to what he wanted from our relationship. It was never about us. It was only about Brad, and how Luca fit into his life. I believed that he truly loved me, but only on his terms.

His treatment of his son reinforced my perception of him. When Michael came out, Brad was cruel and thought only of how it affected him. His concern centered on Michael's earning potential and social standing. I just couldn't understand his lack of compassion. I would have thought that he could relate to his son by recalling his own struggle. Where was his empathy and love? That day in his parlor, when all hell broke loose, I felt a chill; it was as if his heart had turned to ice. It was striking how little warmth he showed toward his own son. Perhaps I am being too harsh. I knew that he had grown and that there was a great deal of good in him. But I bore too many scars to see it anymore.

After that day, Brad continued to support charitable causes in my diocese with active enthusiasm. He and Michael mended their relationship and developed a closer bond. I saw positive change in this man that I loved so ardently, but deep down, I knew I would always doubt the authenticity of his actions. Part of me would never forgive him.

My cell phone rang, startling me from my reverie. I was delighted to see Michael's face appear on the screen. Although we spoke often, it had been several months since we'd seen each other.

"Michael, carissimo. How wonderful to hear from you, my friend. How is everything?"

"I'm happier than ever, Bishop Luca. Sorry I haven't been in touch lately. There's no excuse."

"I'm just glad that we're talking now. Tell me what's going on in your life," I prompted.

"Well, I have good news. Of course, you remember Marco?"

"How could I forget? You gush about him each time we meet!"

"Well, we've been dating for almost a year. It's getting serious," Michael said with excitement.

"Well, that is good news," I responded.

"Bishop Luca, he's like no one I've ever been with. He inspires me to be a better person and he treats me like gold. At times he sounds just like you. It's surreal. I know you will love him," he said with great enthusiasm.

"That's great, Michael. It sounds like you're in love. I am so happy for you."

"I am, and I want to spend the rest of my life with him."

"How wonderful! Well then, when do I get to meet him?" I asked.

"That's one of the reasons for my call. Can we set a date for the three of us to have dinner?"

"I would love to, Michael. But it will have to be sometime this week. I fly to Rome on Sunday night."

"Oh, well then, we can definitely make that happen. Wait, why are you going to Rome?" he asked.

"To be honest, it's all very exciting. It has to do with my advocacy for the LGBTQ community. I can tell you all about it at dinner."

"Wow, you're getting even more important, aren't you? Will we be calling you Cardinal De Santo soon?" he teased.

"I don't know about that, but I'm very passionate about our cause, and elated that they are finally listening. But of course, I do need to temper my expectations."

"So, not to pour salt on a wound, but have you seen my father lately?" Michael asked, changing the subject tentatively.

"Strangely, I haven't. We used to run into each other at fundraisers, and he is still an active donor, but it may have been over a year since I've seen or heard from him. Why do you ask?"

"No reason. It's just sad that you've become so distant."

"After that scene at their house when I went to speak to him about you, it's been very strained. Perhaps it is for the best," I said with candor.

"I'm sorry to hear that. You were always spoken about with great reverence in our house. In fact, that's what gave me the courage to come speak to you after the LGBTQ Mass. I knew you could help."

"I don't know, Michael. I think I may have made matters worse for you."

"No, no. Absolutely not! If not for our conversations, I would never have had the courage to come out to him. And maybe that blow up was what finally broke the dam and released what we were holding inside. No, Bishop, you did not make matters worse. Dad and I have come a long way in our relationship since then, and you made that happen."

"You made that happen, Michael," I said. "Your strength and determination led to that healing. You're an amazing young man—anyone would be proud to call you his or her son. I would be proud to call you my son."

"Now you're going to make me cry. Bishop Luca, in many ways you have become a second father to me. I wouldn't change a thing. Let go of that guilt, please," Michael said earnestly.

"Well now, Michael, that's a bit of a role reversal. You sound like a priest. Thank you, I am very moved by that."

After checking our calendars, we settled on a date for dinner. "OK, so we're on for this Thursday at Positano. I can't believe you're still going there after all these years," Michael teased. He was more and more comfortable with me and I loved it.

"Well, there's something to be said for constancy, Michael." We laughed and said our goodbyes. His phone call lifted me from my over-analytical musings. I rose from my desk and decided to take a walk along St. Mary's by the Sea. I deserved a break, after all.

+++

I was really looking forward to seeing Michael again. When Thursday came, I arrived at the restaurant early. I asked for my usual private table, and while I pensively sipped my red wine, I wondered what Michael's boyfriend would be like. When I looked up, the most handsome couple was walking toward me, and I stood to greet them. Michael and I greeted each other with an affectionate embrace, and he kissed me on the cheek. A new level of intimacy, I thought, how very sweet.

"Bishop Luca, this is Marco," Michael said.

"How wonderful to meet you, Marco. Michael was very excited for us to meet," I said, placing my hand affectionately on his shoulder.

"Same here, Bishop De Santo. Michael has spoken about you so often during this past year, I feel like I already know you."

"Please, let's dispense with the formality. I am Michael's friend and now yours. You should both call me Luca."

We sat down as the waiter offered them both a glass of wine. I was looking forward to getting to know Michael's boyfriend. "So, Marco, tell me a bit about yourself," I began.

"Well, how do I start? I went to Boston College, and then went on to join the Jesuit Volunteer Corps. They ruined me for life, as they say."

"That's a great program, Marco. Where did they send you?" I asked.

"Billings, Montana. The middle of nowhere for a guy from the South End! I worked with drug-addicted youth. It was eye-opening, to say the least."

"I'm sure it was. That must have transformed your life, Marco."

"Yeah—so much so that he wanted to become a priest." Michael interjected.

"Yeah, so shortly after that I entered the Jesuit novitiate. I felt I had a vocation to the priesthood."

"Hmm, sounds familiar. So what changed, Marco?" I asked.

"I fell in love... again, and again. It was clear that I needed to follow a different path."

"Thank God you came to your senses!" Michael chimed in as we all laughed.

"We can plan all we want, but in the end, God brings

us where we are supposed to be–often to places we never dreamed of," I said. "So what do you do now, Marco?"

"I've been teaching Social Justice at Jesuit High School in New York City. The guys are as bright as can be and at times, a real challenge. I love it there."

"That's a great school, and we need dedicated teachers like you," I said. "Michael, it sounds like Marco is going to keep you on your toes. Are you ready for that?"

"Luca, when I am with Marco I am happier than I've ever been. Like I said on our phone call, he makes me a better person. In fact, I am a better version of myself than ever before." He leaned over and gave Marco a kiss.

"Well, a healthy relationship should always bring out the best in each individual. I am so happy for you boys," I said with genuine affection.

The rest of the evening was just as delightful, and I didn't want it come to an end. We must make a point to remain in closer touch, I thought. By the time dessert came, Michael placed his hand over Marco's, looked up at Bishop De Santo and said, "So, we have an important announcement to make."

"Ah, this seems serious. Go on, Michael, please don't keep me in suspense."

"Marco and I are planning to get married," he said looking directly into Marco's eyes. When he turned back to face Bishop De Santo, he could see the tears welled up in Luca's eyes. De Santo reached across the table and took each of their hands in his.

"I couldn't be happier for you two. If our brief time together this evening is any indication, your lives together will be rich in love." And with that, he stood and pulled them up into an exuberant bear hug. The three of them were laughing and crying with joy.

Marco pull away first and said, "Bishop, we have a request. You have been such a significant influence on Michael and in turn on me and our relationship. It would be a great honor for both of us if you would give the toast at our wedding reception?"

"Gentlemen, it is I who should be honored. However, I have to be very careful in my position. My appearance at such a significant public event would certainly make a few waves. Public perception of my blessing a gay wedding would have devastating repercussions. I regret that I will have to decline."

"Luca, you have to be there. I can't imagine getting married without you looking on. Besides, it's not going to be a big New York event," Michael said.

Then Marco jumped in. "No, not at all. We're hoping to do something relatively small. Isn't that right Michael?"

"Absolutely. I asked Dad if we could have a private ceremony at the house in Greenwich, looking out over the Sound. Dad is thrilled that he doesn't have to invite all his rich buddies. We want only our immediate family and friends there. We would be the only ones who would know that you're a bishop. Honestly."

"Well, that certainly paints a different picture. In that case, I would love to be there for your most special day."

Driving home from Positano, it occurred to me that although my reunion with Brad had caused so much renewed pain and struggle, it also created a most wonderful consequence: my friendship with Michael, and now with Marco as well.

✝

CHAPTER 30

BISHOP DE SANTO
SUMMER 2018

It was a warm summer afternoon on Long Island Sound. The gazebo was decorated with lavender and white bunting. Flowers of similar colors flowed from every direction as I walked to the edge of the water. A chamber orchestra could be heard playing their classical repertoire, and the waitstaff were handing out wine and champagne as each guest arrived. Everyone was milling about with eager anticipation. There were no more than 20 to 30 chairs facing the gazebo, and the water glimmered just beyond. I was immediately relieved by how intimate a gathering this would be, and that I could let myself relax and enjoy this wonderful occasion.

Wendy was the first to greet me. She placed her right hand on my chest while she looped her left arm through mine in one smooth gesture. We strolled toward the small group now gathered by the gazebo.

"Luca, I am so happy that you were able to join us today. Michael loves you a great deal and your presence means the world to him," she said, almost apologetically.

"Thank you, Wendy. I am grateful that he has become an important part of my life. And thank you for welcoming me into your home again," I added.

Without breaking her stride, Wendy turned to me and said, "Luca–you, Brad, and I are bound together by a complicated history. I can't ignore it like I did when we were younger. I've accepted it and I'm moving forward. We've all made our choices and our commitments, and the consequences of those choices impacted the rest of our lives. I can live with that. But I tell you truthfully, what you have done for Michael fills my heart with such joy," she said, her face lighting up. "I have witnessed a wonderful transformation in him. His happiness and self-confidence are overflowing, and I give you a great deal of credit for allowing him to blossom. I will never forget what you've done for him." She turned and kissed my cheek just as a waiter offered us glasses of champagne. She reached out and grabbed a flute for each of us and said, "Now let's toast to our wonderful boy."

I was startled by her candor but moved by her words. It took a lot of courage for Wendy to say all that she did. I was impressed by how genuine she was and that she didn't gloss over our struggles. I realized how little I knew her after all these years. In my mind, she was always the person that Brad deceived into marriage–how terribly unfair of me.

The ceremony had a greater impact on me than I had expected. When I looked up to see Michael and Marco facing each other, hand in hand, I began to cry. I cried for their joy and love for each other. I cried for all those LGBTQ Catholics who could never marry in their own church, and finally I cried for me, for what might have been.

Wendy was right: we had each made our choices, and there had been many life-giving results because of them. In my fantasies, I often asked the question, "What if?" What would my life be like if I did not become a priest? What if Brad and I had worked through our pain and conflict together? I dreamed of what life would be like with my one true love.

As the tenor soloist began to sing "One Hand, One Heart" from West Side Story, I was pulled from my imagined life and became self-conscious about my crying. But as I looked around me, I found that I was far from the only one. I didn't have all the answers to my "What if?" questions, but I could clearly see that there was a great deal of love on that beach, and I was glad to be a part of it.

Following the ceremony, I was relieved to discover that the dinner was casual. With high top tables dotting the lawn, many of us mingled as we nibbled. Being unsure about the guest list, I was grateful to discover a couple of my college friends to pal around with. As was our custom at class reunions over the years, we regaled each other with endless tales from St. Robert's. There was no one to impress and no need to schmooze with the influential players. I felt completely at home, and I relaxed and laughed with my old friends.

When the moon rose over the water, I was mesmerized. I wandered away from the party and stood at the water's edge. The gentle lapping of the waves mingled with the festive music from the reception. Being in a particularly reflective mood, I thought about all the wonderful opportunities that had come my way during this past year, and said a quiet prayer of thanks. Out of my internal silence, I heard footsteps approaching.

"What are you thinking about, Luca?" Brad asked as he took his place by my side. We had only said a perfunctory hello when he was greeting his guests.

"Brad, hey. I was just thinking how grateful I am," I answered honestly. "It's been an eventful few years, hasn't it?"

"That's for damn sure—especially for you. I hear congratulations are in order," he said, catching me off guard.

"Why? What do mean?" I asked.

"Come on Luca, your move to Boston," he replied with mock annoyance.

"Are you kidding me? How did you hear about that? It's not even public yet," I asked.

"You know that I've always had my finger on the pulse of those in power," he joked.

"That you have, Brad. I should have learned by now not to underestimate you," I said with a smile. "To be honest, the idea of moving away from Connecticut makes me very sad. This has been my home for many years."

"Boston is not very far away, Luca¬—and if I'm not mistaken, the Archbishop of Boston has always been raised to Cardinal. Am I right?"

"Brad, you really are in the know. Yes, there has always been a Cardinal in Boston, but there are no guarantees. Pope Francis follows a different set of guidelines. He chooses men who 'smell like the flock': those who are serving those most in need, not necessarily the bishops who raise the most money."

"Well, Luca, it's a good thing that you have always done both," he replied.

"Perhaps I have, but I am happy to serve in whatever way he asks," I said with exasperation.

"Now you sound like a company man, Luca. It's just us here. You are allowed to revel in your success. You've always had trouble with that."

"You're right, Brad—and yes, I have been briefed about the Pope's intentions. I'll likely be raised to Cardinal at the next go-around. Who would have thought?"

"I would have, Luca. You are one of the most faithful and dedicated men I know. You deserve to be recognized for it." He put his arm around me and we stood looking out over the water.

Eventually, I broke the silence and asked, "How did it feel to witness your beautiful son marrying a man, Brad?"

Brad was silent for a moment. "Sad. Sad for what I could have had," he finally said, opening up. "But happy for him. I love that boy with all my heart."

"Brad, if not for your marriage to Wendy, you wouldn't have those two beautiful children. It's strange to think about things that might have been. But it all worked out in the end, didn't it?"

"It did." He paused for a moment and looked at me. "Luca, my greatest regret is the pain I caused you. I hope you know that I have always loved you, just not as I should have. I am truly sorry for what we lost." Tears streamed down his face and I pulled him closer to me as we stood side by side, gazing at the moonbeams dancing on the water.

Eventually, we rejoined the celebration. This evening had been packed with emotional revelations, I thought. In the end, I couldn't have been more grateful for all the twists and turns our histories had taken, because ultimately, they brought us to this moment.

When the time came for me to give my toast, I held none of my emotions back. I stood at an angle so that I could look directly at the happy couple as I spoke. At that moment, they were the only people that mattered.

"Michael, I love you as if you were my own son. Marco, I suppose that makes you my son-in-law." We all laughed, and then I continued. "Your love and care for each other is clear to anyone in your presence. Many of us can only dream of having a love as profound as yours. As you begin your married lives together, continue to support one another in striving toward your goals. Lift each other up in times of struggle and pain. Always share your innermost fears as well as your hopes and dreams; it's the only way to make those dreams come true. For together, you can overcome any obstacle, and you will be stronger for it. Show your love often, and most of all, always act with kindness toward one another." With tears streaming down my cheeks, I lifted my glass and said, "To Michael and Marco, may their love grow ever stronger."

As the three of us embraced, we laughed and we cried. "I love you too, Luca. Thank you for being my second father," Michael said through his tears. At that moment, I realized that my heart had never been so full.

For the remainder of the evening, I watched the sheer joy and exhilaration flowing from our two grooms. What struck me about Michael and Marco was how kind they were to one another. They were genuine in their expressions of love, and they seemed completely relaxed with each other.

They knew how to laugh and play with each other. It was heartening to watch Michael dote on Marco: he held out his chair, poured his wine, and tried to anticipate his every need. Although Michael had inherited his father's drive to succeed, he was completely different in how he expressed his love. He was generous with his love and care, showing genuine concern for Marco, as well as his friends. He didn't place himself before or above others.

Oddly, the more I got to know Marco, the more I came to realize that he was so much like me as a young man—a dreamer seeking to save the world. And Michael, on the other hand, was everything I wished Brad could be. I smiled a satisfied smile. They say history tends to repeat itself, I thought. Perhaps this time, they'll get it right.

✙

Acknowledgments

I would like to thank all those who supported me in the writing of this book. Drawing from the collective experiences of many friends who have shared their stories of coming out, I've created characters that reflect a greater reality of the journey toward self-acceptance. Thank you to Katie Naum and Eileen Pollack, who took on the task of copy-editing and proofing. Your probing questions and candor helped to further develop the storyline. To Anne Gardener and Matthew Speiser, your feedback and encouragement during the early stages of writing inspired me and helped transform my meandering thoughts into a story of self-discovery and human struggle. Thanks to my nephew, Matthew Roberts for his graphic expertise and help with the cover design. He turned my concept into a piece of art. A final thank you to my husband, Jim Alexander for his continual support and for his creativity in coming up with the title.

Photo credit: www.matthewdavidroberts.com

As chair of the music department and ethics teacher at an independent school for girls in Manhattan, Mario Dell'Olio conducts the Concert and Chamber Choirs. Dr. Dell'Olio is responsible for all Liturgical celebrations for the Lower, Middle and Upper Schools. He leads the Choirs on annual international and domestic concert tours and has released numerous albums on iTunes and Amazon.com. Dr. Dell'Olio was director of music at Mission Dolores Basilica in San Francisco, California, from 1990 - 2000. He led the Basilica Choir on its first international concert tour to Italy in June 1999. Dr. Dell'Olio holds a Doctor of Sacred Music, a Master of Music in Vocal Performance, and a Masters in Religious Education. He pursued postgraduate work in Theology at the Pontifical Gregorian University, Rome, Italy. https://www.mariodellolio.com/

Also by Mario Dell'Olio

Coming About: Life In the Balance

A mid-life crisis, a sailing adventure, and a rescue at sea, Coming About tells a story of survival and inner-strength through a foundational loving relationship. Coming About is a memoir of Mario and Jim who, at 40, quit their jobs and sell their home in San Francisco to follow their dream. They buy a 50-foot sailboat and move to St. Thomas, Virgin Islands where they discover many quirky facets of adjusting to life on the island as well as its many cultural idiosyncrasies. During the maiden voyage from the US mainland to St. Thomas, they encounter treacherous weather conditions and a series of life-threatening events that lead to a rescue at sea and the destruction of their dreams of retirement in a Caribbean paradise. Battling relentlessly crushing waves and shark-infested waters, their lives hang in the balance. Their struggles are vividly recounted as they search for meaning in the near loss of their lives and the shattering of their dreams.